The Shift Key

Quite unexpectedly, Basil Goodsir exploded.

Leaping to his feet, he roared, 'He stole a sheep! That violates the sacred laws of property! I say he must be hanged, right now, in public!'

His co-magistrates, and the clerk, strove in vain to quiet him.

'I won't be silent!' he raved on. 'Where in God's name is the executioner? *Take this wicked fellow out and hang him by the neck until he's dead!* Then let his body rot upon the gallows! To steal from your own son – I mean your father – is the most heinous crime conceivable! It's worse than murder, worse than blasphemy!'

An awed silence had by now pervaded the court, apart from certain officials who were conferring softly by the door through which the accused were brought in. By degrees even their voices hushed, and all eyes turned on Basil.

Who gradually seemed to realize what he'd said.

'But stealing sheep . . .' he forced out under that massed accusing gaze. 'I mean: it is a crime that calls for hanging, isn't it? I mean: I know it is!'

By the same author,
available from Methuen

The Compleat Traveller in Black

John Brunner

The Shift Key

A Methuen Paperback

A Methuen Paperback

THE SHIFT KEY

First published in Great Britain 1987
by Methuen London Ltd
11 New Fetter Lane, London EC4P 4EE
Copyright © 1987 Brunner Fact & Fiction Ltd
Printed and bound in Great Britain by
Richard Clay Ltd, Bungay, Suffolk

British Library Cataloguing in Publication Data

Brunner, John, 1934–
    The shift key.
    I. Title
    823'.914[F]   PR6052.R8

    ISBN 0–413–14920–X

I

Victor Draycock awoke to the taste of excitement.

Last night he had been restless. Despite the swirl of autumn mist that filled the valley of the River Chap, he had had to take a midnight walk in order to unwind. Later, though, in sleep, it seemed his subconscious had been working overtime. He had figured out precisely how best to phrase an article he had been planning for the past two months, publication of which in the *Chapminster Chronicle* had been as good as promised.

In the village of Weyharrow Goodsir, where he lived with his wife Carol and their six-year-old son Tommy, a dispute was raging about the two kinds of visitors it attracted, especially during the summer. There were prosperous tourists lured by its picturesque site and handsome stone buildings; they met with the grudging approval of the local gentry because they did nothing more disruptive than take photographs, uttered properly admiring comments, and lunched or dined expensively at the Bridge Hotel, whose landlord was chairman of the parish council. Then there were the others, mostly under thirty, mostly shabby, drawn here for entirely different reasons, who were more likely to sit shirtless and barefoot on the car-park wall of the pub across the road. They met with no approval at all from the gentry, though some from the young folk of the village, to whom they constituted a welcome diversion in a generally boring existence – and likewise from Victor, who prided himself on siding with the younger generation and had made himself immensely unpopular with the officious ladies of the Weyharrow Society by referring to the second type of visitors as 'pilgrims'.

His article was intended to dot the said ladies one in the

eye, haul them over the coals and otherwise leave them discomfited.

All of a sudden he saw it complete, as though he had read it in a dream and remembered it word for word.

He glanced at the bedside clock. Over an hour remained before the regular time to rouse/wash/dress/feed young Tommy and get him off to school. But the light beyond the bedroom curtains indicated that last night's mist had melted, leaving – for October – a fine morning. This was too good a chance to miss.

Beside him Carol still lay peacefully asleep. Moving gently so as not to disturb her, he eased his bony frame out of bed, detoured to the adjacent bathroom to pee – he left the loo unflushed for fear of waking Tommy – and brush his teeth and comb his lank black hair, then made himself a mug of instant coffee. Balancing it with care, still in pyjamas and dressing-gown, he scrambled up the counter-balanced ladder that gave access from the upstairs landing to the cubbyhole above the eaves where dwelt his pride and joy, his computer cum word processor, safe for a year or two from the inquisitiveness of his son. (How long before the boy grew tall enough to reach the dangling rope that hauled the ladder down?)

He was delighted with the machine that here reposed on a desk he had botched together out of scraps. He had owned it for barely three months, but it had proved as simple to use as the salesman had promised, and working on it had become second nature in next to no time. His old typewriter, on which he bestowed a scornful glance in passing, was gathering dust because he kept forgetting to bring up a plastic bag to wrap it in.

Its successor, on the other hand was lovingly protected under half an old sheet. Bundling that up, he switched on, loaded the necessary floppy discs, and began to thump the keyboard in the grip of white-hot inspiration.

Countless people [he began] who have never visited the west of England know the name of Weyharrow Goodsir, the historic village that straddles the River Chap between Chapminster and Hatterbridge, a few miles south of Trimborne.

Most, no doubt, recognize it because it has featured in so many publications of the British Tourist Authority. It's a village of classic form, centred on a triangular green. On one side stand the church, the parsonage and the village hall; on the second, a line of houses punctuated by the primary school; on the third, more houses some of which have been converted into shops, concluding with a petrol station whose pumps and workshops are customarily excused by residents showing visitors around on the grounds that, though they are a bit of an eyesore, one has to pay the price of progress. Perhaps it's indicative of Weyharrow's world view that its people have been saying much the same since 1926, the year the garage was erected . . .

On a rise overlooking the valley of the Chap, catching the morning sun a fraction earlier than the houses below, stands Weyharrow Court: a stone-built manor house dating back to the fourteenth century but much modernized and added to.

The Court has seen many changes in the village apart from that intrusive garage. Farms that once abutted the green have long been built over; the ancient ford has been replaced by a bridge – shivering now under the burden of traffic it was never designed for – thanks to which, between the wars, the 'new estate' of incongruous brick houses sprang up on the other side of the river; and, of course, the woods that formerly fledged the valley's flanks have been cut down, to the considerable profit of the Court's proprietors, the Goodsir family, who still own about half the land in the area, including most of what's been built on.

Noticing the name of the village, most people assume it must have been in the possession of the same family since time immemorial – or at least since the Norman Conquest, to which we owe so many similar names (Norton Fitz-warren, for example, and the Fitzpaines to be found further west).

Not so. 'Time immemorial' in this sense reaches back no further than the age of a Masonic lodge.

Proud of that little gibe, Victor paused to savour it, sipping his coffee. He reviewed the previous paragraph, altered 'in the possession of' to 'held by' without needing to consult his instruction manual, and resumed.

True, Weyharrow stands on a most ancient site. Its ford marked an important crossing-place, used by Roman legions and Saxon traders, and ultimately what financed its replacement by a bridge – timber in the fifteenth century, stone in the seventeenth – was the toll levied on drovers taking cattle, sheep and even geese by road to London.

And it is also true that it formed part of an estate granted by William the Conqueror to one of his retainers. His name, though, was nothing like Goodsir. If a faded inscription at Hatterbridge is to be believed, it was Odo de Beyze, but he died before Domesday Book was compiled.

In any case, for some reason he studiously neglected this corner of his land. It may have been because the river marked its border, and his neighbour was a powerful rival; it may have been, as we shall see, for a subtler reason. At all events, at his death the estate changed hands, and continued to do so at frequent intervals for the next five or six hundred years.

Victor paused for more coffee and amended 'land' to 'lands'.

By the eighteenth century there was little to be seen at Weyharrow save the church, the manor house (now the Court), a few wattle-and-daub cottages, and a number of scattered farms whose occupants enjoyed a widespread reputation for debauchery and ungodliness.

And one other important and substantial building, adjacent to the ford – not the modern Bridge Hotel, but the inn, then called the Slaking House ... where, presumably, one slaked one's thirst (though some claim it had to do with processing lime).

This was known far and wide as not just a tavern but a rendezvous for riff-raff. Smuggled goods were traded there; robbers and highwaymen begged refuge from a succession of corrupt landlords who, for a price, were prepared to guide them to hideouts in the then-dense woods, and many local farmers sheltered them in barns or sold them horses to help them on their way.

Romantic as such a situation may now seem, that was not how it struck the Reverend Matthew Goodsir, of Northumberland, when – thanks to a distant cousin dying childless – he inherited the lordship of the manor.

He was an enthusiastic supporter of John Wesley and the Methodists; indeed, he had been stoned out of his pulpit in Northumberland for heresy and his patron had deprived him of his living. He took the coincidence between his own name and the tag that had already come to be applied to Weyharrow as a divine omen, moved to the Court – which he found partly ruined and which he restored – and set about purifying the morals of those unexpectedly fallen into his charge.

However, his plans met with an obstacle at once.

He wanted, naturally, to close the Slaking House, that den of iniquity. The incumbent landlord, one Jacob Fidger (a name still found in the village), figuratively thumbed his nose, and with impunity. Almost alone of the people in the area, he rejoiced in freehold possession of the ground his tavern stood on. At some point in the previous century the lord of the manor had needed funds to send his eldest son to court, and the taverner had supplied them against title-deeds in perpetuity.

'Tell you what, squire,' said Landlord Fidger – so the story goes. 'I'll meet you and your Methodies half-way. I'll change my sign. Instead of being called the Slaking

House, from now on 'twill be the Marriage at Cana!'

'That's blasphemy!' fumed the Reverend Goodsir, but there was nothing he could do, and the countryside resounded with laughter at his expense.

He would have been even more put out if he had known a few of the facts that modern scholarship has revealed.

His half-full coffee-mug was growing a greyish skin. Victor ignored it. He had hit his stride and the words were pouring out as fast as he could press the keys.

Specifically, he would have been mortified had he known that the coincidence between his own surname and that of Weyharrow had nothing to do with the family connection that led to him inheriting. It is, though, probable that he went to his grave without realizing that 'Goodsir' in the West Country has no connection with the 'goodsire' or 'gudesire' (godfather or grandfather) from which his own northern patronymic derived, but is rather a variant of 'Goodman', meaning the Devil. 'Goodman's Plot' and 'Goodsir's Piece' are still to be found as field-names, implying that the land is so poor only the Devil himself could scrape a living from it.

As to what would have happened had he known the true meaning of 'Weyharrow' ... Well, that boggles the imagination.

The reverend gentleman fancied himself as a bit of an antiquarian – what we would nowadays term an archaeologist. But, like most such in his period, he preferred to conduct research not in the field but solely from books. (Incidentally, to his credit does stand one achievement: he founded the great library at Weyharrow Court, long a mecca for historians, although alas threatened with being broken up by the present owners. So priceless a collection deserves a better fate than being peddled abroad for private gain.)

Old Matthew was doubtless aware that there were many ancient remains in the vicinity. What he certainly did not know – this is attested by a surviving letter – was the literal significance of the village's name.

'Wey' or 'Wye' occurs frequently all over the south of England, often if not always with the meaning 'pagan god or idol'.

And 'Harrow' means 'site of a heathen temple' . . .

Victor remembered his coffee, took a sip and found it cold and nasty, set it by and carried on, fingers flying.

Members of the Weyharrow Society are forever boasting about how they 'keep up local traditions' – yet they are vociferous in their objection to the crowds of young people who for several summers past have descended on the village from all over Britain and even from the Continent, many arriving on foot like the pilgrims of old.

However much one disagrees with their talk of 'dragon power' and 'ley lines', it is they who are truly keeping up the local traditions – traditions far older than the Goodsirs' day. They come to Weyharrow in search of the mystic forces that impelled our long-lost ancestors to choose Weyharrow as the site of a temple housing an idol whose fame survives in the very name of the village. It is they, rather than the residents who imagine that history began with the arrival of Reverend Matthew, who –

'Vic! *Vic*!'

It was Carol shouting at the top of her voice from the landing below.

'Vic, don't you know what time it is? Tommy will be late for school, and so will you!'

'Coming!' Victor answered with a sigh.

He would have liked to add his point about how Odo, a devout Christian, must have steered clear of Weyharrow thanks to its pagan associations, but it didn't really matter. Albeit a trifle long, what he had written was good, and he knew it. And even though he hadn't had time to print it out or even make a backup copy, it would be safe on the disc.

'VIC!'

'Coming!' he called again, and entered the 'store' and 'shut-down' commands as he had done already countless times. The screen blanked, and he reached for the power-switch.

And froze.

The VDU had lit again. Now it was displaying the bland message:

TEXT DELETED.

What?

But he had hit – he *knew* he had hit – precisely the commands he always used!

He sat with jaw agape, confronted with the need to reconstruct everything he had written from scratch ... but his inspiration was fading even as he thought about it, fading like dew in morning sunshine, fading as completely as a dream, as the words he had consigned to his machine.

From below came the sound of Tommy squalling at the top of his lungs, and another, now despairing, shriek from Carol. Slowly, fighting the grip of paralysing disbelief, Victor rose from his chair and turned towards the ladder.

But I know I used the right command, I know I did. I know!

In most respects, apart from the unseasonable brightness of the sunshine, Weyharrow Goodsir's day had begun quite normally, to the accompaniment of crowing cocks and barking dogs and growling tractors.

What had happened to Vic Draycock was merely the first of many signs that that was not how it was due to end.

2

Stick – his name was Simon Bember but everyone had called him Stick for so long he'd forgotten why – yawned and rubbed his eyes and found he was asleep on the living-room couch. Eventually he decided he was wrong. Actually he was awake on the living-room couch, and cold because the window was ajar. He looked at his watch. It had stopped. The hi-fi was on, though – had been all night, since he dozed off listening to his much-worn copy of Terry Riley's *In C*. He switched to radio and twisted the tuning knob until he hit a station which was giving a time-check.

Early, thank goodness. Sheila was never in the sweetest of moods when he overslept.

He swung his legs to the floor, yawning hugely, and ran his fingers through his gingery beard and hair. His jeans and T-shirt looked none the worse for being slept in. But then, they never looked otherwise than as if they had been.

All the doors in the flat were open, as usual. Still yawning as though the top of his head wanted to detach itself and fly away, he made for the loo, passing the bedroom where Sheila lay asleep. Having tossed her covers aside in the night, she was bare to the waist, her pale back stranded with her long dark hair. He blew her a kiss. He liked Sheila Surrean, with whom he had now lived for nearly half a year – had known he would the moment he saw the hand-written sign she'd taped to the door of her riverside flat above what had formerly been a boat-store, converted now into rented garages. It read *Wearystale*.

'Because it's unprofitable?' he had suggested. He had met her that evening in the Marriage, and although she had

9

agreed to let him see her home he had been expecting at best a kiss and cuddle at her door. Weyharrow was, after all, a village chanced on a long way from the London that he wanted to escape.

'Nobody in this damned place ever got the point before!' was her reply. 'Come in!'

He'd stayed ...

Much to the annoyance of sundry local folk, both old and young.

And found a job into the bargain, though luckily one they didn't envy. Tending the village green and cemetery, raking dead leaves and trimming hedges, and generally tidying up, might not appeal to everyone, but it suited Stick to perfection, especially since it meant he had access to a patch of land where the old war memorial had stood until they moved it in 1946, neglected ever since. He wasn't much of a gardener, but there was one thing he was very good at growing and it flourished there.

Moreover it had broken down some barriers. Even certain young men – married and unmarried – who had set their sights on Sheila now talked to him politely.

And this year's crop, as he had proved last night, was quite exceptional ...

Opposite Sheila's room, which had become his as well, was the one where her children slept in twin bunk-beds. It was time to wake them.

No, let them wait a minute longer, while he attended to an urgent problem in the minuscule bathroom adjacent to the equally exiguous kitchen.

Emerging, he called over his shoulder as he headed for the electric kettle, 'Sam! Hilary! Time to get up!'

Water run, flex plugged in ... no sign of movement.

'Hilary! Sam! Didn't you hear me?'

Teapot rinsed and tea spooned into it, still nothing. Time to come the heavy non-father. He marched into the kids' room, tramp-tramp as loudly as feet in socks permitted, and whisked the covers off them both.

Aged eight and ten, they slept in T-shirts, baggy from repeated washing. Blinking, he stared down.

He'd got the names right – crayoned signs at the head of each bunk said HILARY and SAM, though to the second one was appended a footnote he did not recall: 'PLEASE DONT ADD THE ANTHA I DONT LIKE IT.'

Funny! I could have sworn that Sheila's kids were boys.

But what the hell? He'd always liked girls better.

Having made sure they were awake, he returned to the kitchen just before the kettle boiled in search of milk and cereal and bowls and spoons.

After smoking grass like what he'd raised this year, one never knew quite where one's head was likely to be at.

The Reverend Patrick Phibson entered the vestry of St Matthew's Church and prepared to don his surplice for the morning service. His eyes were sore and his belly was rumbling; he had been out until midnight comforting Mrs Lapsey who – not for the first time – had been convinced she was at death's door, but had only called the doctor at his insistence. He had missed supper, and the sandwich he had forced down on his return still lay heavy.

He looked with jaundiced gaze on the church, as usual. Ever since his appointment to this living, which would be his last before retirement, he had felt that in spite of its respectable antiquity there was something tainted about any such edifice that had been re-named owing to the vanity of its incumbent. Precisely that had happened at Weyharrow. Before Matthew Goodsir moved in and imposed his own name, it had been dedicated – ecumenically, as one might say, and very sensibly in a period of wars of religious intolerance – to All Saints.

But, of course, as he was always forced to admit to himself, albeit with a sigh, there had been times when one must distinguish between saints and 'saints', that was to say the heretics who held that once received into the community of the elect whatever they did must necessarily be right, for they were permanently cleansed of any taint of sin . . .

Much of this church dated back past the days of the Great Plague to those of the Black Death, when such notions had been rife. Part, some people claimed, especially of the crypt, must be far older – relics of the age when this had been not a Christian but a pagan centre of worship . . .

Enough! Enough! Much more of this and he was likely to find himself agreeing with that awful Victor Draycock who argued that the dirty amoral mob who nowadays invaded Weyharrow each summer were heirs to a spiritual tradition with deeper roots than his own creed –

Stop!

Garbed in the prescribed manner, having recited by pure reflex the appropriate prayers, Mr Phibson realized it was more than long enough since the morning bell tolled from the tower. He drew a deep breath and thrust aside the vestry door.

As usual at this hour of seven-thirty, the congregation was negligible: seven people, five of them women and one of those his housekeeper. There was no organist on weekdays. How much more impressive it would have been had a swelling voluntary rung out . . .

Yet and still, it was a service to the Almighty. He composed his features into a suitably cheerful expression and went forth to utter the customary comforting phrases that – as he had known for years – properly began each daily act of worship.

'I, Patrick, a servant of the Father, bid you welcome in His holy name, and that of the Mother, and the Child!'

With the assurance due to having performed the same rite countless times, he turned his back on the altar (had someone been meddling with it? It didn't look the way it should according to his own recollection of the calendar, but he had barely glimpsed it and in all humility one must admit the possibility of being wrong) and spread his arms.

'Come hither and embrace me, as the Mother once embraced Her Child! Let us exchange the Kiss of Peace as the apostles did, passing from lip to lip the touch of our immortal Parent!'

Abruptly he realized that all the faces gazing at him were locked into the same expression: stony, appalled.

Had heresy taken root in Weyharrow again? The triune He and She and It forfend!

He tried again, this time wheedling. On average, his listeners must be fifty or sixty, but of course a sense of frustration was apt to strike at just about that age – as he himself had been made only too aware when Maud died.

'Beloved, I know there are some who resent the fact that contact of a more intimate kind with skin that touched the skin that touched the skin – and so back and back to Intercourse with the Blessed Child, Man and Woman blended in one sacred Flesh – should be reserved to those in holy orders. But our wise and patient guide, the Church, has so decreed because above the waist the brain, the seat of judgment and intelligence, is sovereign. Below the waist, only faith may transmute the blind operation of instinct into a holy act of worship, and it is given to few to . . .'

His words died away. The members of the congregation were rising, but not to exchange the Kiss of Peace with him or one another. They were shouting at him, trembling with fury – or maybe horror. He stood bewildered. How could they possibly object to such an orthodox exposition of their common creed?

It hadn't been like this yesterday morning, he was sure of that.

Ursula Ellerford caught sight of her reflection in the window above the kitchen sink, and reflexively tidied back a strand of her brown hair. There was more grey in it than there had been a week ago, she thought. No doubt there were also more wrinkles on her face and neck. Coping by herself with two demanding teenage sons was proving more than she could bear. Last night Paul and Harold had been out God knew where until God knew what time, and she'd waited up for them as usual, terrified of the phone call that might tell her they had had an accident, or got in a fight and been arrested.

But she hadn't wanted them to know what a watch she kept. Though she had wandered round and round the garden in the midnight mist, she had darted up to her bedroom as soon as she heard their cheerful voices on the street.

She hadn't even left them a reproving note.

If only Ted had been spared . . . But he'd developed cancer, taken enforced retirement, died a lingering death. If, equally, he had left enough for something better than this cramped house – best of all, enough for a servant of the kind they had enjoyed when working in Hong Kong . . .

All the time she was rehearsing her pointless private litany of might-have-beens, she was boiling a pan of water, throwing in a handful of rice, laying out rice-ware bowls and matching handleless cups and hunting for the tea she was sure ought to be in *this* cupboard. No. That one?

She remembered to shout at the boys to hurry up or they would miss the school bus. Older than eleven, children in Weyharrow had to go to Powte, near Chapminster. If only Ted had left enough for them to board at his old school, as he had always dreamed . . .

Her sons came clattering into the kitchen and sat down. She set the steaming pan before them.

'What's this?' they demanded as one.

'Breakfast, what else?' she snapped.

'It looks like yucky muck to me!' countered Harold, and his brother said the same, adding obscenities.

Ursula stood there blankly. She said in a faint voice, 'You never said you didn't like it before.'

'That's because we never had it before!' – from Paul.

But it's congee – rice soup! Like in Hong Kong . . .

The words died unspoken. Sometimes it seemed they were determined to torment her every waking moment. Dully she turned away, while they exchanged shrugs and helped themselves to packet cereal. After all her trouble . . . !

But she managed not to cry until they'd gone.

Tom Fidger rolled the smoking ancient bus out of the forecourt of the garage that he ran in partnership with his brother Fred. It was a family business; their grandfather had founded it, and their father Jack still helped out in the office now and then.

He turned around the green to the bus shelter beside the churchyard gate, where his usual passengers were waiting: boys and girls in blue and grey school uniform. Thursday was never a busy morning. It was pension day, and the older folk must collect their money from the post office before they could go shopping away from the village.

He thought wistfully of times past, when Fidger's had run a proper service with three buses and hired drivers. Back then, they hadn't just ferried shoppers and schoolkids, but all sorts of passengers. Every morning they'd taken a dozen people to work at the pharmaceutical factory up the valley in Trimborne, and brought them back in the evening. Then, though, the managers had introduced automatic machinery, and the few staff they kept on became able to afford cars, and the demand dwindled. Now literally no one from Weyharrow worked at the factory any more, and even this rump of a service barely broke even except during the school term, despite weekend holiday excursions . . .

Still, there were people who without it would never be able to get out of Weyharrow at all. It was a public good, and worth preserving for as long as possible.

Braking, opening the door, he called good morning to those waiting. He felt fine, despite having been up late. A tourist coach had broken down on the main road, and it had been his turn rather than his brother's to go and help. He hadn't got to bed until nearly midnight.

Everybody was aboard. Shutting the door, he engaged gear. And hesitated with his foot on the clutch.

Something really ought to be done about the siting of this stop! Why in the world was it on the wrong side of the road? And there was a car coming!

He waited until it had gone by, then swung over to the right and set off for Powte. Three near-collisions later, his screaming passengers finally made him believe that in Britain one drives on the left.

Shaking and sweating, he obeyed, and delivered them to their destination with no further mishap.

But he had been so sure! He'd *known*! And in his heart of hearts still felt it wrong!

Leaving his boots at the back door, Harry Vikes crossed the stone-flagged floor of the farm kitchen and sat down gloomily at the big scrubbed wooden table.

His wife Joyce bustled over from the solid-fuel range with a mug of tea in her red-knuckled hands. 'Here you are!' she said. 'I'll get your breakfast directly.'

Harry had been out late last night tending a sick calf, and up again at six as usual for the early milking and to drive the cows to pasture.

His only response was a grunt.

'What's amiss now?' Joyce demanded. 'Did the calf die?'

'No.' Not looking at her, he spooned sugar into his tea.

'What then?' And added suddenly: 'Where's Chief?'

The door was wide open, but there was no sign of Harry's constant companion, his black and white collie cross.

'By the gate, looking like a hundred devils got at him.'

Indeed he was. Joyce spotted him through the window, hunched down to the ground, tail low, eyes wide.

'What did you do to him?'

'It's more what he did to me,' Harry grunted. 'And 'tis all the fault of they damned Pecklows!'

The Vikeses and the Pecklows had long been neighbours, but propinquity had never made them friends.

'Know what they done this time?' Harry went on. 'Put the piece I rent from Nigel Mender down to turnips – in the night, just like that! 'Course I drove the cows in anyway, but Chief went mad. I had to kick him 'fore he'd leave off snapping at me.'

Joyce sat down very slowly. She said, 'What piece that you rent from Mr Mender?'

'The one in Fooksey Lane, o' course!'

'Harry,' Joyce said in a faint voice, 'that was last year. This year Ken Pecklow has it. He outbid you. And it is down to turnips.'

'That's what I said!' he burst out. 'And it warn't yesterday! I remember clear as I see you now!'

'And you drove our herd into it ... No wonder the dog tried to stop you! Seemingly he has more sense than you!'

The phone rang. She forced her heavy body to her feet.

'That'll be Ken, I reckon,' she said in a dull tone. 'And after we get this lot sorted out, you better go and see the doctor.'

'What are you rattling on about, woman? It's the calf that's sick, not me!'

'You think you're not sick?' she flared. 'When you're saying that Ken spent all night setting full-grown turnips in a field you grazed our cows on yesterday?'

'I told you! I remember clear as I see you now ...'

But the words trailed away. He turned his leather-brown face to her, and it grew pale. Beads of sweat started to run down his forehead, and his hand shook so much that tea slopped from his mug.

The phone was still ringing. Wearily Joyce moved to answer it.

Dr Steven Gloze did his best to look cheerful as he came downstairs for morning surgery, but Mrs Weaper the receptionist was doing the opposite, as though the name she had married into had permanently conditioned her expression. She informed him tartly that there were patients waiting, as though that were somehow his fault. But the first appointment was at nine, and only now was that hour clanging from the church clock.

Steven sighed as he collected the patient records. He had undertaken not a few engagements as a locum since his graduation, but they had mostly been in or around London. The idea of spending a month in a West Country village, especially in a practice where rumour hinted that Dr Tripkin, the incumbent – currently on holiday in Spain – was seriously considering retirement, had greatly appealed to him.

However, he was being made to feel distinctly unwelcome. Last night, when the parson had called him to attend Mrs Lapsey, the old bag had snapped at him as though he were some kind of unreliable quack.

Still, he had only been here since Monday. More than three weeks remained.

Riffling through the documents he had been handed, he discovered that the first patient was one William Cashcart, whom he had not previously met. An intercom linked the consulting-room with the waiting-room; he pressed the button and called him in.

Mr Cashcart, who was forty, said he was employed by Wenstowe's the builders and that his right wrist was hurting even though he'd bought a navvy's bracer to put round it. A

18

brief examination revealed he was most likely suffering from chronic but as yet low-grade arthritis. Well, that meant a good plain start to the day. It didn't seem worth sending him for an X-ray. Steven wrote out a prescription, told him to take it across the green to the chemist's, and called for the next patient.

She was just leaving when the phone rang. He picked it up. It was Mrs Weaper.

'Mr Ratch wants you!' she said sharply.

Steven's heart sank. Mr Ratch was the pharmacist, and he seemed as suspicious as anybody of this intrusive young stranger to whom the health of Weyharrow had been entrusted.

'Put him on,' he sighed.

'Dr Gloze? Lawrence Ratch here. Since when have newly-slaughtered chickens been available on the Health Service?'

'What? But it's standard treatment – has been since Lord knows when!'

'I have no idea' – frostily – 'what in the world you're talking about.'

'But surely . . .' Steven sought words through a haze of incomprehension. 'All he has to do is plunge his hand into the chicken while it's still warm, and keep it there until it's cold. The vital forces – '

Then, slowly, a vision of Mr Ratch's shop, which he had visited on Monday morning, took form in his mind. Indeed, it was not the sort of place where one would find live chickens. But why not, when their use was a commonplace? In town perhaps one might not obtain them so easily, but in the country . . . ?

He forced himself to say politely, 'Don't you have an arrangement with a local butcher? Or a farmer?'

'Dr Gloze! If this is a joke, it's in very poor taste! Mr Cashcart obviously has arthritis. I'm taking it upon myself to let him have something suitable, and I trust you'll sign a revised prescription straight away! Be so good as not to play such pranks again!'

The phone slammed down, leaving Steven in a state of indescribable bewilderment. There was a rack of medical texts above his borrowed desk; he snatched at each in turn, searching for the treatment he was so sure he had been taught to use.

It wasn't there. It wasn't there. It wasn't there . . .

And then the phone rang again and Mrs Weaper announced that he was needed urgently to tend two farmers who'd been fighting.

At least, her scornful tone implied, he must be up to applying bandages and sticking-plaster.

But by then Steven himself was far from sure.

3

Jenny Severance backed her dark-blue Mini into its usual space in the yard outside the offices of the *Chapminster Chronicle*. She was trembling. Partly that was due to the near miss she had had when leaving Weyharrow (what could have possessed Tom Fidger to drive his bus around the green on the wrong side of the road?), but far more importantly it was because she had a really tremendous story to file, and it would only just be in time. Publication day was tomorrow, and the presses were due to roll at noon.

Maybe she should have filed it with one of the nationals last night. . . .

But somehow it hadn't occurred to her. She had no idea why not, even though the meeting at Hatterbridge that she'd been sent to cover had dragged on far later than intended, and then fog had delayed her, so it had been midnight when she got to bed.

Sometimes she wondered whether she did really have the makings of a reporter. Ian Tenterwell, her editor, had often voiced the suspicion in his thin sarcastic tones.

But she was determined to prove herself.

Inevitably, as she jumped out and locked the car, half a dozen male passersby whistled and catcalled at the sight of this plump but pretty blonde of twenty-five. She pretended they weren't there.

In spite of that, too, she was determined to prove herself.

Rushing into the building, fending off still more would-be admirers, she hastened to her desk and rolled paper into the elderly manual typewriter which was the best – so Ian claimed – that funds would stretch to.

Maybe so, since the *Chronicle*'s was still a 'hot metal' operation.

And, speaking of Ian . . .

Here he came, when she had written scarcely more than a dozen lines.

'Well, well!' he said, swinging his leather briefcase. He affected dark suits and striped ties, the businessman look. 'Good to see you hard at work before I got here – for once! How was the meeting?'

Gritting her teeth, Jenny forced a smile.

'It'll be this week's lead.'

'What?'

'Just wait till you see what I've got. It'll make international headlines!'

Uncertainly he said, 'Jenny, are you feeling all right?'

'Stop trying to put me down!' was her cross reply. 'I'll bring it in as soon as it's ready. Then you'll see!'

And went back to pounding the keys. Ian shrugged and passed on.

The story was complete in a matter of minutes. Waving three pages in triumph, Jenny leapt up from her chair and marched straight into the office whose glass door was branded with the gilt word 'EDITOR', heedless of the fact that Ian was involved in deep discussion of galleys with chief sub Dennis Dewley. The latter looked at her reprovingly over his bifocals.

'Here you are!' she exclaimed. 'And it's all ours! None of the nationals sent so much as a stringer!'

And then, in the nick of time, she realized what Ian was about to read.

'Hal Awnham, MP for Hatterbridge, has finally revealed in public what so long has been suspected. The US government plans to launch an all-out nuclear attack on Russia next year, and British forces will be involved from the very first strike . . .'

22

She snatched the pages back in terror. She could imagine precisely what Ian was bound to reply, his voice acid with scorn.

'He can't have said anything of the sort, or there'd have been a bloody riot! He went to address a meeting of Hatter-bridge Peace and Disarmament Group, right? For a Tory, that's playing Daniel in the lions' den! He can't possibly have uttered such a load of claptrap! If he had, the disarmers would have made sure every paper in the country – and the BBC, and TV-AM! – headlined it this morning. Have you seen the papers? Did they have to call the police because the audience was trying to lynch him? Isn't that what you'd expect if he had said this?'

Suddenly, terrifyingly, there was a gap in her memory. She remembered the hall, the restive audience, the look of boredom on the chairman's face – he was a local vicar . . .

But no riot.

And, logically, there should have been.

I am not going to be weak and womanly. I am not going to break down and cry . . .

It was no use. Clutching the pages to her, she spun on her heel and ran out of the room, out of the building, leaving Ian and Dennis to exchange patronizing shrugs and carry on.

Vic Draycock knew it was a bad habit in a teacher to take out his own snappishness on his pupils. Today he couldn't help it. Instead of what he had planned to do with his morning history class, he set them an essay. They were to describe General Wolfe's attack on the Heights of Abraham. He gave them twenty minutes, and himself a chance to brood over his own stupidity in deleting his article.

When he called their papers in, the top one – last to be collected, of course – was from Harold Ellerford, who had kept scribbling until the latest possible moment. He and his brother Paul made an unlikable pair, forever hinting that they were somehow 'better' than their companions, and ought never to have wound up in a lowly state school like this.

Victor had intended to tell the class to study the next chapter of their history book while he glanced through what they had written, then spend a few minutes at the end of the period passing comments.

But the moment his eye fell on Harold's essay he felt beside himself.

'Harold!' he barked. 'Stand up!'

'Yes, sir?' – in the meek but defiant tone he and his brother seemed to have been coached in by their mother. (She was a leading light in the Weyharrow Society, as might have been expected.)

'Would you tell me what in heaven's name you meant by writing this from the point of view of Montcalm's soldiers? And, what is more, *in French*?'

Someone at the back of the room giggled. Goaded beyond endurance, Victor roared, 'You're making mock of me, you little devil!'

Alarm crossed Harold's face. 'Sir!' he protested. 'That's what you told us to do! Yesterday! I remember clearly!'

Brandishing the blackboard eraser, Victor stamped down to confront Harold, shaking with fury, wanting to beat him about the head until he moaned and blubbered.

'I did nothing of the kind!' he shouted. 'Ask the rest of the class!'

Uncertainty supplanting his alarm, Harold said, 'But, sir, I'm absolutely sure you told us yesterday . . .'

'Did I?' Victor rounded on the other pupils. 'Well?'

Two or three voices confirmed that he had not.

'I hadn't even thought of your assignment before this morning!' Victor bellowed, bethinking himself too late of the risk that such an admission might further undermine his precarious authority. 'For telling lies, and most of all for playing the smartass bastard, you're going to see the Head! Come with me! The rest of you, carry on reading!'

Dropping the eraser, snatching up Harold's essay, he marched the boy out of the room.

The meeting with the Head, of course, was a disaster. Brushing aside the question of lying to a teacher, he pronounced himself favourably impressed by what he termed Harold's initiative and enterprise ... but not by Victor, whose ears he made burn privately during morning break.

At which juncture Harold's younger brother Paul was standing alone, very puzzled and increasingly angry, in one of the music-rooms, deserted at this time of morning. He was absolutely certain that he'd made a date last night with Eunice Hoddie, from his class, whom he'd long lusted after. They were to meet here and snatch an hour of bliss.

Well, fifteen minutes, anyway.

Shortly before the bell rang to mark the end of break, he lost his temper and marched back into the corridor. Spotting Eunice chatting with a group of friends, he rushed over to corner her.

'What do you mean by standing me up?' he shouted.

She was his age but, like most girls in comparison with boys, far more sophisticated. She tilted back her head, crowned with a punk-dyed crest of spiky hair, and seized the chance of sweet revenge for all the times in the past when Paul and his brother had disdained the company of their 'inferior' fellow-pupils.

'Stand you up?' she said, with a wink at her companions. 'If you mean what I *think* you mean, I'm not sure I'd want to try. After all, you don't look like you could!'

The bell sounded, and she and the other girls swept away

amid a gale of laughter. Paul was left white-faced and shaking.

Eunice had promised to meet him in the music-room! She had! She HAD!

But ... when?

By lunch time, naturally, the joke was all around the school. The Ellerford boys being regarded as 'snooty', it became embroidered as it passed from mouth to mouth. During the afternoon it underwent still further transformations and elaborations.

Meantime, back in Weyharrow, sundry other events had come to light which those involved would have paid an arm or a leg to conceal. The village being, however, like all such small communities, a factory for gossip, they were public currency within hours, although nobody would ever have admitted passing on their private knowledge ... save maybe to close friends, who had pledged utter secrecy.

So how on *earth* – ?

A good few relationships were strained that day, and many snapped.

The first disaster to 'go public', as it were, was the case of Phyllis Knabbe.

Some time very early – it was still too dark to read the bedside clock – Miss Knabbe rose in answer to the squalling of her tomcat, called Rufus for his ginger fur. Until the year before last she had lived by herself, apart from a succession of cats, since the death of her parents. They had died when she was thirty-six; now she was forty-two.

But the little cottage, not fronting on the green, which the price of their larger but much-mortgaged home in Wedget Minor had sufficed to buy, cosy though it was, had often felt lonely. Cats were not enough.

Thank goodness, Miss Knabbe thought drowsily as she

padded to the kitchen door in dressing-gown and nightie, for the arrival of dear Moira when she had to let a room.

Moira O'Pheale was her own age to within months, and had been widowed, though not tragically. What she had recounted about life with her husband – miraculously, they had remained childless – had done nothing but reinforce Miss Knabbe's own feelings concerning single blessedness.

On the other hand, she was having vague second thoughts about the companionability of cats, especially whole toms like Rufus. Last night she had wandered the garden until some unconscionable hour, not daring to call his name out loud because the windows of nearby houses were in darkness – and, besides, dear Moira had already gone to bed. It had been midnight at least before Rufus condescended to return, to lap some milk and purr around her ankles, for all the world as though he had done nothing disobedient.

And now, at this chill darkling hour, he wanted to make off again . . .

She was standing beside the back door. It was ajar and he was gone. Very well! That settled it! If not tomorrow, then next week, he must be taken to the vet, to rectify that fault she would herself have liked to set right in her father – who had, as her mother had if not said outright then frequently hinted, inflicted his lusts on her in most disgusting fashion.

As for what Declan O'Pheale had done to Moira, who had married him in dazzlement for his tallness and good looks, only to find he was a drunkard and a lecher . . . !

Images of what Rufus might by now be up to mingled in Miss Knabbe's imagination with their human-to-human equivalents. She closed the door on her decision and found her way back upstairs by touch. She had refrained from turning on the lights lest Moira be disturbed.

Herself already in the clutch of Morpheus again, she groped for a door-handle, turned it, entered the room, let fall

27

her dressing-gown, and slipped into a warm and welcoming bed. Her hands encountered smooth nylon, and groped beneath it as she sighed with pleasure. What a relief it was to live with Moira now, instead of that horrid – randy – Rufus, that disgusting *male* . . . !

'Mary Mother of God! What do you think you're up to?'

A cry, almost a shriek. The bedside light snapped on. Moira was sitting up, the shoulder-straps of her nightie drawn down to expose her breasts.

And crying, 'Phyllis! Are you mad? Get out of here!'

Miss Knabbe fought back the tide of sleep. 'Is something wrong?' she ventured.

'What the hell do you mean? I'll bloody say there is! *Get out of my bed!*'

'But . . . !'

But this was the bed the two of them had shared since Moira came here. Miss Knabbe knew it was, she knew it in her bones. Had she done something wrong?

She asked that very question, ready to apologize – and Moira slapped her cheek.

'You must be bloody mad!' she cried, magnificent with her mop of brown hair tousled round her face, snatching back the nightgown-straps that Miss Knabbe had dislodged. 'If I'd known you were bloody queer I'd not have spent one night beneath your roof! *Get out!*'

'But this is our room!' whimpered Miss Knabbe, raising her arms as though to ward off the kind of blows Moira had said her Declan rained on her.

'Our room? You *are* mad! It's mine and I pay rent to keep it private! Yours is the other side of the landing! Get out! Get out! Get OUT!'

'What have I done?' Miss Knabbe heard herself moaning as her sense of contented certainty evaporated.

'Got rid of me!' was Moira's bitter answer. 'In the morning I'm going to advertise for safer lodgings!'

28

'But, darling Moira . . . !'

Her expostulations were of no avail. Moira did not recall what she recalled – what she'd have testified to on her Bible oath – that they had shared this room for two whole years . . .

Preparing to offer incontrovertible evidence, she gestured at the dressing-table, meaning to point out her own belongings on it, such as the silver-mounted toilet set she had been given for her twenty-first birthday.

They weren't there. Nor was anything of hers.

Sobbing, Miss Knabbe fled as she was ordered to the other room across the landing, and switched on the light. There they were, all her possessions: shoes on the floor, dress and underwear across a chair . . . And the covers on the rumpled bed had been thrown back.

The hideous suspicion crossed her mind: she might be wrong.

And yet she could not make herself believe it. Her memories were much too real.

She wept until the sky outside was light and there were no more tears. Distantly she heard Moira descending the stairs, going to the kitchen, moving around. At last she plucked up the courage to go down herself and beg forgiveness.

It was to no avail. Moira was pulling on her coat, her face a frozen mask.

'I'm going to tell everybody what you did!' she promised. 'And find a *man* to share my bed, if someone must!'

And marched out, slamming the door.

She kept her word.

Outside the primary school, in the shops, in the post office (which doubled as the newsagent's, tobacconist's and confectioner's), in the Marriage at Cana and the bar of the Bridge Hotel when those opened at mid-morning, rumours took root, and sprouted, and bloomed. Not in living memory had the people of Weyharrow had so much to talk about – not even when, last Midsummer Day, the police had descended on the hippies who had come here believing it to be a pagan site more ancient than Stonehenge, and taken off a bunch of them for drug offences. That had involved outsiders. It had been petty compared to the Knabbe scandal and the fight between Ken Pecklow and Harry Vikes.

With deep content the local folk discovered they had sex and violence on their doorstep.

It was to the general mood of excitement that Mr Jacksett, proprietor of the general store, ascribed his lapses in filling orders for his regular customers, all of whom seemed to have been given the wrong items. Shaking his head over the task of changing them, he wondered whether in fact it might rather be because he was worried about Boyo, his boxer dog, who had been missing since yesterday noon. He had been out until midnight calling and whistling. Presumably the brute had picked up the scent of a bitch and would return in his own good time, but the kids were crying for fear he might have been run over.

All morning similar incidents kept cropping up, though some went unregarded, like the one at the Bridge Hotel.

At the moment the hotel had no guests in residence – it seldom did after mid-September save at weekends – but last night the bar had been busy with the remnants of a birthday party. Having played the affable 'mine host' until his eyes began to cross with all the drinks the customers had stood him, Nigel Mender descended grumpily to the kitchen at ten-thirty, to find his chef, Tim Wamble, demanding why he couldn't lay hands on the stocks he needed for today's luncheon special. He was convinced they must have been thrown out with yesterday's midnight garbage.

'Today's special?' the landlord rasped, having heard his

complaint. 'What do you mean, "today's"?'

Tim – he was a slightly vague young man, but a hard worker, who had been hired to help out with the summer rush and agreed to stay on for the winter for lack of any better prospects – Tim spread his hands.

'Yesterday's was Spanish prawns and rice. Today's is hot game pie.'

'So what does it say over there?' growled Mr Mender, pointing to the list he himself had chalked on the blackboard that each day at opening time was hung in the porch, and brought in overnight. 'It says Wednesday, doesn't it? And hot game pie? Today is Thursday, which means ham in cider, peas and chips! Prawns is tomorrow! Lord, I'd have thought you knew the drill by heart by now!'

Not staying for an answer, he swept past into the bar, as yet not open, to serve himself the Bloody Mary that would have to do in lieu of breakfast.

Tim stood there agape, whispering, 'But I remember! I do remember! Prawns was yesterday!'

Miles to the east of Weyharrow, tour guide Ella Kailet sighed with relief as the coach drew in sight of Stonehenge barely half an hour later than the schedule called for.

Last night had been purgatory. It was never much fun conducting forty or more Americans on a whirlwind trip around the history-beset West Country. But when the coach broke down, so that they had to put up with a snack in a transport café instead of a square meal at their overnight hotel as they'd been promised, and then it broke down *again* barely ten miles from that hotel, and took another two hours to fix . . . !

At least, however, the mechanic who had turned out from Weyharrow Goodsir seemed to have cured the trouble. She had been none too happy about his competence when he showed up, nor about the state of mind of her tourists; the night was chilly and they had stayed huddled and grumbling inside the coach – as had the weary driver, who claimed he had no help to offer; that was going to earn him a bad report when they returned to London! – while she stood shivering in mist and badgering the mechanic to get a move on.

Still, here they were at last, and she knew this part of the drill by heart. She rose to stand beside the driver.

'Ladies and gentlemen!' she told the microphone, forcing an air-hostess's smile to her weary face. 'We are now approaching Stonehenge, perhaps the most famous of all prehistoric monuments. It was here that visitors from outer space landed in flying saucers to bring to the primitive inhabitants of Earth the arts and skills that came to be reflected in the pyramids of Egypt and South America.'

The driver was tugging at her skirt. She slapped his hand away and ploughed on doggedly.

'Later, of course, other similar landing sites, with their great dolmens that served as interstellar beacons, were constructed – *keep your paws off me, you oaf!* – were constructed as far away as Brittany and Scotland . . .'

Her mouth grew dry. The tourists were staring at her. Some of them had begun to mutter.

Oh, no! There wasn't going to be another crisis, was there? What on earth could have gone wrong now?

'Sarge?'

Constable Joseph Book was in Weyharrow's only public phone box. He lived in Weyharrow, in a police house, but there was no actual police station here; the nearest was at Chapminster, and he spent most of his time patrolling the area by car or on foot. He preferred the latter.

'Oh, it's you,' said the phone. 'I thought you must have got lost in last night's fog . . . Sorry, only kidding. Someone said you had a spot of bother. Ken Pecklow and Harry Vikes again. Wasn't Joyce threatening to have Harry put away?'

'She gave up on that one, thank goodness ... But don't poke fun, Sarge – please! This time it's serious. Ken bust a tooth and the doctor sent Harry to hospital with a broken nose. It's all in my notes and I'll be in as soon as I can to make out the incident report. But ...'

He hesitated. Impatient, the sergeant prompted him. 'Well?'

'That isn't all,' Constable Book said slowly. 'There's something very funny going on.'

'Come and tell me about it, then!'

'I'm not sure it wouldn't be better if I hung around' – with dogged persistence. 'You know I've lived here seven years. That's enough to get the feel of a place, isn't it?'

'I would say so ... Come to the point!'

Bridling: 'Sarge, people keep stopping me and telling me the weirdest stories!'

'I know, I know' – with a sigh. 'They've been ringing here all morning.'

'Did they say what Mary Flaken did?'

'I don't think so ... No, we don't have that name in the log. What happened?'

'Seems she got up, same as normal, found she'd run out of eggs and popped down the road to buy some for breakfast. But when she came back she didn't go home. She went next door to Bill and Hannah Blocket's – '

'Where exactly do you mean?'

'They live across the river, on the new estate.'

'I wonder when they're going to stop calling it that. It was there before my time, or yours ... Sorry, go on.'

'Well, she tried to open the back door. It was locked. She banged away till Hannah came to answer. Then she went spare! Marched in, yelling that Bill was her husband, not Hannah's, and wound up throwing the eggs all over the kitchen! They got her back home in the end, but I swear we haven't heard the last of that one – not by a long chalk!'

There was a pause. Eventually the sergeant said heavily, 'Sounds as though you're right, Joe. Something very odd indeed is going on.'

4

At Weyharrow the valley of the Chap broadened out; its water purled on pebbles. Two miles higher it tumbled over rocks; that was at Trimborne. Allegedly the name meant 'where the river is made neat', and certainly its stone-sided mill-race must be ancient, for the mill was named and priced in Domesday Book. To the Norman Odo, first lord of this once-enormous manor, Trimborne doubtless seemed far more precious than Weyharrow and its ford.

But the days when the mill had been a constant source of income, because the owners of the nearby farms were compelled to bring their grain for grinding and pay taxes for the privilege, were far in the past. Not in living memory had that or any other yearly rent from Trimborne brought much profit to those who nominally held the land.

With the arrival of Helvambrit Pharmaceuticals matters had admittedly taken a turn for the better. The company, a Swiss-based international conglomerate, had been among the first to decide that dingy urban sites assorted poorly with its claims to be promoting public health; moreover, bad though unemployment was in cities, in the countryside it was often relatively worse, implying that plenty of cheap labour was to hand. Add in a touch of conservation, by restoring the facade of a historic mill – that had in fact not been a corn mill for over a century, but by turns a snuff mill and a gunpowder mill and even an engineering works – and hey presto! A major public-relations coup! If heavy lorries had to lumber up the narrow lanes nearby, forcing tractors to back out of the way and walkers to seek shelter in the hedgerow, that was a petty price to pay.

Petty price . . .

Indeed Helvambrit had paid one! Pacing the library of Weyharrow Court, Basil Goodsir brooded on the fact. How could he have been duped into letting his father Marmaduke sell the Trimborne mill instead of leasing it? The old fool must have been both greedy and short-sighted! Why, they'd certainly have paid by way of annual rent ten, even fifteen per cent of the price they'd paid for the freehold, so the mill could have been furnishing a steady return – to be continued for the foreseeable future.

Of course, when the matter first arose, his son Cedric had just been sent to boarding school, and he and Helen had been faced with all the attendant expenses . . . Even so, it had been unfair of Marmaduke to take advantage of his own son's temporarily straitened circumstances! If the old fool had had an ounce of wit left in his addled pate, by now the deal would have been showing an enduring profit!

And to think that just a couple of years' revenue from that source could have set him on his feet again, maybe placated Helen who now nagged at him so constantly . . .

Basil Goodsir was forty-seven. His straight black hair had started to recede and his complexion was florid, with a tracery of broken veins on his nose and cheekbones. His face was set in an expression of permanent discontent, for he had been brought up to expect that he would make a success of his life, with the implied assurance that if he didn't there would always be some financial cushioning from the family.

That assurance, though, had come from his mother, who was dead, and had left her personal money not to him but to his sisters, now both married and living abroad. So far Basil had inherited nothing, for at seventy-five his father obstinately clung to life. As for his own career, it was pockmarked with failed business ventures. Currently he was drowning in debt, and the vultures were closing in. And here he was surrounded by priceless heirlooms but forbidden to capitalize on them! It was high time to make the old dodderer see sense!

About this library, for example. He remembered with a start why he had come in here this morning. It was his intention to list a few of the prizes that he had once – oh, he had to admit the fact, if only to himself – dismissed as so much waste paper, fit chiefly for a Guy Fawkes bonfire, because so many of these splendid leather bindings covered nothing more remarkable than reprints of sermons.

But great-great-grandfather Abel had been a notorious opponent of Darwin, and collected scores of books about the evolution dispute, and now there were all these colleges of 'Bible Science' breaking out in America like a rash. What might people like that not pay for a first edition of, say, Gosse's *Omphalos*, that famous study of all the reasons why Adam must have been created with a navel?

At least, that was what Basil assumed it must be about. He was wrong, not having read it. As a matter of fact, he had read precious few of the books in here, even as a child. Reading had never been his 'thing'.

Nor writing, come to that. But determinedly he gathered pencil and notebook and set about tabulating the items he thought might fetch the most on the American market.

'Good morning, young fellow!' wheezed Marmaduke from his velvet-backed armchair at the head of the dining-table. The days were long gone when at breakfast time the sideboard groaned with kedgeree and chops and devilled kidneys; he was eating porage because that was what there was, bar cereal or toast and marmalade. Still, he seemed to be thriving on his reduced diet; his eyes were bright above his wrinkled cheeks and sparse white beard.

'Morning, Gramps!' said Cedric, making for the coffee-pot. He was twenty and should have been at university again this year. However, there had been a regrettable disagreement with his tutors, and . . .

Cedric didn't mind. He enjoyed living at Weyharrow Court, above all because of his grandfather, whom he liked infinitely better than either of his parents. Besides, during the summer at least the village was always full of fascinating people of his own age, if not his social class. His fondness for them annoyed his parents so deliciously . . .

'Where's your father?' Marmaduke inquired.

Loading a slice of toast with ginger marmalade, Cedric shrugged. 'In the library, I think. At any rate I heard someone muttering in there as I came past, and it can scarcely have been anybody else.'

'The library. I see.' Marmaduke pushed aside his bowl and drained his cup. It held tea rather than coffee, and left a tealeaf on his bewhiskered upper lip because he abominated tea-bags and would only have his morning beverage brewed in the traditional fashion. 'You do know what he's up to, I suppose?'

Cedric nodded. Around a mouthful of crumbs he said, 'He wants to carve up the library and sell it to America.'

'That's right. He can't get over the fact that neither the house nor its contents belong to him, although he treats them as though they do.' A heavy sigh. 'Sometimes I wish, you know, that I hadn't let his mother keep him under her wing – '

'Far past the proper time,' Cedric supplied. 'Yes, *Gramps*. You have told me before, and I've always agreed.'

'Then what about yourself?' – eyebrows bristling. 'You evidence no great desire to flee the nest!'

'Oh, I live in hopes. One of these days I'll probably pack a bag and hitchhike round the world.' Cedric's tone was light; it was hard, even for his grandfather, to know whether he intended to be taken seriously.

'Damned young escapist!' Marmaduke rumbled, though there was a twinkle in his eye. 'And suppose while you're away the lightning strikes and he and I and your mother all

38

get carried off?'

'I'd come back at a run, and make this place into a pilgrims' refuge. Have you heard that phrase? Vic Draycock, who teaches history at Powte, applies the term "pilgrim" to the young folk who come here in the summer – '

'Don't talk to me about them!' his grandfather barked. 'They're a bunch of lazy, drug-addicted layabouts! Most of them have never turned their hands to honest work!'

Cedric concealed a sigh. He said placatingly, 'You must remember how few alternatives are open, what with unemployment at an all-time high – '

'There's always some work needing to be done!'

And more under our present lords and masters than under most we've had before . . .

But Cedric bit that back. Seeking politer turns of phrase, he was saved by, if not the bell, a shout. It was his mother, Helen, in the entrance hall.

'Basil! *Basil!* You're sitting at Chapminster today – have you forgotten?'

'Coming!' was the loud reply, and doors were slammed. By then Cedric had worked out what he most wanted to say and what, he thought, his grandfather would best accept.

He said daringly, 'Would you rather see me keeping up a front like Dad, sitting on the magistrates' bench and pretending that everything's all right when in a juster world he'd be in court himself? He's the next best thing to bankrupt, isn't he? Would you really like me to turn into the same sort of hypocrite?'

Marmaduke seemed uneasy, and evaded his grandson's eyes as he hunted for a proper reply.

'You mustn't think he's unaware of his responsibilities, you know,' he said at last. 'Why, only last night I heard him pacing up and down the river-terrace, right below my window, worrying aloud about his problems.'

'One of which,' said Cedric softly, 'he calls – you.'

For an instant he feared he'd overstepped the mark. The old man's mouth set in a thin accusing line, and behind the curtain of his beard his Adam's apple bobbed on his stringy throat, sure harbinger of an explosive outburst.

At that moment, though, in strode Helen, tall and lean. She had been a model when Basil met her a quarter of a century before, and never given up the habits she'd been trained to. Not a wisp of her blonde hair was out of place above her strong-boned face; her make-up was flawless; red ovals flashed on all her fingertips. As befitted a country setting, not the town, she had donned a V-neck pullover, its neckline filled in with a bright silk scarf, and jeans . . . but designer jeans, of course, their label prominent on her still-shapely bottom.

As usual, Cedric thought she looked ghastly, like one of the living dead. But he had never said so. He only went on wondering privately, as he had for years, how many of his father's debts were due to keeping up her wardrobe.

'The bloody coffee's cold,' was all she said before she drank it anyway and set about a bowl of mushy health-food.

Watching her eat, Cedric found himself fascinated – not for the first time – by another private question:

Does she not know what a three-time loser my old man is? Or is it rather that she knows and is avoiding the risk of being told by someone else who's noticed? Gramps has. It hasn't been a secret between me and him since I was – what? – sixteen, I suppose.

But today, for the first time ever, a third possibility stole under Cedric's guard, and he contemplated it with vast dismay.

Or could it be that she does know – has known for years – and wants to take advantage of the fact? What? How?

The idea was so disturbing he had to excuse himself on the pretext of sending off an urgent letter.

Of course, that wasn't his real reason for biking down to the village. What he actually wanted was some of Stick

Bember's current crop of grass, and he detoured via the amusingly-named Wearystale Flat to pick up enough for a dozen spliffs. But he believed in backing up his lies, if he ever needed to tell any, so he took the precaution of carrying along a genuine letter. Therefore it was at the post office that, waiting patiently behind a score of old folk queueing to collect their pensions, he first heard of the strange goings-on in Weyharrow.

Something else, equally peculiar, happened not long afterwards in Chapminster Magistrates' Court.

Jenny Severance had got over her hysterics. She hated to admit that that was what they had been, but how else could one describe sobs and moans that stemmed from remembering something that couldn't possibly have happened? She had come so close to letting other people know . . . !

Still, everyone had been remarkably kind, even Dennis Dewley, even Ian, who had muttered something about her being overtired because she had worked extremely hard since joining the paper, and stressed the need for her to get back on the job like the pilot of a crashed plane, who must fly again at once to stop the rot from setting in.

The upshot was that she'd been sent to cover the morning session at the magistrates' court. Of course she wouldn't have anything to show for it; the paper closed for press at noon, and Ian had looked over the roster of cases due to be heard and told her not to get her knickers in a twist about filing a story before lunch. But just in case anything did show up that might still be live next Friday . . .

Grateful, appalled at herself, afraid of going mad, amazed that she had been given this reprieve, she took station on the press bench.

As usual, she was alone. Now and then, if a juicy case was on the docket, the locals were crowded out by stringers for the national press or even visitors from Fleet Street, but that

41

had only happened a couple of times so far this year, the latest back in June when a few hippies camping at Weyharrow had been arrested for possessing cannabis.

Today there was nothing so newsworthy offered to the three magistrates: one fight – both parties bound over to keep the peace and barred from the local pubs for a year; one arrears of maintenance – adjourned for reports from a social worker; one road accident with injury – the driver concerned electing to go before a jury . . .

As noon approached she was trying to stifle yawns, though her pencil still flew over the pages of her notebook. After making such a spectacle of herself this morning (Why? Above all, how had she escaped so lightly?) she needed to get back in her editor's good graces.

Before he repeated the comment she had not been meant to hear, made behind his hand to Dennis, concerning her need to consult a doctor, or better, a psychiatrist –

What was that?

Abruptly she was alert again. This latest case was nothing special, yet it seemed to have aroused the ire of one of the magistrates. For the moment, Jenny realized in horror, she'd forgotten who he was, apart from being a local bigwig. She was leafing frantically through her papers in search of today's court schedule when memory came to her aid.

Of course! How could she not know Basil Goodsir? Wasn't he the person Vic Draycock kept accusing of planning to break up the library at Weyharrow Court?

The magistrates were conferring with the clerk of the court, as was usual when they needed to know the extent of their legal powers. Why, though, should they do so for such a trivial case? A teenage boy was arraigned before them, charged with stealing a sheep from his father. The latter was estranged from his mother and now lived with another woman on the farm where the boy had been raised. The father's evidence had been riddled with vindictiveness and

42

contradictions, while the son's defence had been – just a second . . . Jenny shuffled her notes, for she had taken down the last lot more or less subconsciously.

Yes! It sprang back from lines of neat shorthand. His defence was that the sheep he was alleged to have stolen was one he had been given, a stray lamb he himself had tended and even named, that knew him and came when called. On any other day but Thursday the *Chronicle* might well have found space for it as a human-interest item . . .

Turning, she caught the eye of a police constable who had earlier given evidence. They shrugged and smiled at one another, both at a loss to know why the magistrates were making heavy weather of a case that ought not to have been brought at all.

And then, quite unexpectedly, Basil Goodsir exploded.

Leaping to his feet, he roared, 'He stole a sheep! That violates the sacred laws of property! I say he must be hanged, right now, in public!'

His co-magistrates, and the clerk, strove in vain to quiet him.

'I won't be silent!' he raved on. 'Where in God's name is the executioner? *Take this wicked fellow out and hang him by the neck until he's dead*! Then let his body rot upon the gallows! To steal from your own son – I mean your father – is the most heinous crime conceivable! It's worse than murder, worse than blasphemy!'

An awed silence had by now pervaded the court, apart from certain officials who were conferring softly by the door through which the accused were brought in. By degrees even their voices hushed, and all eyes turned on Basil.

Who gradually seemed to realize what he'd said.

'But stealing sheep . . .' he forced out under that massed accusing gaze. 'I mean: it is a crime that calls for hanging, isn't it? I mean: I know it is!'

Dead pause.

'Well, it always used to be . . .'

'Adjourn!' shouted the senior magistrate. 'Adjourn! Get this court cleared!'

Jenny did not obey the order, but sat white-faced with pencil poised above the next sheet of her notebook, convinced that what she had just heard was as chimerical as her memory of Hal Awnham's speech last night.

Coming up, the usher – who had grown friendly with her since she joined the *Chronicle* – said chaffingly, 'Pity that's too late to make the paper this week, isn't it? I mean, what a story for you! "Local JP goes off his rocker in public! Demands death penalty for stealing sheep!"'

'Even though you heard him say it,' Jenny whispered, 'even though everybody else did, too, I wouldn't stand a prayer of making my editor believe it. Not after what I almost did to him this morning . . .'

Jumping up, she went to drown her sorrows in a pint of lunch.

But when she came back to the office, Ian Tenterwell met her with a brow like thunder.

'Were you in court when Mr Goodsir lost his marbles?'

'Of course!' – raising one hand as to defend herself.

'And you didn't phone me right away?'

'I thought you wouldn't believe me!' Jenny cried.

'Christ!' He seemed not to have heard. 'We had a reporter on the spot and still we had to get the news from someone who phoned it in on spec! Christ, there would have been time to make the front page over! With so many witnesses . . . !'

Drawing a deep breath, he clenched his fists.

'Now, Jenny, you get one thing straight – once and for all! When I send you to cover a story I expect to *get* the story, clear? From this moment you're back on probation! One more *damned stupid cockup* like the two you've managed so far today, and you'll be out on your backside, hear me? And I don't care how pretty it is! If you spent less time wiggling it at

44

people and more time concentrating on your work, I'd not be saying this! Get back to work!'

'I know all about it,' Helen said composedly. Hearing her husband's car ascend the gravel drive, she had ambushed him in the Court's entrance hall.

Pale, shaking, Basil confronted her. He said, 'How?'

'Marge Grewsam phoned me.' She was the junior of his fellow magistrates. 'By now it's all over the county.'

'I swear I don't know what came over me!' he moaned.

'Then it's time you were told.' Formal as a carving, she stood her ground. 'I phoned Ralph Haggledon at once.'

'Why in hell do I need a lawyer?'

'You may think you don't. I do! And a psychiatrist! I asked Ralph to bring one if he can.'

'Helen – !' Basil took a pace toward her. She warned him off with one hand, edge-on as though she knew karate.

'You need treatment. Mental treatment. I've known it would come to this for years. So has your father, who despairs of you! So does our lazy-minded son for pity's sake! *He* knows you're off your rocker! You must be! To be born heir to one of the biggest estates in the west of England and spend every penny you could borrow against your expectations and *still* wind up over ears in debt – from drink, from gambling, from damn-fool "businesses" on which you lost your shirt . . . And now to claim in open court that sheep-stealers should be hanged – ! You've had your chance and blown it, Basil *dear*. You're going to be declared incompetent to manage your affairs . . . and mine!'

'It's a plot!' Basil cried. 'Hatched by you and Cedric and my nitwit of a father! You've been trying to get me put away for years – !'

Outside, once more, there came the grinding sound of car-wheels.

'That will be Ralph, and, very likely, the psychiatrist,' said

45

Helen with the sweetest of skeletal smiles. 'If you hope to convince them that you aren't off your head, you'd better start figuring out excuses. Marge said there was a reporter from the *Chronicle* in court. The paper comes out on Friday, doesn't it? That's tomorrow. Your time, my darling Basil, is running out!'

She went to open the front door, leaving him to mutter over and over: 'But it *is* a capital crime to steal a sheep. I'm sure it is. I'm sure, I'm sure, I'm sure ... And I'm a magistrate, aren't I?'

For the first time since he'd had to hide from bullies at his boarding-school, Cedric was frightened. Kneeling beside Marmaduke's wicker chair in the conservatory, he whispered, 'Is my father really off his head?'

The old man answered in a voice like creaking hinges. 'If he wasn't before he married your mother, she was enough to tip the balance.'

'Does this imply she can get him put away and – ?'

'Enjoy his income, what's left of it? Yes, I imagine that's what she has in mind. Beyond that, of course, there's the question of what I'm going to leave when I die.' Marmaduke gave a dry chuckle. 'But I've never liked her, you know. I only put up with her because she bore you. Let her get her claws on my estate? Never!'

Cedric rocked back on his haunches. 'You mean – ?'

'Oh, yes! It's all entailed to you. According to the will she and Basil have seen, not until you're twenty-one, next year. If I die first, that is. But to be on the safe side, when they changed the voting age to eighteen I made a codicil she doesn't know about. Nor does her precious Mr Haggledon, because I did it through a London lawyer. What she hopes to do, you see, is get her hands on the lot before you come of age, and time – she thinks – is running out. This aberration of your father's is a godsend for her. She can't revoke my sale

46

of the freehold of the mill at Trimborne – which, by the way, I did to spite her – but ... Where was I?'

'So Dad was right to say it was a mistake? It could have yielded more if you'd sold them a lease?'

'Of course it could.' Marmaduke's legs were wrapped in a blanket; he lifted one corner to wipe his bleary eyes. 'But your father wasn't fit to be trusted with a steady income. He'd inevitably have borrowed against it and wound up in a worse mess than before. Being already deep in debt, he and Helen leaned on me for urgent funds, offering as an excuse the need to meet your school-fees, so ...' An arthritic shrug.

'You, though!' he resumed with sudden energy. 'You're more like me, or Abel, or even Reverend Matthew who was so deluded when he thought the coincidence between our name and the nickname given to his new parish was a sign from heaven. It looks as though our family's fortunes go in cycles ... Where was I?'

'Saying that I'm more like Abel and Matthew.'

'Oh, yes.' Marmaduke gathered his stiff old limbs into a tidier posture, refusing help from his grandson. 'What I meant was ... Ah, this worn-out brain of mine! What did I mean? I think you probably know.'

'If Mum does get Dad put away, she won't gain any benefit unless I let her.'

'That's right.'

The staggering implications of those two brief words took a while to register in Cedric's head. He said faintly, 'You mean that if I wanted to I could turn this place into what she'd call a hippies' haven?'

Visions of countless nubile girls prepared to bare their breasts to summer sun, and doubtless lie down with whatever stranger offered them a bed, came and went in a flash. For Marmaduke was saying sternly, 'That depends on whether I am dead! And whether, when I am, you will still want to!'

For a second Cedric had been assuming that he was. He

reproached himself . . . and suddenly found the whole affair so damned funny that he burst out laughing.

'I'm right,' his grandfather murmured.

'What? I'm sorry! It just came over me!' Cedric hauled himself to his feet.

'Do you know something?'

'What?'

'The last time I heard Basil laugh was so long ago I can't remember. And I never heard him and Helen laughing together. That's why I realized they weren't fit to be trusted with the heritage.

'You, though!' – fixing Cedric with a spear-sharp gaze. 'I can't remember when I *didn't* hear you laugh! From your cradle up! There haven't been too many jokes in my life lately. But those there have, I think I owe to you.'

For all such talk of laughter, the mood had grown abruptly solemn.

'Now go away and mess up Helen's plan,' the old man said. 'Walk in on them and make a scene. Have fun.'

'You know,' said Cedric slowly, 'that's exactly what I had in mind.'

5

There came yet another knock at the iron-studded oak door of the parsonage – a mansion too large, too gloomy for this modern age, and especially so for a widower like the Reverend Patrick Phibson.

Sitting at the desk where he had been striving to draft a sermon, he buried his face in his hands. Would this ghastly day never end? It was already past five o'clock, and he had to take evensong at six.

To confront his congregation again after this morning's débâcle – ! The prospect was unbearable, even though his memory of what he had said and done had receded to the vagueness of a dream. Yet it had been all too real!

Moreover, people had spent all day descending on him like a plague of locusts, recounting fearful tales . . .

'It's the temporary doctor,' said Mrs Judger from the doorway. She was his housekeeper, and had as usual been one of this morning's few worshippers.

In other words: *she knew.*

Forcing himself to appear calm, Mr Phibson said, 'Please show him in.'

And, during the brief moment between her turning away and the doctor's appearance, uttered another silent appeal for strength.

'Dr Gloze! Come in, sit down! Let me offer you a glass of sherry!'

Taking the chair the parson pointed at, the doctor shook his head.

'Frankly,' he said in a faint voice, 'I'm afraid to touch anything that might disturb my mind worse than has already

49

happened . . . Excuse me. I have no business intruding on you, especially since I'm not religious by conviction. It's just that I have to talk to *somebody*!'

He produced a handkerchief and mopped his forehead. He was in his late twenties, brownish-haired, clean-shaven, with a crop of freckles. He looked awful. Mr Phibson felt a stir of sympathy. He himself had been no older when he first took Orders.

'I prescribe some nonetheless!' he said heartily, and crossed to a corner table where, by force of a routine inherited from his predecessor, Mrs Judger daily filled a cut-crystal decanter and set four glasses next to it. Three of today's were still clean.

As he poured, he added over his shoulder, 'In case you think it paradoxical for a parson to prescribe for a doctor, let me admit at once that I've been thinking seriously about paying you a call.'

Steven tensed, accepting the drink and clutching the glass so tight it risked breaking. He said, 'But after the stupid way I behaved this morning – '

A wave cut the words short as Mr Phibson, his expression grave, sank into a facing chair.

'I did too,' he said. 'And I think we might usefully compare experiences. You see, young fellow . . . I'm sorry. I don't mean to sound patronizing. We hadn't met before last night, had we?'

Steven shook his head dumbly.

'Let me say how impressed I was with your no-nonsense manner. Obviously you realized at a glance that Mrs Lapsey is a self-pitying, self-glorifying fool. I don't have to be a doctor to tell that she has a heart like a horse's. Inside that scrawny frame it's going to pound away for years. Lord, she's buried three husbands!'

Steven took a cautious sip of his sherry. He said, 'I didn't know.'

50

'Why should you? You've only been in Weyharrow a few days. Here's how!'

Mr Phibson emptied his glass at a draught and made to set it on a nearby table.

But it was a bow-legged Victorian relic with a glazed top, and as glass touched glass there came a rattle and a clatter and a final slam. By the time he safely set it down his fingers, and his face, were drained of blood.

It was Steven's turn to offer comfort. Hunching forward in his chair, he said, 'The last patient I saw today said something about – '

'About my having taken leave of my senses?' Mr Phibson suggested bitterly. 'Yes, it seems that during morning service – repeating something I've done literally daily since I was ordained, bar variations due to the changing of the calendar – I made an utter fool of myself! And yet . . .' He clasped his hands together. 'And yet I *knew* as I was doing it that it was right! It was as though I were living a dream. Everything was different. Everything – '

Checking, he looked at his visitor.

'I heard something about you from Mr Ratch. Forgive me for inquiring. But was it similar?'

Steven nodded miserably.

'Even down to it being as remote as though I'd dreamed it all. I couldn't believe what I'd done until I looked up the note I'd written on Mr Cashcart's file. And then the whole horror of it overcame me! You see, I was so eager to make good down here! I've been surviving in locum posts since I graduated. I don't want to go back into the kind of hospitals I trained in, in search of a consultancy. I'd rather be an ordinary GP. And I'd set my sights on a country practice like this one. This seemed to be a chance, a better one than I ever had before. And now I've cocked it up – Oh, excuse my language!'

Mr Phibson rose to pour more sherry for them both. Resuming his chair, he said, 'I feel much the same. There was one mischief-maker in this morning's congregation who took it on himself, or herself, to phone my archdeacon, who then phoned me. Unless I can plead my way out of it, I could find myself arraigned before an ecclesiastical court. What an end that would be to my career, undistinguished though it may have been!'

Steven, cradling his glass, blinked in amazement.

'Do they still do that sort of thing? I mean, heresy trials and all that?'

'I assure you they do. This Church of ours isn't called "established" without reason. But – Ah, you said you're not religious.'

Steven hesitated. At length he muttered, sounding embarrassed, 'I lost my faith when I first had to tend an injured baby. She was in a car that crashed and caught on fire. She went on crying till her strength was spent, and then she died.'

'Hearing you say that,' said Mr Phibson, 'brings to mind not so much the heretical beliefs that this morning I felt convinced my congregation shared, as the conclusion I find myself being driven to this evening, concerning the all-too-concrete reality of evil as a Power.' He contrived to make the capital letter audible. 'I plan to address that subject at evensong, and again on Sunday when I can expect a somewhat larger – ah – audience ... But you didn't come to hear my plaints. It is clear that you are deeply troubled. Though a weak unworthy vessel, can I help?'

Gazing at the carpet, Steven said, 'Did Mr Ratch explain exactly what I did?'

'He said something about telling someone – let me see – to plunge his hand into a new-killed chicken.'

'That's correct.' Steven drained his glass with a gesture like a blow to an enemy. 'Later, though, I remembered where I got it from! It's real!'

Mr Phibson stared. 'What do you mean?'

'It *isn't* a real treatment for arthritis! But it *was*! It was prescribed for Schumann! I was listening to a concert on Radio 3 yesterday, and the fact was mentioned. That's what made me think of it when Mr Cashcart turned up! But how on earth I could have been so – so deluded . . . That's what I can't understand!'

There was a pause, silent save for the ticking on the mantelshelf of a Victorian clock in a carved ebony case.

'I don't know much about music,' Mr Phibson said at last. 'It's one of your interests, is it?'

'I suppose you'd say so.'

'Then you should be introduced to our choral group, if they haven't cornered you already . . . Excuse me: I'm digressing. But, you know, everything you've so far said confirms me in the view I've tentatively reached.'

'Which is – ?'

'Let me offer a little more evidence before I explain in detail. Were you called to attend Mrs Flaken this morning?'

'I haven't been called to attend anybody today,' was Steven's bitter answer. 'Word of my ridiculous mistake got around so fast, thanks presumably to Mr Ratch and/or Mrs Weaper – Wait: that's not quite true.' Suddenly he seemed fully alert. 'I did have to wipe the blood off a couple of local farmers who'd been fighting. I sent one of them to hospital; his nose was broken.'

'That would have been Ken Pecklow and Harry Vikes,' the parson said. 'I heard about their – their contretemps. But you weren't told about Mary Flaken?'

'I never even heard the name.'

'Scarcely surprising . . . But suppose I were to say – Oh, this wasn't in a confessional context, and besides, dozens of people must have heard her say the same by now. Suppose I were to tell you that she came to me in tears at lunchtime and admitted being plagued by jealousy because her oldest friend from school married the man she'd set her own heart on . . . and now lives next door.'

53

He was pacing his exposition according to the reaction he read on Steven's face.

'And woke up today convinced that she and this man were married and his wife was an intruder.'

Steven sat with mouth ajar.

'She came to me because she needed to admit to somebody impersonal and in authority that she had attacked Hannah Blocket and her husband Bill – pelted them with eggs, to be exact – and it wasn't until her real husband Philip showed her their marriage certificate that she could make herself believe she'd been mistaken.'

There was a terrible solemnity in his voice.

'After what happened to me, and her, and you – and, as I am informed, certain other persons in Weyharrow, or who live here or nearby, such as our JP, Mr Basil Goodsir, who reportedly disgraced himself today in court at Chapminster – I feel driven to an inescapable conclusion. I don't imagine it will meet with your approval, but my vocation requires me to maintain a more open mind than most people do in this corrupt and secular age.'

Steven sat immobile as a statue. Eventually he husked, 'Go on.'

'Are you familiar with Mr Draycock's theories about the name of our village?'

Steven licked his lips. 'I don't believe so.'

'Well, there's no reason why you should be. Suffice it to say that he's been sowing discord in the Weyharrow Society with his claims that Wey means "pagan idol", Harrow means "site of a heathen temple" and Goodsir is a nickname for the Devil!'

'I don't know much about the history of place-names,' Steven muttered.

Mr Phibson rose and replaced his glass on the tray next to the decanter.

'He's right, it seems to me, in one sense at least. And, in

54

passing, I have the suspicion I may have been unintentionally misleading when I said earlier that I had it in mind to call on you. I meant: I felt in duty bound to do so owing to Dr Tripkin's absence abroad. You see, this was undoubtedly an ancient pagan site, a haunt of the being whom we term the Evil One. And, for what reasons we may not even guess, the Father of us all has chosen now to turn him loose again! Maybe it's owing to our laxity in morals, our tolerance of the wicked who infest the village every summer . . . Wait! That's it! It has to be!'

Standing up slowly, Steven ventured, 'You mean . . . ?'

'I mean we are being assailed by the armies of evil – *and our defences are already breached!*'

There was another pause, during which countless half-formed answers flashed through Steven's mind. He had no time to utter them. Having waited only a few seconds, Mr Phibson glanced at the clock.

'Now you must excuse me. Duty calls.'

Steven rose. 'I didn't mean to take up so much of your time. I'm afraid I wasn't thinking. You see, there's no evening surgery on Thursday, only on Monday, Wednesday and Friday . . .' He realized he was gabbling, and broke off.

'No need to apologize!' the parson said, escorting him to the door. 'I've found this discussion very helpful. What were the memorable words Marlowe put into the mouth of Mephistopheles? Ah yes: "It's sweet to have companions in adversity!" And our affliction is a dreadful one!'

Steven ventured, 'Don't you think that before mentioning your theory to – uh – in public, you ought to consult somebody else? You mentioned your archdeacon. Wouldn't he – ?'

'No need! The evidence is incontrovertible! The signs are all around us!'

Abruptly it dawned on Steven that Mr Phibson must have been consoling himself from the decanter before his own arrival at the parsonage. He said, 'But – '

' "But me no buts!" ' – with hand upraised and gleaming eyes. 'The Evil One is at work in Weyharrow, and we must fight back with all our force. I'm right. I know I'm right. You'll see!'

Grey clouds had closed overhead during the afternoon, broomed along by a chilly wind. The change in the weather matched Steven's mood.

Despite the cold, however, he noticed that an unusually large number of people were heading towards the church for evensong. What on earth were they likely to make of Mr Phibson's claims about a visitation from the Devil?

Maybe they just wanted to see him lose his mind again. It wasn't every day a priest went crazy ...

Lord, how come this village was making him so cynical so soon?

Dead leaves rustled around his feet as he trudged across the green back to the Doctor's House. During his stay he had the use of the family's guestroom, fending for himself in the kitchen of a morning, taking a snack lunch at the Bridge Hotel and his evening meal with Mr and Mrs Weaper, who lived half a mile from the green on the Fooksey road.

Mrs Weaper was far from an outstanding cook. But it was not the prospect of indigestion that made Steven so apprehensive about heading for the Weaper's now. It was the reception he could picture in his mind.

Should he brazen things out with affected defiance? After all, if a parson could blame his lapse on the Devil, a doctor ought to be able to find some equivalent excuse. Suppose, for instance, he were to bark: 'Mrs Weaper! Kindly do not remind me again of the fact that both Mr Ratch and yourself seem to be woefully unacquainted with certain medical techniques of, I must say, respectable antiquity!'

(By that time, with luck, she would be blinking at him

behind her glasses, totally at a loss.)

'Gaining the patient's confidence in what one prescribes is half the battle! I can hardly expect Mr Cashcart to feel much confidence in me after a mere pharmacist took it on himself to overrule my judgment! Be so kind as to inform him that he doesn't know everything!'

For a second he convinced himself that it might work. Then the picture in his imagination wavered and blurred, and he heard the sound of mocking laughter.

Sighing, he felt for his door-key.

At that moment, however, a car pulled up behind him, and a clear high voice called, 'Excuse me!'

He turned to see, getting out of a blue Mini, a blonde girl wearing a denim jacket, jeans and a black sweater.

'You're Dr Gloze, aren't you? Look, I know I haven't made an appointment, and I'm not even a patient here – I go to Dr Grail in Chapminster. But . . .' She hesitated, twisting her ring of car-keys round and round. Then, in a rush: 'I've got to talk to somebody! I'm afraid of losing my mind!'

Oh no. Not another of us!

Steven had been about to say, by reflex, 'I'm sorry, but there's no surgery this evening.' He cancelled the words because by this time he had taken a proper look at her. She stood some five foot three, with bright blue eyes and short and curly hair. Her round face was innocent of make-up, which he hated. She was not so much plump as – he sought the right word – chubby. His hands desired at once to curve around her . . . *Stop!*

There had been something familiar about her voice. He said slowly, 'You know who I am. May I know who you are?'

'My name's Jenny Severance. I work for the *Chapminster Chronicle*. Actually we spoke on the phone on Monday, do you remember? I put a bit about your standing in for Dr Tripkin in this week's issue. It'll be out tomorrow.' She was talking much too fast, and her hands kept folding and unfolding round those keys.

Suddenly Steven felt reckless.

'Miss Severance, how long have you been imagining that you might be losing your mind?'

'Well' – a pass of a delectable pink tongue over equally pink lips – 'only since this morning, to be honest. I did something stupid that I scarcely remember. Now, it's as vague as though I'd dreamed the whole thing. But I didn't! It's left too many traces in reality!'

'And what, as a doctor, would you expect me to do for you if I did have a surgery this evening? Send you to hospital? Listen to you for a while, pretending not to yawn, and pack you off home with a bottle of tranquillizers? Or what?'

His tone was sharper than he had intended. She turned away with a sigh.

'I'm sorry to be a nuisance. Like I said, I just need to talk to somebody. I don't know many people here – I'm in lodgings – and I blotted my copybook at work, so I wasn't inclined to discuss my trouble with anybody in the office. I suppose I might try Mr Phibson. Excuse me.'

Steven called after her, 'He's in church! And in any case you wouldn't get much sense out of him – Damn. I had no business saying that.'

Hand on the door of her car, she turned back with a puzzled expression. She said at length, 'We had a lot of very weird phone-calls at the paper today.'

'Were any of them about me?' Steven grated.

'As a matter of fact, yes.' Straightening, she gazed at him defiantly. 'And others were about Mr Phibson!'

'I see.' Steven felt suddenly calmer. 'Yet you decided to appeal to me anyway, or him instead. Why?'

'In the hope that I might turn out not to be the only person living in Weyharrow who lost their marbles today. I mean, I don't see how I can be. Not after what happened to Basil Goodsir. Did you hear about that? I was there!'

'Mr Phibson said something ... But no. Not in detail.'

She recounted the story of her day in crisp terms, concluding, 'And my editor had the gall to tick me off!'

A sense of certainty grew in Steven's mind. He said, 'Miss Severance, I can't believe there's anything worse wrong with you than there is with me, or the parson, or this magistrate you just told me about. I need to talk to someone, too. I prescribe a long chat over a few stiff drinks. At the hotel? Or the Marriage?'

'Isn't it a bit irregular for a doctor to – ?'

'Nonsense! You're not a patient of mine, or even Dr Tripkin's. And I know even fewer people in the area than you do. What about it?'

A haunted look came and went on her face. At last she said, half-inaudibly, 'All right ... But what did you mean about my not getting much sense out of Mr Phibson?'

'I shouldn't have mentioned it. Forget it.'

'No. Wait.' Light was dawning in her face. 'I've met him plenty of times since I moved here. And if what that person said who phoned the paper is to be believed ...'

She drew a deep breath.

'Never tell me he thinks the Devil is at work in Weyharrow!'

Steven started. 'How on earth did you guess? This very moment that's what he's telling his congregation! At least, that's what he was threatening to tell them.'

'You're right. A drink *is* called for. Jump in.'

'Do you mind if we walk? I need the fresh air.'

'Okay. Just let me lock the car.'

6

No one any longer called the Marriage at Cana by its full name, though it was still to be read on the sign fixed to the wall facing the road, and that sign still depicted a jovial rustic wedding-party spilling gallons of purple wine over a long trestle table. Countless attempts had been made, especially in Victorian times, to change its name back to the Slaking House, or to anything else, but the villagers had resisted on stubborn principle. An unspoken compromise had eventually been reached: the sign had been repainted, and repainted and repainted, with no attempt to portray Jesus among the company, and 'Marriage' had been made larger and the other words smaller.

Nowadays, anyway, not one customer in ten would have recognized the reference.

Tonight there was an air of gloom in the pub, totally out of keeping with the jollity portrayed on the sign. On a high shelf a colour television played a quiz game against itself, unheeded. Among a bunch of cronies at one end of the room sat swollen-lipped Ken Pecklow, recounting to everybody who would listen how Harry Vikes had turned cattle into his field of turnips, and how he was going to have the law on him. At the other end sat Harry, a triangular mask of plaster supporting the bridge of his broken nose, with two or three companions who had as much reason as he did to dislike the Pecklows. The feud between the families went back so far, not even they themselves had any clear idea of how it had arisen.

In between, on stools at the bar, were people with no axe to grind one way or another, but problems of their own to brood about. They included Tom Fidger, trying to live down the fact that he had driven his bus on the wrong side of the road; Roy Jacksett, who had sent people items they hadn't ordered; Phil Flaken, whose wife Mary – so he said – was crying non-stop and making their home unlivable; and his old friend and neighbour Bill Blocket and Bill's brother Jerry whom he'd asked along to show there were no hard feelings; and Moira O'Pheale, who was still extracting a succession of free drinks from men who wanted to find out *exactly* what Miss Knabbe had tried to do when she got into bed with her . . . not that they were learning much.

Behind the bar, alert for trouble, hovered Colin Jeggs, the landlord, and his fat wife Rosie, who was long past the stage where one could call her merely plump. Now and then they conferred in quiet tones. So long, though, as they could keep the rate of drinking down, and the Vikes and Pecklow factions separated by a neutral zone . . . If only a few more uninvolved customers would show up!

Colin brightened as the door swung wide and just the kind of folk he had been hoping for came in: Jenny, the young reporter, and the temporary doctor. He positively beamed as they sat down at the one remaining empty table in the dead centre of the room and lapsed into deep and private conversation.

He'd taken the precaution of phoning Yvonne Book, to warn her that Joe might have his evening's telly-watching interrupted, but with luck it wouldn't happen after all.

Pleasantly tired after his day's work, Stick headed for the entrance to the Marriage. He was coming to like his job more and more, even though he got precious little money for it and still less thanks. People didn't seem to realize what a chore it was on a windy afternoon to gather leaves into neat heaps around the green, then wheel them off by barrowloads to rot for compost. Someone had even asked him – yesterday? the day before? – why he didn't pile them on a bonfire, and he'd had to spend half an hour explaining why the slow fire of nature was better for the land.

It had done no good. Around here they still burned their stubble in the autumn, regardless of how many hedges caught alight, how many cars collided when their drivers were blinded by the drifting smoke . . .

Time, though, for a jar in here, his usual evening pint of local cider. And he could afford to take a flagon home to Sheila, too, which they would share when the kids were safe in bed. He didn't hold with giving children alcohol.

Thinking of children: how *could* he have imagined that Hilary and Sam were boys? He must have dreamed it!

'Evening all!' he called as he walked in.

And checked in mid-stride.

Everybody seemed to have stopped talking simultaneously save for two people at a table in the middle of the room. He knew one by sight – the fair and pretty girl who worked for the local paper – but the man with her . . . ? Oh, of course. The locum standing in for Dr Tripkin.

Stick had his own opinions about modern medicine, but he believed in everybody doing their own thing. He wouldn't hold that against the guy.

'Usual, please, Colin!' he said breezily.

When the golden pint was handed to him, he looked around for somebody to chat with. But the ranks had closed. Backs were turned whichever way he looked, except at the doctor and reporter's table, where there was the one remaining vacant chair.

'Mind if I join you?' he said.

'Ah . . . !'

'Don't worry, I'm not here to play gooseberry! I just want a chance to rest my legs while I sink this lot.' He kicked the chair around and settled on it with a sigh of gratitude, adding as he gulped his drink, 'Cheers . . . ! I'm Stick, by the way. I try to keep the village clean. You wouldn't believe how much junk people can generate in a small place like this. It makes me glad we haven't got a fish-and-chipper. Greasy wrapping-paper blowing down the road – Excuse me, I didn't mean to drive you away!'

Blinking, as the young doctor rose.

'It's all right,' he muttered. 'It was your mentioning fish and chips. I need to make a phone-call. Won't be a second, Jenny.'

And he headed for the phone at the end of the room.

Stick sank a third of his pint, glug-glug. And looked at Jenny.

'What's wrong with everyone tonight? Any idea?'

She shook her head, looking troubled.

'You're a reporter, aren't you? Keeping your finger on the pulse of the neighbourhood . . . Oh!' Inspiration dawned. 'Is it anything to do with Ken and Harry?'

He looked warily to left and right.

'Well, things seem to be calm enough right now, though of course it does take a while for that sort of thing to blow over. Is that what's making you so worried?'

'If you must know' – coldly – 'no, it's not. It's something that I'd rather not discuss.'

Stick shrugged. 'As you like. Never let it be said I meddle in people's private affairs . . . Excuse me, squire!' – tilting back his chair as Steven returned.

'Anything important?' Jenny ventured.

Steven shook his head. 'Not unless you consider Mrs Weaper's plastic food important. I rang to say I won't be back for supper.'

'Oh, I'm keeping you – '

'Not at all, not at all! I'm enjoying myself! Insofar as one can enjoy talking about this sort of thing . . . Shall we step across the road and have a bite at the hotel?'

'I'm driving you out!' Stick exclaimed, raising his half-

63

empty glass. 'Didn't mean to! Sorry! I'll be on my way soon as I've got rid of this lot!'

But, when the cider was still poised in front of his mouth, there was a grand commotion.

The door was flung wide and in marched a ruddy-faced, sturdily-built woman in a drab grey coat, clutching a black leather handbag. She looked around in search of a particular target, at first failing to spot him. Everybody fell silent anew.

'Who's that?' Steven whispered.

Stick was prompt to answer. 'It's Joyce Vikes – Harry's wife. Come to fetch him home, is my guess. Bit early, though. She isn't usually around till after nine.'

On the table, Jenny's hand sought Steven's and clasped it tight. The pressure communicated without words: *this doesn't look like an ordinary case of wife-drags-husband-home-from-pub*!

His answering squeeze implied: *You're right*!

'So there you are! I knew it, I knew it! Boozing with your mates again, you vial of wickedness, you vessel of the Anti-christ!'

Stick's eyes were sparkling. 'Just listen to her!' he whispered. 'When she hits her stride it's what they call "a proper education!"'

Joyce was advancing down the room, slapping aside with her bag hands that tried to delay her.

'What made me fool enough to marry you, with the brand of Babylon upon you? And now you've lured the Evil One to Weyharrow! Yes, you!'

On the final word she swept her bag across the table her husband was sitting at, knocking over two half-full glasses whose owners were not quick enough to snatch them out of the way.

'Been at the gin again,' Stick said with a shrug. 'It's always the same! Whenever she and Harry have a row, she heads for the good old bottle. Then of course she comes over all pious.

Used to go to a pentecostal church in Hatterbridge, I hear, before she kicked up so much fuss they threw her out. See, her and Harry got no kids. He says it's her fault and she – '

The rest of his words were drowned out. Joyce had begun to belabour her husband with her bag, while Ken Pecklow and his chums at the other end of the room burst out laughing. One of them was heard to say clearly, 'Sometimes I think I'd trade hell-fire for life with Joyce, you know!'

But she caught the words and swung around with eyes aflame.

'Who said that?'

Colin, raising the bar-flap to intervene, paused in mid-movement as Rosie touched his arm.

'Who said that?' Joyce repeated, advancing the way she'd come. 'Whichever of you fools it was, you don't know what you're talking about! Don't you realize this village is in the grip of the Evil One?'

'Oh Lord,' Steven whispered. 'She must have been in church and heard old Phibson's rantings . . .'

Stick gave him a curious glance, but had no time to say anything before Joyce blasted on.

'That's what made Parson talk so odd at meeting! That's what made my Harry act the way he did – and you may stuff *that* down your busted gob, Ken Pecklow! Best farmer in the county, is my Harry! 'Spite of all!'

'Joyce!' – from landlord Colin.

'You be quiet! You're a vessel of evil yourself! This place is curst! You and your drink corrupt even those who seek the godly Light! You're a limb of Satan!'

Colin's plump-jowled face grew red. He said, 'If that's so, why did you beg me for a bottle of gin today? *And* on tick!'

Harry had been rising slowly from his chair. Now he ran forward, but too late. Joyce's temper had reached fever pitch.

She screamed: 'The Evil One is loose in Weyharrow! It

must be true! The parson told us so! Get thee behind me, all thou forces of Babylon! Put on sackcloth and ashes and beg forgiveness – *ness* . . . Haraharcha wumble cloturanid orgle-fopsy premble prow!'

'Hmm!' Stick murmured. 'That must be what they call "speaking in tongues". She used to do it a lot, they say, over at this church they threw her out of.'

But by now Joyce was not content with speaking. Set on repeating her coup with that tableful of glasses, she made to sweep her handbag along the bar. Just in time, Rosie caught her wrist in a grip that belied the pulpy plumpness of her arm.

'Harry,' she said calmly, 'I think you'd better take her home.'

'I will!' Harry seized his wife. 'Come along!'

'No! No!' Joyce shrieked. 'I have to tell everyone what Parson said! I have to tell how Weyharrow is infested with devils and you were the first to fall into their trap! I must! I –!'

The door slammed on her cries, as Harry's friends helped him to lead her away.

There was a dead pause. Ken Pecklow broke it with a roar of laughter.

'Well, all of you heard that, didn't you? That'll be their defence in court, no doubt, when my case comes to be heard against them! But who's going to believe Harry was led by the Devil to turn his cows into my turnips? Don't Old Nick have bigger fish to fry? We'll see Harry in the looney bin before we're through – and Joyce as well!'

Abruptly he realized that no one else was laughing.

'Well,' he concluded awkwardly, 'I best get along too.'

As the door closed behind him, Stick remembered that his glass wasn't empty yet. Reaching for it, he said, 'And I'd better do the same. Carry on talking among yourselves. I didn't mean to interrupt –'

'Hang on,' Steven broke in, his face very pale. 'Stick – did you really say Stick?'

'That's what I generally get called.'

'You seem to know a lot about the people here. Far more than I do, at any rate. I'd like to talk to you for a bit. Have another. Or something else?'

'Same again, and thanks!'

'Jenny?'

'Yes please!'

While Steven was collecting fresh drinks, conversation resumed among the rest of the customers. Jenny's eyes darted hither and yon, fixing at last on a brown-haired woman on a stool at the bar who had earlier been talking animatedly with a succession of young men. Now they all seemed to be leaving in the wake of Ken and Harry, she – Moira – was looking extremely miffed.

From the doorway one man glanced back and cocked an eyebrow. Though clearly less than eager, she gathered her bag and gloves, emptied her glass, and followed him.

'I won't ever make it as a reporter,' Jenny muttered under her breath. 'I keep overlooking the obvious . . .'

'Sorry? What did you say?' – from Stick.

'Never mind . . . Steve, you wanted to ask Stick something, didn't you?' – as he set glasses on the table.

'Well, I would like to ask a few questions,' Steven agreed, resuming his chair and drawing it an inch closer to Jenny's.

'Plough ahead, squire,' Stick said expansively. 'I won't guarantee to answer, but what I can't tell you I'll happily invent . . . Sorry. I didn't mean that. But what is truth? – said jesting Pilate, and would not stay for an answer . . . Anyway, here's peeping up your kilt, *señor*!'

He sank half the fresh pint of cider, brushed drops from his moustache, tilted back his chair and looked expectant.

'Well, you see,' said Steven, 'some very odd things have apparently been going on here today. Excuse me; I do now realize who you are, though we never met before. I've seen you at work, haven't I? I'm Steven Gloze. And you know Jenny Severance – Jenny?'

She was rising, her face a mask of determination.

'Excuse me. It's my turn for the phone.'

'What about that bite to eat?'

'In a little while, maybe. My phone calls come first.'

She departed. Looking uneasy, Steven followed her with his eyes for as long as she remained in view, then turned back to Stick.

'I was about to say: there have been some odd goings-on in Weyharrow today, haven't there?'

'Well . . .' Stick folded his hands together, seeming to find the intertwining of his fingers endlessly fascinating. 'Well, if you'll forgive me for mentioning it, I heard one very funny thing about yourself.'

'From – ?' Steven steeled himself.

'From a mate of mine called Willy Cashcart.' Stick glanced around. 'He sometimes drops in here of an evening, but I don't see him. He said the chemist refused to give him what you said he ought to have – just some ordinary pills. He's tried pills. None of them ever worked, and some of them made him feel sick.'

To his incredulous relief, Steven realized he was talking to someone who wasn't going to mock him for his error. Nonetheless, he said hastily, 'I hope he realizes that –'

'You prescribed something a bit unorthodox? Sure he does. But I told him straight out: he ought to give it a whirl, at least, and he said he would. Said he'd buy a cockerel from one of the local farms. You see, me, I've always believed that all these damned pill manufacturers – like the ones at Trimborne – they're on the wrong track! Oh, I grant that when it comes down to epidemic diseases like syphilis or TB they've discovered plenty of effective treatments. But if you want to *be healthy*, that's to say avoid degenerative conditions like

68

arthritis and cancer and MS, you have to lead a healthy life and eat the right food. The trouble I have convincing the lady I live with to give her kids a proper diet . . . !'

Slurp! And the cider-glass was emptier by another inch.

'Which reminds me. You were talking about odd things happening round here.'

Steven nodded. His mind wasn't really on what Stick was saying. He had been preparing an orthodox defence of orthodox medicine when Stick forestalled him by admitting its efficacy in particular cases. He took another sip of his drink. He'd chosen white wine because he had already had so much sherry at the parsonage, but he seemed to have absorbed a remarkable number of glassfuls.

'Well, I had one happen to me today,' Stick said, cheerfully oblivious. 'When I got up, I could have sworn that Sheila's kids – that's Sheila that I'm living with – I could have sworn that they were boys. I pulled the covers off to rouse them, and they aren't.'

'You mean – ?'

But before Steven could complete the sentence Stick had added, 'Of course, after the way I got stoned last night I couldn't be surprised. I – Oh, shit. I didn't mean to say that.' He tensed. 'You're not going to shop me, are you? Isn't what you tell a doctor under a seal same as the confessional?'

Steven wasn't listening. His attention had been caught by something being said up at the bar. While he and Stick had been talking, many of the clientele had changed. The customers now present were gathered around the section of the bar where Tom Fidger sat, conversing in low tones with Colin and Rosie. From time to time one or another of them glanced around as though afraid of being overheard.

'Look, squire, I – '

'Shh! Isn't it Mr Phibson that they're talking about?'

And, clear into a transient silence, rose the words:

'Like it or bloody not, he is our parson, ain't he?'

Simultaneous expressions of alarm crossed Colin's face, and Rosie's.

And then, astonishingly, as though that had been the key to clinching a debate, half the drinkers turned away from the bar, not even emptying their glasses.

'Good night,' one of them rumbled.

'Off to say your prayers, are you?' Colin attempted in a bright tone.

But the joke met with such burning disapproval that the rest of the men joined the move towards the exit.

And were gone, leaving nobody at the bar except Tom Fidger, stirring uneasily on his stool. But he had a full pint before him and was reluctant to waste it.

'What's happened?' Steven whispered.

'Search me!' was Stick's reply. 'I never saw the like. 'Course, I've only lived in Weyharrow a few months, but ... Colin! Rosie! What's up?'

'By the sound of it,' Colin rumbled, 'Parson's gone off his head.'

Steven jumped to his feet. 'Did he really say, at evensong, that the village is being invaded by the Devil?'

'Didn't you hear Joyce? She said as much!'

'Yes, but ...' Steven clenched his fists. 'I thought that must be due to too much gin. I – '

'Wasn't just Joyce,' Rosie chimed in. 'The word's got around. And small wonder. Did you hear about the chef at the hotel?'

Dazed, Steven shook his head.

'We didn't have anything like that happen here, did we, Colin?' – glancing at her husband for confirmation. 'And that's what makes it all so odd, you see. If this were truly a stink of iniquity –'

'Sink!' Colin cut in.

'Stink!' she countered indignantly. 'A sink is a clean place, where you wash clothes and dishes! Not that you ever lend a hand for that kind of work, do you?'

Detecting a gleam in Colin's eye that harbingered the resumption of what sounded like a long-established quarrel, Steven stood up hastily.

'Well, thanks very much for your hospitality. I hope everything will be back to normal tomorrow . . . Ah! Jenny!' – with vast relief as he saw her returning from the phone. 'Did you get through?'

'Yes.' She wore a smug little smile. 'And my bloody editor is never again going to be able to accuse me of not filing a story when I find it under my nose.'

A dreadful sense of chill invaded Steven's belly. He tried to say what had been foremost in his mind; he shaped the words: 'Well, how about that dinner we were talking about? It's after nine, you know! I hadn't realized how much time had slipped away while we were chatting. But I don't suppose they stop serving much before half past.'

They remained unuttered. All of a sudden Tom Fidger, elbow on the bar, had said, 'That's her! Turn up the sound!'

And pointed to the television set, on which was displayed the face of a pale woman in horn-rimmed glasses, about forty, wearing a navy-blue jacket with gold-braided lapels.

Nervous, but exact, Rosie hit the set's remote control. At once a smug announcer's tones rang out, tinged with patronizing amusement.

' – tour guide Mrs Ella Kailet. Over to our interviewer at Victoria coach station!'

'Mrs Kailet!' – in a crisp light female voice. 'According to what we've heard, your tourist group ran amuck because you told them that Stonehenge was a beacon to guide down flying saucers, and the Tower of London was built by giants from Mars. What have you to say to that?'

Suddenly it was apparent that, behind her glasses, tears were streaming down this woman's cheeks, while the camera held her fixed in its merciless gaze.

'All I can say is that it's what I've told other tour groups,' she forced out, her voice reduced to a whimper. 'No one ever complained before.'

'And what if we confront you with the person who trained you as a guide?' The screen displayed a middle-aged man in a dark suit, brows drawn together, lips tightly pursed. 'Vincent Chank will tell a different story!'

The camera panned away to show in the background a coach with half its windows smashed.

'That's the one I fixed!' Tom Fidger roared, slamming his fist on the counter. 'I knew it was her!'

'What the hell do you mean?' Colin barked.

'Last night! On the main road! That was the coach they called me out to! Dirt in the fuel-lines, that was all it were in the long run! Took me an hour to track it down, though, 'cause she – that one you just saw up there – she kept saying they'd been blown through so it must be due to something else! I got chilled to the bloody marrow!'

'Shht!' said Rosie. But it was too late. The news-item was over, and the two presenters were sitting back and grinning at each other.

'Well, if they're going to watch telly, I'm leaving,' Stick said, rising with a sigh. His glass was empty. 'I hate the telly ... Nice talking to you, though, Doc. And you, Jenny. See you around.'

'Wait!' Steven cried. But Stick was out the door, clean forgetting about the flagon of cider he'd meant to share with Sheila.

Jenny was practically beside herself. Effortfully, Steven turned his attention back to her, and said, 'Did you get the point of all that?'

'Of course!' She jigged up and down. 'Didn't you?'

'No! Except that that man at the bar seemed to recognize the woman, and her bus ... Jenny, what about that meal? Aren't you hungry?'

72

'Yes, but I'm going back to my lodgings.' She rose and laid a hand on his shoulder. 'I'll make do with an egg or something. I left my number, so I'd best be there when the calls start coming in.'

'What calls?'

'Lots, I hope. And you'd better be around in the morning because they're bound to want quotes from you. Thanks for the drinks.'

'Who's going to want quotes from me?'

She looked vaguely surprised. 'Half the British press, I'd say. Who did you think I went to phone?'

A terrible cold sensation gathered in Steven's belly. He said faintly, 'Jenny, you can't mean –'

'Can't mean what?' she flared. 'I told you: no bloody editor is ever again going to tell me I was sitting on a story and lost it! It's Thursday night! The timing's perfect for the Sundays! Like Vic Draycock keeps saying, lots of people have heard of Weyharrow who never came near the place! Now hordes of them are going to show up, and reporters will be the spearhead!'

'Jenny – !'

But she had swung around towards the bar.

'Mr Fidger! Tom!'

'Yes, young lady?' was his prompt reply as she caught him by the arm.

'That woman on the box just now!' She pointed at the TV. Rosie had cut the sound again because news had given way to the weather forecast. 'She was on the coach you were called out to last night?'

'That's right! And if I'd known her tourists were likely to start rioting and smash its windows I'd have asked Joe Book to stand on guard! Any idea what it takes to break the glass of a coach like that? They must have been carrying hammers in their handbags!'

'Thanks, that's exactly what I wanted to hear.' Jenny

73

rounded on Steven. 'See what I mean? Thanks for the dinner invitation, but – no thanks. I must get next to my phone . . . Oh, shit! I'd forgotten! I have to walk back to my car first, don't I? Good *night*!'

She marched out, leaving a baffled silence.

'Well!' Colin said at last. 'All I can hope is that nothing worse happens between now and closing time . . . Dr Gloze, isn't it? Would you care for another?'

His wife cut in. 'Or would you like something solid? I couldn't help gathering that you were hoping to take the young lady to dinner. It's not the same, but I can have a Welsh rabbit ready in two ticks. We keep some frozen, for the microwave. That all right? With a salad, maybe?'

'Yes please,' Steven sighed. 'And you'd better lay in extra stock. For all these journalists, you know . . .'

7

'Surely you're not going out at this hour, Mrs Judger – not when it's pouring with rain!'

In the hallway of the parsonage Mr Phibson confronted his housekeeper, an umbrella tightly clutched in both her white-knuckled hands.

'After what you said about being taken over by the Devil, I'd rather not spend the night under this roof. So I'm going to my sister's. I've left your breakfast ready, and you only need to boil the kettle.'

'But –!'

'I'll be at morning service, same as usual. Whether I continue in your employment, though, is up to you.' She gave a dismissive sniff. 'Such nonsense I never did hear! Pardon the liberty, but I know where your devils hail from – out of that decanter that you empty *much* too often, even when you don't have guests!'

A dreadful suspicion invaded Mr Phibson's mind. He whispered, 'Was it you who telephoned the archdeacon?'

'Someone needed to!' Mrs Judger snapped. 'At first I had my doubts, but after what you said at evensong . . . Shut up in your study, inventing pious phrases for your Sunday sermon, you haven't heard what's going on in the village. You've set the people by the ears, you know. It's going to be a scandal. A *grand* scandal! I promise you, if there's any more such nonsense, it won't just be the archdeacon I get on to, but Mr Marmaduke! He may be old, but according to what I hear he's kept his wits about him better than that no-good son of his who went as mad as you today, and likely for the same identical cause.'

Mr Phibson stood in bewilderment. He'd rarely heard her make so long a speech before, and every word was like a blow. But resolution and opposition were growing in his mind. He countered sternly: 'So you don't believe the Evil One has power?'

'I just know how much you drank this afternoon!'

'But Dr Gloze had some of it!' Mr Phibson argued. 'You can ask him – he'll say I was prescribing it to him, like a medicine . . . No, Mrs Judger, the Evil One *does* have power, and it seems he's made a conquest of your heart! Repent before he makes a conquest of your soul!'

'Good night, Parson,' Mrs Judger said, turning with a sigh to the door and opening it to the rattle of raindrops. 'I'll be in church tomorrow morning, like I said.'

She marched into the dark.

Mr Phibson found his right hand raised, and the words of an anathema on his lips. In a ludicrous posture he hesitated for a long moment. Could she conceivably be right?

But to accept that she was also meant accepting that he himself was deranged, either through over-indulgence – as she claimed – in a harmless and refreshing beverage to which he'd been accustomed since he was an ordinand, or because the Lord had chosen to afflict him with a disorder of the mind. He was no Job, the heavens knew! But was it not enough that both his children, whom he seldom saw, had rejected the Church? Was it not enough that Maud, his helpmeet, had been carried off by emphysema?

It had to be enough! The Almighty could never punish a faithful servant with such viciousness!

He drew a deep breath and pronounced the anathema on Mrs Judger, concluding: 'And may you never darken my doorway again!'

Afterwards he felt a curious sensation of relief. When he went to bed, wearing around his neck a crucifix he had been given as a memento of his ordination but neglected for at least

76

twenty years, he slept exceptionally deeply, without dreams.

At Wearystale Flat there had been a bit of an upset, Stick having forgotten to bring home the flagon of cider he had promised. Into the bargain, the kids were trying to stay up long past their proper time.

But a hug and a kiss, plus a promise of some interesting gossip – she was a great one for gossip – and a whispered reference to the new crop of grass, which she hadn't yet sampled, sorted Sheila out in next to no time, and a bit of ranting and roaring did the same for the kids while Sheila dressed a salad for her and Stick's supper. When the girls came to say good night, teeth brushed, faces washed, everything seemed back to normal.

It must have been the second pint of cider, the one Dr Gloze had bought him, which made Stick look pointedly at the hems of their T-shirts and say, 'You know something funny?'

Anxious for yet another stay of bedtime, the girls exclaimed as one, 'What?'

'I'm sure you were boys yesterday!'

'Oh, *Stick*!' – from Sheila, half-choking as laughter met tomato-pips.

'Do you like it better being girls?' Stick continued imperturbably.

'You'll kill me with your silly jokes one of these days, you know!' Sheila reached for her water-glass and gulped a mouthful. 'You really mustn't make cracks like that while I'm eating . . .'

And then she, and he too, realized that Hilary and Sam were exchanging peculiar glances. They fell silent. Now and then kids just waited for the right juncture to say something crucial, and this felt like such a moment.

'*I* think I was a boy yesterday,' Sam said abruptly.

Hilary crowed with laughter.

77

'Yes. she must do! Know what she did at morning break? Went into the boys' toilet!'

Flushing beetroot-red, Sam muttered, 'I made a silly mistake, that's all.'

'I know! You can't tell left from right, can you? Or read the "BOYS" sign –'

Sam's face was crumpling. Sheila said sharply, 'That will do, Hilary! I'm sure you've done things just as silly as that!'

'Including today,' Sam muttered resentfully.

'Such as?' Stick put a comforting arm around her.

'When Miss Wimford told the boys to sing in music class Hilary joined in and sang louder than any of them!'

'I didn't!' Hilary cried indignantly.

'You did you did you did!' – breaking free of Stick and jumping up and down.

'I just thought she said all of us were to sing this time!' Hilary, to the grown-ups' astonishment, sounded on the verge of tears.

Stick flickered an eyebrow at Sheila. It meant: *a bad day in school today?*

Her answering grimace confirmed it. He rose. Time to play the heavy non-father again.

Well, they seemed to expect it from him . . .

'So what was all that about?' Sheila asked as he resumed his chair, this time bringing the old tobacco-tin in which he kept a minimal quantity of grass for making spliffs – just in case of a visit from the fuzz. It wasn't Joe Book they were worried about; if by this time he didn't know who in the village was dealing, he had no business being on the force, and ditto-ditto if he hadn't figured out that at a party the guests who smoked cannabis were more inclined to doze off in a corner than start a fight like the ones who got tanked up on booze, so he and his mates ought to be bloody grateful.

But harder stuff kept drifting in from Chapminster and Hatterbridge and the south-coast ports, and people who had sampled it kept pestering Stick for speed and even cocaine, which he would have no truck with, so it was inevitable that sooner or later one of his disappointed would-be customers would shop him. He was resigned.

What had Sheila just said . . . ? Oh, yes.

Dexterously loading a skin and twisting it into a tube, he said, 'It's true. When I woke up today, I was convinced your kids were boys. I must have had a vivid dream.'

'Hmm!' was her sharp retort. 'If they were they'd stand a better chance! Men stay out at the pub instead of –'

'Oh, *Shee*!' He leaned towards her coaxingly, proffering the first spliff, neater-rolled than those he would make later. 'We've been over that, and I told you I got held up by the new doctor and the girl from the *Chronicle* –'

'And I still don't think you have any right to call her a girl! Would you call a man of the same age a boy?'

Proffering a match, Stick chuckled inwardly. They had been this road before, and every time it had concluded with them intertwined in bed. He looked forward.

It worked out. There was only one false note, and that a strange one. Suddenly, for no apparent reason, Sheila said, gazing past his shoulder at the ceiling, 'Did you ever dream of being a girl?'

'What . . . ? No, not that I recall. But if reincarnation is true, next time I want to come back female and find out what I've been missing!'

Seeming not to have got the point, she said, 'I never dreamed of being a boy. Why should Hilary and Sam? Has their consciousness been raised that far already?'

'We can ask them in the morning' – his breath hot in her ear. 'Or on Saturday . . . *But not right now!*'

The phone rang. They ignored it. And again later.

Ursula Ellerford sat in the high-backed leather chair that had been her husband's. Her sweat-moist fingers were clenched on its arms and she was striving not to cry.

All around her – and she knew it, she knew it, because she could hear phone-bells ringing either side of this poky narrow house, and across the road as well – all around her was flying the information, the gossip, the *news* that should have kept her in touch the way the other members of the Weyharrow Society were kept in touch, so that at each monthly meeting they were in the swim while she, who was the voluntary secretary, who organized their visiting speakers and made sure expenses were met and told the publicity group how much they could afford for posters and reminded them to mount their fund-raising wine-and-cheese parties when the bank account was low and cleared up the mess after the members' sons, drunken louts that they were, had upset glasses and dropped lighted cigarettes or even vomited . . .

She was left high and dry, ignorant of what was going on, because of course if anybody invited her, a widow, to one of the almost nightly get-togethers in this village, any wife might imagine she was out to snatch the said wife's husband, so it was safer not to ask Ursula.

Even if they did call her 'poor' Ursula . . .

And tonight was intolerable. *Her* phone was ringing now and then, maybe because some kind soul or other – Phyllis Knabbe, for instance, who had not a grain of malice in her body – was trying to bring her up to date.

But she was being forbidden to answer!

Her two man-tall sons were glowering at the TV, watching a programme she didn't want to look at and apparently not one they would normally have stayed in for, either. But each time the phone rang one or other ordered, 'Leave it alone! It'll be about us. The yobs are after us again!'

Ursula had asked over and over, 'But what have you done?'

So far the answers had always been simultaneous: 'That stupid git of a teacher!' and 'That lying Eunice!'

It had taken her some time to make sense of the overlapping words. Once she had done so, she requested further details, and was met with grunts and curses.

In the end she cowered in her chair, realizing by slow degrees how afraid she was of her sons. Even more slowly, but with the inevitable grinding of a glacier, she began to realize she had been equally afraid of her husband . . .

And what her sons were doing was treating her as he had.

She decided that the only safe thing to do was remain absolutely still. Even though the phone was clamoring again, and more insistently, she must not betray that she had noticed it. She took a deep breath and made a heartfelt resolution, and sat *still*.

In the hallway of the Doctor's House the phone shrilled. Upstairs Steven was about to undress, gloomy after his extraordinary evening. Who would have thought that a girl like Jenny Severance was prepared to magnify an aberration on the part of the local parson into a national scandal? It was unworthy of her! Mr Phibson, obviously, needed treatment. How could he be persuaded – ?

Just a moment! If the phone was ringing here, instead of in one of the practices at Hatterbridge or Chapminster which provided emergency cover – Steven knew what night duty he himself was committed to, having taken special care to check after a bad experience in London when he found himself on call night after night without relief – it meant that someone was ringing the private number . . .

Jenny?

Steven rushed downstairs and shouted, 'Hello!'

But the voice that answered was male, unknown to him, saying: 'Doctor? This is Paul Ellerford. It's about my mother. She won't move. She won't say anything.' He was panting, and it dawned on Steven that he must be very young – at oldest, in his teens. 'We were watching telly and she just passed out!'

A shout in the background, which Steven heard clearly: 'She isn't dead! I felt her pulse! She just won't move!'

Steven heaved a deep sigh, wondering whether he had all the right items in his bag.

'Very well. Give me your address, and tell me how to get to you . . .'

After his departure the phone rang again repeatedly. At the local exchange had recently been installed an automatic device to re-route doctors' calls at prescribed times, referring them from number to number until it struck lucky. Some-one, however, had forgotten to instruct it that once a doctor had accepted a call there was a chance he might be out for a considerable while, so it should default to the emergency mode and try someone else.

Instead, it was under the mechanical impression that once a doctor's phone had been answered that was proof that he would be there until further notice. Tearful and on the verge of hysteria, other people rang, and rang, and rang . . .

Mr Jacksett nearly did, not so much for himself as for his wife Judy. Right up to closing time people had been either phoning or coming back in person to ask indignantly why their request for canned sardines had been met with tuna, or self-raising flour with wholemeal, or long-life milk with apple-juice. Couldn't he get anything right, when his prices were already higher than the supermarkets' in Chapminster and Hatterbridge?

Besides, their kids were fretting dreadfully, because Boyo the dog still had not come home . . .

What with that, and the prospect of sorting out the re-turned goods and replacing them on the shelves – *and* re-flashing everything with the proper price, for they added a penny or two to the cost of items for home delivery to cover what they paid Peter Lodd, the boy with a bicycle who took them round the village after delivering morning papers –

both of them had lost their tempers. Judy had accused her husband, one of the soberest men in Weyharrow, of being drunk because he had taken off a bare half-hour to go to the Marriage where, he said, he hoped to catch and apologize to a few of their regular customers. But it was true that during his absence she had carried on with the job, and he'd stayed out longer than he had promised, and by the time he got back she was ranting about all the food they'd have to eat that would otherwise be spoiled . . .

Roy Jacksett, being a stolid kind of person, and used to scenes of this sort if not on such a scale, kept trying to calm her throughout the rest of the evening, to such effect that she drank a second cup of the coffee he had brewed from a jar of instant returned by a customer who'd ordered a decaffeinated brand . . . and then said she couldn't get to sleep, so he must bring one of the sleeping-pills Dr Tripkin had given her.

It had been months since she last asked for one, and the label Mr Ratch had stuck on the bottle said the capsules were only safe until March of this year. Now it was October. Having grown used to discarding stock when its time expired, Mr Jacksett pointed out the fact.

It was the resulting row that made him try and phone the Doctor's House; he could see a light on. But there was no answer, and when he went to make apologies to Judy, she was snoring. Much relieved, he joined her.

But it was a long time before he got to sleep. Where *was* that bloody dog?

Business was slack this evening at the Bridge Hotel. Mr Mender decided to close the dining-room early and told Tim Wamble the chef he could clear up.

Having done so, and changed into ordinary clothes, Tim slipped into the bar for a nightcap. The landlord gave him a look of annoyance – he didn't approve of his employees mixing with the clientele – but said nothing. Staff were hard to find, and apart from his peculiar lapse this morning Tim had proved hard-working and reliable.

There were a couple of customers Tim didn't know talking together in low tones, man and wife by the look of them, and another that he did, Mr Ratch the chemist, a roly-poly man with thick glasses and a shiny bald pate. Most uncharacteristically, he was indulging in a succession of pink gins that had unlocked his tongue.

'I can't get *over* it!' he kept exclaiming, and then proceeded to describe what it was he couldn't get over. By the weary expression on Mr Mender's face, Tim deduced that this was far from the first time he'd said the same thing in more or less the same words.

'I mean, in a village like ours, if you can't trust the doctor and the parson, who can you trust? In the old days you'd have said the squire, I suppose, but with poor old Marmaduke Goodsir in the state he is, and Basil having behaved in that extraordinary fashion . . .'

He grew aware that Mr Mender's attention was wandering, and cast about for a fresh audience. Spotting Tim, he twisted around on his stool and demanded, 'What do *you* make of what's going on?'

'I'm afraid I don't know what you mean,' Tim answered diffidently. 'I've been in the kitchen all day.'

'You mean you haven't heard that the locum tenens sent me a prescription for a still-warm chicken on the Health Service?' Mr Ratch was delighted, and moved to the next stool, closing the gap. 'You haven't heard about Mr Phibson being possessed of the Devil, or what Basil Goodsir said about hanging people for sheep-stealing? No? Well, let me bring you up to date!'

Listening, while in some relief Mr Mender collected used glasses for Megan the barmaid to wash, Tim felt a stir of private anxiety. He'd had that strange conviction about the day's special, hadn't he? It had given him a very odd feeling to discover that Mr Mender was right and he was incontestably wrong, despite his inner certainty. Not to be able to feel you could trust your own memory . . . Had Mr Mender mentioned it?

Seemingly not, for if he had Mr Ratch would certainly have included it in his long list of inexplicable events. To the ones already mentioned he added what Mary Flaken had done to the Blockets, and what Miss Knabbe had allegedly tried to do to Mrs O'Pheale, and some very odd stories that his children had recounted when they came home from school, the younger who went locally chuckling about the behaviour of the Surrean girls, the older who was at Powte laughing inordinately about some trick that had been played on one of those stuck-up Ellerfords . . .

'Take all that together,' Mr Ratch concluded triumphantly, 'and what does it add up to? Does it sound to you like the Devil making mischief? Well, that's what Mr Phibson's saying, in so many words!'

Tim shook his head in polite wonderment, asking himself the while whether what had happened to him felt like a prank played by the Evil One. He decided that it didn't, and drained his glass.

'Well, I'm sure it'll all blow over,' he said, slipping down from his stool. 'And now, if you'll excuse me . . .'

The moment the door swung to behind him, Mr Mender leaned confidentially on the bar.

'Something just struck me,' he said. 'You know that boy's my chef? Well, he was acting very strangely this morning. Though he seems to have got over it. Still, it was extremely odd.'

Mr Ratch was preparing to listen with interest when a siren sounded on the bridge. All eyes turned to the rain-smeared but uncurtained windows facing the street, and Megan paused with a wet mug in her hand to ask the air, 'Fire engine?'

'Ambulance,' Mr Ratch said authoritatively – and there it was, rushing by with its blue lights flashing. 'Hmm! I wonder what's up. Mind if I use your phone, Nigel?' – to Mr Mender.

'Help yourself.'

He was back in a few moments, looking puzzled.

'Apparently it's Mrs Ellerford. Collapsed, or something.'

'Mrs Ellerford? Do I know her?'

'Secretary of the Weyharrow Society. Doesn't mix much otherwise.'

'Oh, yes. I recognize the name . . . Do you suppose she'll be all right? I mean, after what you've been saying about the locum –'

'At least he's had the sense to call an ambulance. She'll be taken care of. That's another funny thing, though, that I forgot to mention earlier. According to my oldest, her sons arrived at school today complaining about the way she acted at breakfast. Gave them some kind of slimy muck and insisted it was what they always had. It wasn't. They said they'd never seen it before.'

He wagged his balding head solemnly back and forth.

'Devil or no Devil, Nigel, you can't deny there's something very fishy going on.'

'Joe, where are you going?' Yvonne Book demanded, leaning over the banisters. She was ready for bed, in a pink nylon nightie, slippers trimmed with nylon fur, and a quilted blue dressing-gown. Leaving the bathroom, she had expected to find her husband undressed also. Instead he was in the hall buttoning his jacket and reaching down his rain-cape from its peg.

She added suddenly, 'Has there been another phone call that I didn't hear because the bath was running out?'

'No,' Joe sighed. The evening had been one long succession of phone calls, mostly reporting the fact that the Doctor's House wasn't answering and the callers weren't being transferred. But he'd got on to the exchange and sorted that one out. 'No,' he said again. 'But while you were upstairs I heard an ambulance go by. I think it stopped on the green. I'm just going to check up.'

'Must you?'

'I think I'd better. I'll be as quick as I can.' He blew her a kiss and hastened out into the rain.

Left alone, Yvonne wondered glumly whether she'd been right to marry a policeman.

Particularly since, now they were older, their kids were getting an awful lot of stick from their school-friends ...

But they were lucky that their father had a job. Any sort of job. So many of the other children's fathers were unemployed. Probably it was mainly jealousy.

A little comforted by the idea, she made for bed.

'Won't it come right?' Carol Draycock said anxiously, cutting off the TV sound with the remote control.

Returning to the sitting-room from the attic where he had spent the evening struggling to reconstruct the article he had written this morning with such fluency and impact, Victor scowled and shook his head.

'I don't understand what can have gone wrong!' he said for the twentieth time. 'I know all the main commands by heart! The only ones I have to look up any more are the rare ones that I scarcely have a use for. And I could have sworn I knew that one as well as my own name!'

'Did you check it in the manual?'

'Of course I did!'

'And – ?'

'And it's not the way I remember it!' He slumped into an armchair, shaking his head bewilderedly.

Carol looked at him steadily for a long moment. At last she said, 'You do so hate being wrong, don't you?'

'Show me someone who enjoys it!' was his curt response.

'Well, I think you ought to get used to the idea that you're bound to make mistakes now and then.'

'Haven't I had that abundantly demonstrated today? First the bloody machine, then the bloody Ellerford kid, then the bloody Head – I've had a day full of bloodies!'

'No need to snap at me, though . . . ! I'm going to make some hot chocolate. Want some?'

'Yes, please – No, even chocolate might keep me awake, the state I'm in. Bovril and milk, please. I didn't eat much supper, did I?'

But after his drink he sat brooding for the best part of another hour before she could persuade him to turn in.

Phyllis Knabbe lay sleepless and weeping, alone in her cottage. Moira had not come back. Doubtless she had carried out her brutal promise to find a man for the night. At any rate she had repeated it when she set off for the pub.

Oh, the looks on the faces of the people when Miss Knabbe had finally ventured out this afternoon to do some necessary shopping . . . ! The children had been worst. She had passed the bus-stop on the green just as Tom Fidger was bringing them back from school. How word had reached them, she could scarcely guess, but obviously it must have (had Tom told them? Would he have?) for they were grinning and passing mocking remarks, and she knew without needing to be told that they concerned herself. Why, Ursula Ellerford's boys, who were normally quite polite, had brushed past her without a glance of recognition. Wasn't that sufficient proof?

She had rung Ursula repeatedly. There had been no reply. She too must be shunning the idiot who had done so scandalous a thing.

And she didn't even have the company of Rufus. He had not come back all day. Not even when the rain started.

At last she forced herself out of bed and went into the

bathroom. There was a nearly full bottle of sleeping-pills in the medicine cabinet. She filled a cup with water and shook two of the tablets into her palm. Having gulped them down, she hesitated for a moment, then reached a decision.

She shook out another, and another, and another, and swallowed, and swallowed, and swallowed . . .

In the small hours Rufus squalled his lungs out at the kitchen door. Miss Knabbe was far past hearing, and for good.

Ken Pecklow was laboriously writing out a description of the damage done to his turnips, chuckling now and then at what Mr Haggledon the lawyer had suggested he should try: put in an insurance claim and leave the insurers to get the money back from the Vikeses. He was a smart one, that Mr Haggledon! He'd never have thought of it by himself.

But now and then he paused, looking worried.

Harry Vikes wasn't crazy. Or at any rate he'd never acted crazy like this before. Bad-tempered, maybe – given to drinking a bit too much now and then, though nothing like what overcame Joyce from time to time. There might be no love lost between the two families, but this wasn't the same. This was different, and very strange.

And it wasn't as though it was just another stage in a good live quarrel, either.

But . . .

Now and then in the *Farmer's Weekly* he'd seen mention of harm that could come to people using certain kinds of chemical spray. Well, everybody used them – the insecticides, the herbicides, the fungicides – and you never heard about anybody dying, or falling ill, not really. Oh, there had been that case on telly the other week, but that wasn't a farmer, just someone who'd been cycling past a field while it was being sprayed, and it hadn't been on their kind of level because the stuff came from a plane.

On the other hand, Harry had bought that new insecticide and boasted about how much it had cost and how much it was going to save him in the long run. Boasted in Ken Pecklow's hearing at the Marriage, more than once, knowing he couldn't afford any this year.

Could that have something to do with – ?

No. 'Course not. If the stuff was that dangerous, the government would never allow it to be sold. Besides, Parson had said . . . and if you couldn't trust Parson, who could you trust?

He went back to his slow and unaccustomed task, promising himself that he would attend church on Sunday. He hadn't been since Christmas.

Now and then his tongue sought out his broken tooth. It had been a small price to pay for punching Harry's nose.

Harry Vikes had put Joyce to bed, where she lay snoring like a pig. Alone in the kitchen but for Chief, he supped home-brewed cider and reflected on the day, wishing he could scratch his nose under its tent of sticking-plaster.

Everything had been a disaster. He had even failed to save the sick calf; when this afternoon he'd had to call in Mr Backery the vet, she was past help. That meant a stiff bill and nothing to show by way of benefit.

Harry could well believe that – like Parson claimed – the Devil was at work in Weyharrow. It wasn't natural, what had happened. He *couldn't* have forgotten that the piece he'd used to rent from Mr Mender belonged to Ken this year. Nonetheless, there was proof that he had . . .

But on the other hand, Joyce was religious, yet her ranting and quoting from the Bible hadn't helped them, had it?

In the end he drowsed off, head cradled on his arms, and only Chief barking to be let out aroused him in time to set about the morning milking.

When he came back Joyce was up and dressed, apparently

no worse for wear, insisting that he come with her to church.

Resignedly, he went to change and shave.

To the annoyance of the retired couple she rented a room from, the phone whose number Jenny had given to her Fleet Street contacts kept ringing almost as often as the Books' throughout the evening. After her landlord and landlady went to bed – they being early risers – she waited beside it in the hall, to snatch it up at the first tinkle.

She was becoming a little worried about the response she had evoked. On any ordinary day an item like the parson of a West Country village going off his head would at best have rated a couple of paras down-column on an inside page. But it seemed that the national Sunday papers were looking forward to a drab weekend, particularly the popular ones that didn't care to lead off with disarmament debates at the United Nations or news about Britain being censured in the European Court of Justice. A crazy parson in a village being attacked by the Devil was right up their street.

When at last a quarter-hour had elapsed without the phone-bell sounding, she remembered she had eaten nothing this evening. Stealing into the kitchen to make tea and toast and fry an egg, she thought regretfully of the meal Steven had offered to buy her.

At least, though, she had made one sound decision, by approaching the Sundays and not the dailies. Had she done the latter, the whole story could have been spoiled by a brief advance mention in a few down-market papers, no doubt in joky, mocking style, and she herself would have gained no credit. Moreover there was a good chance that, seeing Weyharrow thus pilloried, the locals would have pulled in their horns and presented a united front of denial to all reporters including herself.

As things stood, she was instructed to phone in updates tomorrow to at least two popular Sundays, to be paid for at union rate, with the virtual promise from one of them that if they couldn't spare a reporter on Saturday they'd take a story from her and splash it. Exactly what this would do to her relations with Ian Tenterwell, she hadn't figured out and didn't much care. After barely more than half a year working for the *Chronicle* she was bored and frustrated. This looked like the best chance she had so far had to break into the big time.

Her one real regret, as she slipped into bed, was that she hadn't pumped Steven sufficiently about his own weird experience this morning. It was all very well to spread the story about the Devil to the sensational newspapers; ought she not, though, to have kept in reserve the sort of commonsensical explanation that a doctor might provide? Suppose it turned out to be something in the water, for example . . . or sprayed by a local farmer (two of them had gone mad today, hadn't they?) . . . or, best of all, somebody drugging the communion wine . . . No, that wouldn't fit . . .

She was asleep, dreaming of international fame. The dreams would have been delightful if only there hadn't been a rather gauche young man constantly at her elbow, trying to tell her she had made some sort of terrible mistake.

At Weyharrow Court the evening had been indescribably awful. The din of rain on its resounding roof, spilling from neglected guttering and splashing randomly on the walls and windows, made a fitting accompaniment to the concerto of hatred within. The conductor, of course, was Helen, and Basil was the soloist.

Cedric blessed his good sense in visiting Sheila Surrean today and buying a batch of Stick's fine grass. Not only had it given him an appetite at the dinner-table despite the fact that the main course was some sort of horrid stew; it had insulated him from the vindictiveness of the barbed remarks that flashed continually between his parents, because Ralph

Haggledon the lawyer had *not* turned up with a psychiatrist in tow and had declared himself singularly unimpressed by Helen's claim that Basil was already fit for an asylum. Now and then, to their immense annoyance, he had actually been able to chuckle behind his napkin.

When that happened, old Marmaduke – normally stone-faced and glowering – relaxed his mask a trifle, going so far as once or twice to wink.

A point struck Cedric of a sudden. Could it be . . . ? Of course! It could very well be that the old man, who had talked this morning about the way his grandson laughed, had no idea of the reason. Was he not given to pronouncing strictures about the young people who descended annually on Weyharrow, accusing them in particular of being dirty and using drugs? Cedric would have rebuffed the former charge, but as to the latter . . .

That made him laugh again, this time out loud.

Just as Helen and Basil were turning to glare at him, providentially the phone in the hall rang. Cedric jumped up, tossing his napkin on his chair.

'I'll go!' – and suited action to word.

'It's probably for me!' Helen called after him. 'I'm expecting a call from Marge Grewsam.'

'You mustn't believe a word that old bitch says!' Basil cried.

'Have you forgotten how pleased you were when she put in a good word and got you added to the list of JPs?' Helen countered frostily.

Marmaduke snapped, 'Can't you two talk reasonably?'

'After what he did today – ' and 'After the way she's been treating me lately – '

The old man closed his ears. This one, in the cant phrase, could run and run.

Beyond the door, which he had pulled to behind him, Cedric snatched up the phone.

'Hello!'

'Hi!' said a man's voice that sounded vaguely familiar. 'You're Cedric, aren't you? Is Stick there?'

'Stick?' Cedric echoed through a marijuana blur. 'No, his number is –'

'Shit, man, I got his number, but he isn't answering. I got it the same time I got yours. Midsummer night!'

A flash of memory filled Cedric's mind: flaring torches, dowsers of both sexes – some, to the horror of the local folk, 'skyclad', ie naked – clutching hazel-forks and demanding admission to the grounds of the Court at midnight because they claimed to have traced a ley line that led to the lost site of the pagan temple . . .

But he'd been fairly stoned on that occasion, too, and didn't clearly remember either who the people were that he had met in the confusion, or even how he'd talked them out of achieving their intention. He did, though, recall that for the next two or three days his parents had treated him with unusual cordiality . . .

He said eventually, 'Who is this?'

'Shit, it's Chris the Pilgrim, man! You gave me my *name*, man – and I let you hump my old lady Rhoda in exchange!'

'Oh, wow,' Cedric said softly. It was coming back to him now: a bonfire dying to embers at dawn, someone singing softly to a guitar, a passionate and sweaty body under his . . . and a visit to the Special Clinic at Chapminster Hospital when he remembered what he'd been up to.

Fortunately the verdict was: no harm done.

But that night he must have been – a term that Rhoda had come up with, that made him laugh anew – silver-tongued! He had not only talked the dowsers out of invading the estate; he had lured them away to a spot he himself had thought of as magical when he was a kid, a cup of ground concealed by sloes and hawthorn bushes, and persuaded them that this was a proper place for celebrating rituals. Into the bargain he had

94

conned a burly, bearded man called Chris into accepting a new name and conceding that an act of love between the giver of the name and his own mistress would be right and fitting . . .

A twinge of conscience penetrated Cedric's foggy mind. He sought for proper words of apology. But before he found them, the phone was saying anxiously, 'Hey, man, it's nothing bad I'm calling up about! I mean, Rhoda isn't pregnant or anything!'

Whoops! That was something Cedric hadn't considered, though the interval was about right for paternity to have been ascribed.

'No, I just been trying to raise Stick, and when he didn't answer the third time, I remembered you gave us your number too, and I know you're close, so . . .'

'What exactly can I do to help?' said Cedric, choosing his question with care.

'Well, like . . .' A helpless and confused pause. In the background someone prompted Chris, and there was a muttered exchange too faint for Cedric to hear. Then: 'Yeah, that's right. See, there was this bit on the TV news. Some woman with a coachful of American tourists stopped near Weyharrow last night because the bus broke down. When she got to Stonehenge she started telling the *truth*, man! She said all about visitors from space in flying saucers, following the ley lines –'

An interruption. He resumed angrily, 'Okay, she didn't say ley lines! But she said pretty near the same thing! And there's this guy we know, works for one of the papers. He says they had this weird call tonight saying the vicar's telling everyone the Devil is playing tricks on him, right? You hear about that?'

A dreadful sense of inevitability had come over Cedric. He felt he knew precisely what he had to say, in order to disgrace his hateful father, in order to discomfit his loathsome mother, in order to shock into his grave old Marmaduke, regardless of how likeable he might be. The conversion of Weyharrow Court into a pilgrims' refuge was predestined. When he inherited . . .

He said slowly and clearly, 'Chris, you're right. But of course it doesn't mean what most people mean.'

'What?'

'I mean when most people say the Devil what they mean is . . . Shit, man, you know what I mean, don't you?' He had run out of logic partway through.

'You mean they mean the powers that go back all the way, the powers of the Old Religion. Right?'

'Yes, I do!' cried Cedric gratefully. 'And they're breaking out all over! Why, in court today my own father called for people to be hanged for stealing sheep!'

'Hey, we heard about that . . .' A muted discussion away from the mouthpiece. Cedric waited in frantic impatience.

'You still there, man? We best get off this phone – we borrowed it kind of unofficially . . . But what you said made up our minds. Doesn't matter what kind of power it is, we want to be there when it happens. We're taking to the road right now!'

'Fantastic!' Cedric breathed. 'I look forward to seeing you tomorrow.'

'Same here, man. And same from Rhoda. She says you're a great lay and if you ask again she won't say no . . . Hey, just one more thing.'

'Yes?'

'Does Stick still grow that fine grass?'

'Man!' – in a properly reproving tone. 'Don't you know better than to say that on the phone?'

'Ah, shit. You're right. But I'm pretty stoned . . . You too?'

'Me too,' said Cedric solemnly. 'See you tomorrow. And – hey!'

'Yes?'

'Spread the word! Get everybody here you can!'

'Sure, man! Think we'd keep this kind of news to ourselves? See you tomorrow!'

'See you!' Cedric echoed.

And set down the phone, his whole being atingle with a sensation like an electric charge.

Oh, when Chris and his pilgrims got here . . . and the other people they would undoubtedly rope in . . . Weyharrow was going to be shocked out of its genteel rubber boots!

As for the impact on his family – !

'Wasn't that Marge Grewsam?' His mother was looking out of the dining-room door.

'No. It was a wrong number,' Cedric said composedly.

'A wrong number? And you were on the phone that long?'

'Some wrong numbers,' Cedric murmured, 'are more interesting than right ones . . . I think I'll call it a day. Good night!'

8

Save for the squalling of Rufus the tomcat, who fell silent in the end, the zone around Weyharrow Green was quiet during the early hours of Friday. Several lights stayed on late, because a good few unemployed teenagers saw no reason to get up before noon despite the trap of habit their parents were caught in. Thanks to them, whispers of the BBC's all-night radio broadcast competed with but failed to outdo the clatter of raindrops. For the most part affairs seemed to have returned to normal.

It was about four, just after the rain moved eastward and a warmer drier belt of air replaced it, that a slow and smoky bus crossed the bridge and halted beside the green.

Cries of 'Shush!' and 'Keep your voice down!', plus the noise of luggage being disembarked, ensured that local residents were roused. Some peered through their curtains; seeing a bus, perhaps they remembered that another such had broken down nearby last night, as reported on the TV news, and went back to bed under the impression that Tom or Fred Fidger would turn out and fix it when called for.

Dawn therefore broke – dry and bright like yesterday – before anyone paid serious attention to the change that Jenny Severance had wrought on the fortunes of Weyharrow ... thanks to that reporter in London who had heard about her call and remembered that Chris and Rhoda knew the place.

Producing, to the horror of most of the villagers, who had imagined themselves free until next spring of the folk whom Vic Draycock had nicknamed pilgrims, a mushroom-like copse of tents on the green, followed within the hour by campers with sleeping-bags and ground-sheets on the riverbank beside the Marriage, and during the morning by a further influx that at noon exceeded sixty.

It was around six-thirty that the visitors began to rap on local doors, begging for water because they'd tried the village pump and found it no more than a memorial. Many of them had been to Weyharrow before, if only for the last summer solstice, and they remembered who then had or had not made them welcome. The 'nots' were the more numerous.

One door the visitors tried, behind Miss Knabbe's cottage, proved to be unlocked. Two of them entered circumspectly and filled plastic canisters at her kitchen sink.

On their departure, they let in a cat who came purring round their ankles. It looked as though he must belong here, for he headed straight for a waiting saucer of milk.

Leaving a window ajar so he could get out again, they shut the door carefully behind them and rejoined their friends. By then, other volunteers had built a bonfire. It so happened that Friday was the day for rubbish collection, so there was plenty of fuel. Mr Jacksett's shop in particular supplied many wooden fruit-boxes and cardboard cartons.

After breakfast, which was basically porage, Chris the Pilgrim suggested that they check out the time of morning service at the church, and sit in on the deal just in case. The proposal met with general approval. On the way, the visiting congregation encountered sundry friends and strangers who had hitchhiked from London and therefore taken longer to get here. All of them said that there were many more on the way; some were dripping wet because of the rain blowing eastward and preferred to head for the fire and dry out and maybe share the last of the porage; a few were far past caring about food and wanted only to find the pagan temple site at which enlightenment would come to them . . .

That handful among the visitors (and later Chris the Pilgrim admitted it was a mistake) were turned away and told to find their own salvation. But what the hell could you expect when nobody in charge had had any sleep worth mentioning?

Besides, Chris was expecting to meet Stick and Cedric, and neither had as yet shown up.

The person who did was Constable Joe Book, furious at having to turn out before breakfast. But he'd met Chris and Rhoda before, last summer, and remembered them as being among the least troublesome of the visitors. He took a tight grip on himself as he addressed them before the churchyard's lychgate.

'All right, what brings you lot back?' he said at last. 'It isn't the solstice, it isn't the equinox – not according to my diary, anyway – so what's the excuse this time?'

'Your vicar thinks the Devil is at work here,' Chris said, keeping an absolutely straight face. 'We know better. We've come to tell him so.'

'Really?' Joe sighed. And then, in a different tone: 'Really! Going to kick up a fuss in church, are you? Don't try it, or I'll have you for breach of the peace.'

Rhoda butted in. 'Of course not! We may not believe in the vicar's religion, but we're not intolerant, you know. If that's the creed he wants to follow, we're not going to try and stop him.'

By this time a dozen or more young men and women had assembled, some – of both sexes – wearing papoose-carriers with babies in. Under their combined gaze Joe felt more than a little nervous. He was still in mild shock as a result of what had happened to poor Mrs Ellerford. He'd never seen anything like the way she'd just frozen in her chair, with her eyes tight shut. The doctor said he hadn't either, but then he was, for a doctor, very young. Worse still, though, the ambulance men had said the same. They hadn't even been able to get her to lie down on the stretcher; they'd had to carry her out of the door chair and all, and lift her into the ambulance sitting up.

Weird!

And now this lot had come to plague him . . .

But he couldn't very well prevent them from going into the church, and the bell for morning service was chiming from the tower. He stood back and let them mingle with the local folk who now were also approaching the gate, dismayed to see who would be joining in their act of worship.

Most appalled of all was Mrs Judger, who confronted the policeman with a glare.

'Joe, you're not going to let this lot plague Mr Phibson, are you? You know how he feels about these – these ruffians!'

'There's no way I can stop them,' Joe said helplessly. 'But I'm on my way to phone the station. There'll be a couple of cars here before the service is over.'

'You make sure of that!' she snapped. 'They've started making a nuisance of themselves already, you know, what with the smoke of that fire they've lighted, and banging on people's doors and begging –'

Chris had paused to eavesdrop on the exchange. He called out, 'We've only been asking for water!'

'You can help yourselves from the river!'

'We would if it was safe. But we've seen the way the farmers spray their fields with poison all round here. The streams are full of chemicals, you know!'

Mrs Judger had no answer to that charge. She herself had doubts about modern farming. Instead, sniffing, she clutched her umbrella as though prepared to wield it like a club and pushed past him up the path to the church door.

At some time during the night Mr Phibson had become convinced that among his congregation this morning there would be a spy sent on the orders of his bishop to report whether he uttered any further heretical statements. Accordingly, while the worshippers settled into their pews – to judge by the noise, they were far more numerous than at any time since Easter Sunday – he peeked through the vestry door to see whether he recognized any of the diocesan staff.

He didn't. But the sight that met his eyes horrified him. He was prepared to welcome a lot of local folk whom he hadn't seen in church for months – Harry Vikes was here, for instance, dragged along by Joyce. Indeed, over breakfast he had mapped in his mind a short address, reminding them of what could happen to a community when its citizens neglected their religious obligations and hoping that they wouldn't stay away until there was another example of Satan's meddling to frighten them back.

His carefully thought-out words evaporated like frost in sunlight. What were these disgusting strangers doing here? He'd tried talking with people like them, last summer and the summer before, wanting not to be prejudiced, and found out that they were shameless pagans – amoral, drug-using, promiscuous to the point that some of the mothers couldn't say for certain who their children's fathers were...

Rage claimed him. He slammed wide the vestry door and, as the startled congregation rose to their feet, strode out before the altar, shouting.

'What are you doing in a Christian church? You're not Christians! You're not even heretics! You're servants of Satan, and you have no business in a temple of the One True God! Leave us in peace!'

One of the babies, startled by his outcry, began to wail. In a moment, the three others joined in. But the 'pilgrims' made no move to depart.

Spotting Chris, whom he remembered as a kind of spokesman for last summer's visitors, the parson advanced on him. 'Didn't you hear me? Tell these – these cronies of yours to go away! If you don't, I'm sure the decent God-fearing people of Weyharrow will drive you out, as Jesus did the money-changers!'

Chris glanced around. Several men were nodding grimly.

'It's always struck us as peculiar,' he said in a loud clear tone, 'that nowadays your Church finds plenty of room for money-changers – bankers and financiers, leeches and para-sites on our society. And professional murderers, as well. You can always find a blessing for a soldier! Yet you hate people like us, who lead our lives and hold our goods in common like the early Church. That's why we aren't Christ-ians – *because Jesus and the disciples weren't!* Come on, you lot. Next thing you know, they'll be blaming us for all the people here who went crazy yesterday, even if we were a hundred miles away.'

'The power of evil knows no limits!' Mr Phibson roared.

Chris looked him deliberately in the face. 'So I see,' he answered calmly. 'It's got a grip on you all right, hasn't it?'

A hand seized his arm and swung him around. A fist smashed into his face, jolting his head back and cutting his lower lip against his teeth. Rhoda screamed in terror.

Panting, a man with a sort of tent of sticking-plaster on his nose confronted him. 'You got no call to say that to Parson!' he rasped.

Chris touched his mouth gingerly and looked at the blood on his finger. He said after a moment, 'Why not? Wasn't he saying the same himself last night? Wasn't he saying in so many words that he'd fallen into the power of the Devil?'

Mr Phibson snatched at Harry's arm before he could launch another blow. Alarm at the violence that had ex-ploded in his church had driven away his rage.

'God forgive me,' he said in a broken voice, 'but he is right. I was possessed of the Devil at this time yesterday. Wasn't I, Mrs Judger?' – rounding on her.

She licked her thin grey lips, glancing around for advice. None was forthcoming; she had to make up her own mind. Eventually she admitted, 'That was what you *said*.'

And turned to Chris with an accusing glare.

'How come you knew that? You weren't here. You said you were a hundred miles away.'

'I was. Thanks' – to Rhoda who had passed him a handkerchief. Pressing it against his lip, he went on, 'But you don't think that sort of thing can be kept secret, do you? We heard about it from a friend, a journalist. Have any of you seen the morning papers?'

A unison gasp of horror went up from the local folk. Mr Phibson groaned aloud.

'Probably not,' called another of the newcomers. 'I remember from last summer. The papers get here late.'

'Well, there may be a nasty shock in them for some of you. May even be some reporters dropping by in a few hours' time. Of course, that means some of you may have the chance to make a bit of money on the side, selling your account of how a fight broke out in the church whose parson claims to be a victim of the Devil . . . Please be honest enough to say, at least, I didn't try to hit back! Come on, let's get out of here.'

He took Rhoda's hand and led the way. The congregation parted to let them by.

Outside, Rhoda flung her arms around him. 'Chris, you were wonderful!' she exclaimed. Two or three other voices joined in, saying things like, 'Terrific, man! Outasight!'

But Chris's expression was lugubrious.

'I don't like the vibes around here. Not at all. If they're wound up enough to act like that in church, what are they going to do tonight, after dark? Weyharrow never felt so bad before. Did it, Rho?'

She shook her head. 'We'd better try and track down Stick,' she suggested.

'Right. And Cedric, soon as possible. We just been following a lot of rumours up to now. We need to get some solid facts. Anyone remember how to find Stick's place?'

'Isn't his,' someone pointed out. 'It's hers.'

'Anyone recall the name of his old lady?'

'Sheila,' Rhoda said at once.

'Right, let's see if anyone's around that we can ask.'

*

Moira was distraught this morning. She hadn't really meant to carry out her threat about finding a man for the night, because there were damned few men in Weyharrow that she fancied. She'd just wanted to rub Phyllis Knabbe's nose in the mess she'd created. Then, of course, it had dawned on her that if she went back to sharing the cottage with her, after doing such a grand job of noising her complaints abroad, people were bound to start imagining that they did have an unnatural relationship after all. Having had only a sandwich by way of supper, but accepted drink after drink from men at the Marriage – all of whom seemed eager to help her prove that she was normal, married ones as well as single – she had finally gone home with Bill Blocket's unmarried younger brother, Jerry.

It had been pretty much of a disaster. By the time they quit the pub he was lined up for a bad case of brewer's droop, and she'd been grateful enough when the same happened to her late husband Declan never to have learned any ways of curing that sort of trouble. If it hadn't been pouring with rain she'd have left his bed in the small hours and walked back across the bridge and past the green to the cottage.

Well, she was doing it now, by daylight, because she had no option. All her belongings were there, and she had to get changed and eat some breakfast, because on Fridays and Saturdays she had a part-time job in Mr Jacksett's general store, re-stocking the shelves and the frozen meat cabinet, maybe lending a hand with unloading the wholesaler's van.

She saw few people until she had crossed the bridge, and then she noticed the tents that had sprung up on the green. She halted in mid-stride, then hastened onward.

But as she passed the church a group of untidy strangers accosted her, and she was obliged to stand and answer them, clutching her bag tightly in both hands.

All they wanted, as it happened, was to know where 'Sheila' lived. The only person of that name Moira knew in

Weyharrow was Sheila Surrean, and the two were far from friendly. In her heart of hearts Moira was a trifle jealous; Stick had the reputation of being a very nice person, and Sheila wasn't even married to him, and Declan had been such a brute . . .

She gave the best directions she could, though, and they thanked her quite politely.

When she regained the cottage, she let herself in by the back door, hoping she was unobserved. Fortunately there was no sign of Phyllis – or Rufus either, save an empty saucer and an open window. Moving hastily and quietly, Moira went up to her bedroom, finding the door of the other one shut, changed, washed, cleaned her teeth, made up and brushed her hair. That left just enough time to brew a cup of tea and gobble down some cereal, by which time Phyllis had still not appeared.

Much relieved, she locked and bolted the back door – something neither of them usually did, but with all these strangers in the village it seemed wisest – and left the front way. The school bus was picking up its passengers as she passed; it was Fred Fidger's turn to drive it today. She forced a smile in response to his call of greeting.

Were people going to spend today commiserating about what Phyllis had tried to do?

She hoped and prayed not. At least Roy and Judy Jacksett seemed to have other things on their minds; they set her to work at once restoring to their places goods that had been sent out in error yesterday. By the time they opened the door and the first customers came in at nine o'clock, Moira felt almost normal.

Until she, and they, realized that those first customers were shabby, unkempt, bearded and/or long-haired strangers. Once they'd left, in came the regulars, all of whom seemed to have been told already that news of Mr Phibson's claims about the Devil had reached the papers, and all of whom were poised between relief and disappointment because they couldn't find any mention of it.

Jenny, on the other hand, who had rushed out to buy all the papers as soon as the post office cum newsagent's opened, was very definitely relieved. Even if the story started to make national news tomorrow, it would still be strong enough to stand up in the Sundays.

'So long, Chapminster,' she found herself murmuring. 'Fleet Street, here I come!'

She sang to herself while driving to the office. The only thought of Steven that crossed her mind was a mental note to pick his brains as soon as she got the chance.

Even when facing his first-ever solo surgery as a locum, Steven could not remember being so nervous. Mrs Weaper's taciturn reaction to his offer of a good morning served to make matters worse. She looked so disapproving, it was clear she fully expected him to start cupping and bleeding, or telling patients to dance widdershins around a fire in the dark of the moon.

That last image came naturally. Looking out of the window, he had seen the bus by the green, the bonfire, and the tents.

He asked Mrs Weaper about them, but all she said was that she hoped to heaven they would disappear as quickly as they'd come. Sighing, he retreated to the consulting-room, surprised at the number of patients' records he had been handed – he'd half expected that no one would show up – steeled himself, and called for the first person waiting. According to the notes he had been given, it was a girl called Penny Wenstowe, aged eighteen.

And it was obvious at a glance what her problem was. She had curly brown hair, a shapely figure, a face that was pretty and piquant . . . but she was suffering just about the worst case of acne he had ever laid eyes on.

Riffling through her records, he saw with sinking heart that Dr Tripkin had already prescribed all the standard treatments short of isotretinoin. Was she just here for a fresh prescription? Scarcely; that could have been dealt with by Mrs Weaper making out a repeat form for his signature . . . He adopted his best professional manner.

'Well, young lady! What can I do for you today?'

Her answer amazed him.

'You saw Willy yesterday, didn't you? Mr Cashcart, that works for my dad? Mr Wenstowe the builder?'

Steven's heart quailed, but he confessed the truth.

'Well, he did like you said. Says it helped a lot. He's going to keep on with it. Not every day, like, just when the pain gets bad. My dad says it's probably better than taking all these pills that upset people so, sending them to sleep when they're at work like, or giving them' – she blushed – 'a runny tummy . . . A great one for natural things, my dad is. So what I want to know is this.'

And she proceeded to explain, with many false starts and hesitations, that her granny, who was deaf but hadn't lost her wits, wanted her to try washing her face with urine. It took about five minutes for that simple statement to emerge, and when it finally did her cheeks were glowing fiery red, but Steven sat patiently listening until Penny concluded, 'I did try to tell Dr Tripkin, but before I even finished he said it was all quackery and I must take his pills and use his ointment. And you can see all the good *that* did, can't you?'

Steven hesitated for a long moment. Then, suddenly, the memory of one of his professors at medical school came to his rescue. An unusually open-minded and experienced man, he had been fond of quoting Ambroise Paré – 'I dress the wounds, but God heals them' – and impressing on his students that there were plenty of effective remedies whose mode of operation was still a mystery, but that was no reason not to take advantage of them.

108

He had also pointed out, by way of example, that a good many skin conditions, particularly warts, were reliably reported to yield to autosuggestion or hypnosis.

Steven drew a deep breath. What could he say to make his verdict sound properly professional? Ah!

'Do you smoke, Miss Wenstowe?'

She shook her head.

'Do you drink? Alcohol, I mean?'

'Well – well, sometimes on Saturday I go to a pub.'

'That's all? What about tea or coffee?'

'Not much coffee, but – well – I do like my cuppa.'

Tannin, as a matter of fact, might do some good. Did it survive passage through the kidneys? To his dismay Steven realized he couldn't remember . . . but it didn't really matter, did it? He cancelled the impulse to reach for one of the textbooks above the desk.

'I'm going to be absolutely frank with you,' he said in a solemn tone. 'The suggested treatment is unorthodox, but I can call to mind one condition that it is notoriously effective for, and that's chilblains. Now insofar as your trouble is partly due to poor circulation in the epidermis – that's the outer layer of the skin – because if it were functioning properly the body's natural repair mechanism would be capable of getting rid of these annoying blemishes, and insofar as chilblains are a manifestation of a similar shortcoming in the metabolism . . .'

He was obviously striking the right note: plenty of authoritative-sounding jargon leading up to final approval.

'I can only say that you need have no hesitation in trying it. After all, people suffered from acne long before modern drugs were invented, and a great many of them are known to have recovered. I would recommend particularly that you do it first thing in the morning, and also last thing at night so you can leave it on to dry . . . I must ask one further question; excuse me. I see you're not wearing a ring, but of course in these days ... Do you have – ah – a boyfriend?'

'Well – '

'To be brutally frank: do you sleep alone?'

'Yes,' she whispered, and the single syllable made it very clear that she wished she didn't. Come to that: if she didn't, the condition might well clear up of its own accord. It was notoriously hormone-related.

'Then go ahead along the lines I've suggested. If you feel embarrassed about doing it, there's no need to tell anyone. When the improvement starts to show, which with luck might be within, say, a fortnight, just tell people you're growing out of it, and laugh. How about that?'

'Oh, doctor!' She jumped to her feet. 'If you knew how much better you've made me feel already ... !'

And what do I do if it doesn't help? Well, I shan't be here to find out, shall I? Though I suppose I should have said a month, rather than a fortnight ... Never mind!

That was only the beginning of the story. It seemed as though half the inhabitants of Weyharrow had been put off by Dr Tripkin's curt and bossy manner, and were now hesitantly prepared to bring their complaints to the notice of a doctor they regarded as more open-minded. The surgery ran far past the usual closing-time of noon; it was almost a quarter to one when Steven was able to sit back in relief and say over the intercom, 'That's the lot, isn't it, Mrs Weaper?'

In a tone noticeably more cordial than it had been earlier she replied, 'There's someone else waiting to see you.'

Steven double-checked the papers before him. 'I don't seem to have any more records here –'

'Not a patient,' she cut in. 'A reporter.'

Steven's heart leapt. 'You don't mean Jenny Severance?'

'No, doctor, I don't. He's from London. And he particularly wants to talk to you.'

Clearly audible in the background: 'Ask whether he'd care to have lunch with me, would you?'

110

Steven hesitated. He was reluctant. But it might offer the chance to undo some of the harm he suspected Jenny of causing, even though nothing had been in the papers yet . . .

He reached an abrupt decision.

'Very well. There aren't any housebound cases for me today, are there?'

'I don't think so . . . No.'

'Is there any news of Mrs Ellerford?'

'Yes, we had a call from Chapminster General. They've decided to transfer her to Hatterbridge.'

Steven tensed. 'You mean it's psychological – ? Don't answer that; I'll ring Hatterbridge myself this afternoon.' *And I suppose I'd better call on Mr Phibson too, the poor old so-and-so* . . . 'I'm on my way.'

The reporter was a tubby man with a ginger moustache, wearing a brown open-necked shirt under a safari jacket with all its pockets bulging. He proffered his hand.

'Dr Gloze, I'm Wallace Jantrey of the *Sunday Banner*. If you could spare me an hour of your time I'd be obliged. I've been here long enough to figure out that something odd is going on, but also that I dare not risk taking what I'm told at its face value. Oh – and likewise long enough to be told that the only decent food in town is at the Bridge Hotel. My photographer should be there already. She's been taking pictures of the hippie camp.'

9

Wallace Jantrey and Lisa Jopp – the latter tall and fortyish, with prominent teeth and greying hair – had timed their arrival in Weyharrow for eleven o'clock, when the pubs opened. Wallace was forever saying that pubs were the best place to pick up information.

He had been somewhat discomforted to find that there was only one pub *qua* pub, and it was empty but for Colin and Rosie. Not even the hippie visitors were in there yet, and the landlord indicated darkly what sort of a welcome they would get if they did try and enter. When his wife dared to point out that during the summer they had been at least as well-behaved as any average customer, he countered, 'What customers? I can't see any! I never thought anyone would take Joyce seriously! Sink of iniquity, indeed!'

'It's not just her, is it?' his wife said sombrely. 'It's Parson.'

'Ah, the parson!' Wallace leaned eagerly across the bar. 'Is it true that – ?'

'I'm not saying another word!' Colin snapped.

After vainly trying to draw him out for as long as it took him to down a pint of bitter and Lisa a gin and tonic, Wallace gave up and wandered off in search of other leads. His quest rapidly grew even more frustrating.

The Miss Severance who had fed the story to his paper, he was told firmly when he tracked down the house she lodged in, was at work. But when he phoned the *Chronicle* office he discovered she wasn't there. She'd been sent to cover a wedding, or a funeral, or something, and wouldn't be back until about three. When he asked why she wasn't in Weyharrow the person he was speaking to uttered a sound between a snort and a laugh and put the phone down.

Not a reaction, Wallace thought, calculated to inspire much belief in the story she had recounted last night . . .

No one in any of the shops, not even the post office, was prepared to talk to him; at the parsonage he was met by a stern-faced elderly woman who said sharply, 'Mr Phibson isn't talking to anybody, even me!'; and when in near-desperation he tried some of the hippie visitors he quickly discovered that none of them knew much more than he did, except that the parson must still be off his head because he'd ordered them out of morning service.

That, as Wallace glumly said to Lisa, might make headlines in the *Church Times*, but it was scarcely enough to satisfy the *Banner*.

Eventually, so as not to waste the trip, she wandered off to shoot a reel or two of film before the light turned bad; the sunshine of early morning was giving way, as it had done yesterday, to a wave of dense cloud moving from the west. Disconsolately strolling about on his own, Wallace finally struck lucky when it occurred to him to chat up a fresh-faced, bearded man in dungarees, whom at first sight he had mistaken for one of the outsiders, but who was at work with rake and broom and wheelbarrow.

'I'm Stick!' he announced cheerfully. In his downcast mood Wallace heard it as 'I'm sick!' and flinched away, afraid he'd run across one of the lunatics that government policy was turning out of asylums all over the country. But a repetition reassured him.

'What do you make of these goings-on?' he demanded.

'Oh, *I* don't know!' Stick was carrying on with his job as he talked, and his words were punctuated with the clatter of empty soft-drink cans and the rustle of paper and dry leaves. 'The person you ought to ask is Cedric.'

'Who?'

'Cedric Goodsir. Up at the Court. His old man went off his rocker yesterday, same as Parson. Seems a good few people did, including me. But my trip wasn't serious.'

That made Wallace nervous all over again, but he stuck to his guns.

'Who's his "old man"?'

'Cedric's? Oh, his father. Name of Basil. But I don't suppose he wants to talk to anyone about it.'

'Thanks anyway.'

'Be my guest!'

But when Wallace rang the Court he was met with another blank refusal. Maybe he'd go there in person this afternoon; for the time being, it made sense to pump Stick a little further.

'They won't talk to me. Who might, apart from you?'

'Well, you could try Chris the Pilgrim.'

'Who?'

'That's what he calls himself now. His real name is Utterley, so you can't blame him, can you?'

'Is he local?'

'No, he's one of that lot' – pointing at the camp on the green. Thinking he was waving at them, two or three of the women and children waved back and went on about the task of contriving lunch out of what they could afford to buy plus what they'd rescued before the dust-cart ground away with the week's rubbish.

'Thanks,' Wallace said dryly. 'I tried some of his mates already, and they don't know any more than I do.'

'Well, there's Joe Book, the long arm of the law. Don't get me wrong – he's a decent enough guy. But I haven't seen him around since . . . What time did you get here?'

'About eleven.'

'You'd have missed him, then. He whistled up a couple of carloads of fuzz at breakfast-time – something about a fight in the church, which Chris said didn't really happen, and I believe him, because the fuzz didn't make any aggro about it. Then he went off with them. I don't know where he is now. You could try his wife Yvonne, I suppose, but I think she went shopping in Chapminster. She usually does on Friday. Takes the morning bus with the schoolkids. Hey, you're a reporter, right? Why aren't you talking to Jenny, then – Jenny Severance?'

'I would if I could,' Wallace said crossly. 'Isn't there *anybody* in the village that something odd happened to yesterday who'd like to tell me all about it?'

'You could try Harry Vikes, I suppose,' Stick said in a doubtful tone. 'Though I don't imagine he's in the sweetest of tempers. He got his nose broken in a fight with Ken Pecklow yesterday morning, then one of his calves died, then his wife marched into the Marriage, drunk out of her head, and called him a limb of Satan and knocked a lot of beer over people . . . I was there. I saw that. Any use to your paper?'

'Not really,' Wallace sighed, wondering what his editor would say if he found he'd sent two of his best staffers on the trail of a non-story. 'Isn't there *anybody* else?'

Inspiration dawned on Stick's face. 'Have you tried Dr Gloze?'

'No!'

'Well, he'll still be taking morning surgery, I suppose. In that house over there, see? With the brass plate on the porch? He was one of the people that something peculiar happened to.'

'Really!' Wallace's professional ears pricked up. 'Thanks a million! Hey, Lisa!' – catching sight of her as she emerged from the churchyard and hastening over to arrange a rendez-vous at the hotel.

It did not exactly delight him when a moment later he spotted, getting out of a Ford Sierra with a car-phone aerial that had just pulled up to the petrol-pumps of the Fidgers' garage, one of his colleagues, if not a direct rival. He'd been prepared to bump into fellow-reporters, but why in the world should an up-market paper like the *Globe* think it worth sending Donald Prosher here?

And wasn't his red-haired passenger Wilf Spout, who'd won an award last year for his coverage of those kids in Cumbria suffering from radiation sickness?

Lord! They must know something we don't! But what?

At least this was only Friday. He made a mental note to book a room for himself and Lisa at the hotel before Don and Wilf and everybody else got into the act ...

'I don't quite know how to broach this,' Wallace said with feigned diffidence as he and Lisa, and Steven, handed back their menus to the waitress. 'But I have it on good authority' – he lowered his voice – 'that you yourself were affected by the curious phenomenon that overtook this village yesterday.'

He glanced around. At least Don and Wilf hadn't found their way here yet. But what might they be up to while he was otherwise engaged? Were they maybe heading for the Court, to talk to the Goodsir family ... ?

This was going to have to be a short lunch. Pray that the service would be quick! He composed himself to listen to Steven's answer.

The young doctor was saying, 'Well, I don't know how much I'm justified in saying, to be frank.'

'The truth as you see it,' Wallace countered solemnly. 'That's all I ever ask for. I don't know whether you're familiar with my work ... ?'

A brief apologetic smile. 'I don't see the *Banner* very often, I'm afraid.'

'You and millions of others!' Wallace said heartily, and scowled at Lisa for wincing because she'd heard the line uncountable times. 'But ... Well, let me put it this way. If not tomorrow, then on Sunday at the latest –'

'The name of Weyharrow is going to be splashed all over the papers, and probably our TV screens as well,' Steven cut in, his tone resigned. 'Yes, I'm quite aware of that.'

Wallace blinked. 'May one inquire why you're so sure?'

'Well, given that our local reporter did her best to – No, I oughtn't to say that. It's her job, after all.'

'Are you by any chance referring to Jenny Severance? Is she a friend of yours?' And on the strength of two nods: 'Do you happen to know how I can get hold of her? I've rung her paper and . . .'

Steven was shrugging apologetically. 'I've no idea. I only met her yesterday. Isn't she – ah – following up the story, like you?'

There was a pause full of incomprehension, confusion and bewilderment.

Into it, from the doorway of the restaurant, broke a shrill cry.

'Is the doctor here?'

All eyes turned to see a tall, brown-haired woman with tears streaming down her face, smearing wide greyish lines of diluted mascara across her cheeks. She spotted Steven and rushed over.

'You are Dr Gloze, aren't you? I'm terribly sorry, I don't want to interrupt . . . but I can't get hold of Mr Book, and Yvonne says she doesn't know when he'll be back, and I – !'

She clenched her fists and pressed them hard against her temples.

'She's dead!' she forced out. 'And I wouldn't have had that happen for the world! She's been kind to me for two whole years, kinder than my Declan ever was, and if she did do something silly just the once . . . I can't stand it! I can't believe I drove her to it!'

The room – full by now of lunch-time customers – was frozen for a second. Steven forced himself to his feet, discarding his paper napkin on the table.

'You're – ?'

'Moira O'Pheale,' the woman whimpered. 'I'm Phyllis Knabbe's lodger.'

Oh.

Steven, like everybody in the village, had heard some of yesterday's rumours but, he being a stranger, reports had reached him not at second but more like tenth hand. What he had gathered, though, was enough to give him a scrap or two of background.

'So what has happened?' he invited.

'I didn't see her this morning.' Moira glanced around, spotted the paper napkin and dabbed her eyes with it. 'But I popped back at lunch time – I've been helping out in Roy Jacksett's shop. She hadn't been down to the kitchen. My breakfast things were just as I had left them. So I went up to her room and knocked. No answer. I thought she must have gone out. But when I went into the bathroom, I saw something I must have missed before. This!'

She thrust a convulsive hand towards Steven, who took by reflex what she proffered.

It was a small plastic bottle with one of Mr Ratch's labels on it.

Empty.

With a dead hand closing round his heart he read aloud, 'Thirty Mogadon tablets. To be taken as directed ...'

'When I last saw it, it was nearly full!' Moira moaned. 'So I went into her bedroom, and ... and there she was.'

Steven drew a deep breath. 'Sorry about our lunch, Mr Jantrey. Mr Mender!' – spotting the landlord, who had come to see what the fuss was about. 'Please ring 999 and call an ambulance to Miss – '

'Miss Knabbe!' Moira forced out.

'Miss Knabbe's house. Tell them I'm going there at once. And send for the police, as well.'

Wallace pushed his chair back, exchanging a glance with

Lisa that meant: *it's a sort of a story, at least* . . .

'We'll give you a ride,' he said crisply. 'Come on!'

But before they arrived, there was a crowd already gathered: local folk nearest the house, plus a fringe of visitors diffidently hanging around the edge.

And moving authoritatively among them with a tape-recorder on a sling over his shoulder: Donald Prosher, of course. Where did the bastard get the gall? Wallace had been down that road, and concluded that having a microphone shoved under their noses turned more people off than on. He did carry a recorder, of course, but only a pocket-sized model with a built-in mike that he produced with reluctance when he had to.

Such as now! He moved in, following the doctor as he forced his way to the door, and was dismayed to see Don fall in behind. But he could scarcely argue priorities, since his rival had been on the spot before him, even though he had arrived with the person who had found the –

Body?

Yes: in one of the two poky rooms upstairs. A woman, her face pallid in death, her expression a ghastly rictus that even affected the doctor. As for Moira, she wouldn't come in, but leaned on the banister-rail, heaving as though about to vomit.

'And you are – ?' Don said with professional assurance, proffering his mike.

Ghoul!

Listening with half an ear, Wallace turned the rest of his attention back to the doctor, who was saying, 'There'll have to be a post-mortem, of course, but I'm fairly sure what the result will be.' He was touching the corpse's throat and wrists as he spoke, testing their rigidity. 'Aren't the police here yet? Christ, I wish they'd get a bloody move on. And where's that ambulance?'

He was sweating visibly.

'Where's that bottle Mrs O'Pheale showed me? Someone

119

find it, please!'

On the landing Moira was pouring her heart out. She interrupted herself long enough to say, 'You took it!'

'What . . . ? Oh, sorry. So I did.' Steven retrieved it from his jacket pocket as Lisa squeezed into the room in Wallace's wake, having paused on the stairs to change the film in her camera and mount a flashgun. She took a splendid shot of the dead body.

'Who – ? Oh, it was you, was it? Get out! Get out and take your bloody camera with you! All of you, get out of here this minute!'

'But, doctor – ' Wallace began.

'After what your friend just did, I have nothing to say to you! Nothing! Do you understand? *Get out!*'

'But – '

'*Before I pitch you down the bloody stairs!*'

News that Steven had taken sides against the invading reporters, who were even more cordially detested than the hippies, spread rapidly throughout the village. All of a sudden, within a matter of an hour or two, Weyharrow came to the collective conclusion that their temporary doctor wasn't such a bad sort after all. Even before the hotel dining-room closed at the end of the lunch hour Nigel Mender had been heard to mention that Dr Tripkin was – wasn't he? – talking about retiring some time soon . . .

And after what had happened to Mr Phibson, who himself had not been here all that long, only having accepted this living to fill in time between his wife's death and his own retirement . . . well, it was clear there would be another new parson pretty shortly.

But a village like this needed a few stable points of reference, as it were. And Basil Goodsir was never likely to provide one the way his father had before arthritis got the better of him, poor old chap – especially not after his extraordinary outburst in court yesterday.

No, from the point of view of ensuring what one might call a focus of stability in the area, one could do a lot worse than encourage a young doctor to settle here. It might take him a while to adapt to the way things were done, but given that people were already talking favourably about him . . .

Several influential persons promised that when Dr Tripkin got home from Spain they'd have a private word with him. Meanwhile, how was Basil today, since the name had cropped up? And how was Mr Phibson, come to that?

Dreadful about Mrs Ellerford, wasn't it? And Miss Knabbe – whoever would have thought it? Of course, that O'Pheale woman must know more than she had so far told . . .

Joyously, the wellsprings of gossip brimmed and overflowed. In the midst of abundant rumour, Wallace fumed and offered bribes of drink and money and met blank denials.

While Don Prosher and Wilf Spout were nowhere to be seen . . .

Nigel Mender had already been feeling uneasy. It was alarming to see normally level-headed people falling for old Phibson's senile ramblings about the Devil. In his capacity as chairman of the parish council he had phoned the diocesan office, hoping to talk to the bishop, but that dignitary happened to be away until Sunday. Mr Thummage, the archdeacon, had promised to call on Mr Phibson if he could, but his offhand manner conveyed that he felt the whole thing was a matter of mountains and molehills. Had Mr Phibson, he inquired, been over-working lately? He was of course no longer a young man, and a widower at that . . .

Mention of the fact that reportedly the Marriage had had no trade to speak of today elicited a dry chuckle.

'Well, I gather their sign verges on the blasphemous, does it not? Perhaps the Jeggses' business may pick up again when they finally decide to change it.'

Idiot!

News of Miss Knabbe's suicide brought matters to a head for Nigel Mender. Inspired by the conversation in his bar at lunch time, during the afternoon he phoned as many members of the parish council as he could, to canvass their opinion about calling a public meeting tomorrow. The consensus that emerged was in favour. It should be chaired by himself, and Mr Phibson – unavoidably – must be invited to speak. People would expect it, even those who never went to church. On the other hand, someone must be found to speak authoritatively against him, particularly since it was this rumour about ancient psychic forces that had lured that horde of hippies: over sixty so far by Constable Book's count, doubtless with more to follow.

There's that teacher fellow, of course. He's bound to show up – never misses a parish meeting. Might make a good councillor one of these years. Shame that he seems to be a bit on the mystical side himself. What's his name? Draycock, that's the one. If he hasn't sided with old Phibson already he's likely to, isn't he? So what about Basil?

Not under present circumstances?

Granted, granted. Shame old Marmaduke isn't up to it any more. He always kept a level head on his shoulders . . . And of course old Tripkin is still away . . . What about his stand-in? He seems to have made quite a hit with the peasantry, I'm told – ha-ha!

Well, one can always ask . . .

And so, in the way things are done in English villages, it was arranged.

A deputation of two councillors waited on Steven after evening surgery and invited him for a drink at the hotel. There it was made plain to him that at the meeting – which the council had agreed to organize tomorrow evening in the parish hall adjacent to the church – someone must put the case for rationality, even if it meant throwing poor old Phibson to the lions, ha-ha!

Steven struggled not to tremble visibly. He said, 'But I haven't any explanations to offer. All I know is that some very strange things have happened to a lot of people and one or two have been extremely nasty. I can't deny the facts, can I?'

'Nobody's asking you to, old boy! All we want is to be told that it can't have anything to do with devils. Have another? By the way' – in a lower tone – 'the word is out, you know, that you're making a pretty good impression. And you must have heard that Dr Tripkin is planning to retire . . . ?'

Oh dear, Steven thought. *Oh very definitely dear . . .*

10

Cedric had planned to go down to the village immediately after breakfast. But that had been last night. In the light of day the prospect of re-meeting Chris the Pilgrim and his old lady, and the rest of the troupe who travelled around in that beat-up bus, seemed infinitely less attractive.

Besides, people he detested were bound to corner him and ask after his loathsome father.

He dithered most of the morning until Peter Lodd, who delivered groceries for Mr Jacksett, arrived on his bicycle, puffing and panting after ascending the hill. The Goodsirs bought most of their provisions in Chapminster and Hatter-bridge, and luxuries were sent from London, but they made a token show of patronizing the local shops.

'I'm surprised to see you up here,' Peter said cheekily. (But Cedric had promised himself he would grow out of that sort of response, and be a true egalitarian.)

'Why so?' he returned.

'The village is full of your old mates. The ones you got so chummy with in the summer. Been asking after you!'

Well, in that case . . .

Summoning his courage, he wheeled his own bike out of the garage it shared with his father's Mercedes and his mother's Fiat, and they rode down the hill in company.

When he reached the green, he was indeed saluted as a friend, and plied with questions about what had been hap-pening in the village. He had trouble answering; he hadn't even heard about Mrs Ellerford yet, let alone Miss Knabbe's death or the set-to in the church, so he wound up learning more than he had to tell.

Eager to flee his embarrassing predicament, he glanced at his watch and discovered it was nearly one o'clock.

'What say we move in on the Marriage?' he proposed.

Chris and his friends exchanged meaningful looks.

'The landlord's been turning our lot away ever since he opened,' Rhoda said. 'It's this bit about the Devil. None of his regulars are showing up today, and he thinks if he lets us in they'll stay away for good.'

Cedric blinked, but spotted a way out. He jumped up.

'I'll go and have a word with him!' he exclaimed. 'It's probably against the law!'

'Isn't it your dad that makes the law round here!' one of the group murmured, intending to be overheard.

'Funny kind of law, in that case!' said another.

'Sorry about that, Ced,' Chris muttered. But Cedric shook his head.

'Heard about him wanting to bring back the gallows for people who steal sheep, did you? So did I! And I have to bloody live with him, you know!'

Not waiting for the obvious counter – 'So why not quit and come with us?' – he turned away.

'I'll sort out the Jeggses!' he promised, and strode off towards the river.

On the far side of the green he found Stick laying rake and shovel on his barrow, about to quit for lunch.

'Stick!' he exclaimed. 'Got time for a jar?'

'Sure! Just let me find my sandwiches . . .' He bent to retrieve a plastic bag slung underneath the barrow. 'Colin doesn't exactly love people who bring their own nosh, but by all accounts he ought to be grateful to sell anyone a drink today. Last night he seemed normal enough, but . . .'

'Is he really not getting any custom?'

'I could list by heart the people who make for the Marriage as soon as it opens, and then stay there. Plus the ones who drop in for a quick one before lunch. Plus the others who

125

sometimes drop in after lunch. Plus . . .' He spread his empty hand as he fell in beside Cedric. 'But today, not a one. Not a one. Besides, he's turning customers away! The – uh – the visitors, I mean.'

'So Chris and Rhoda told me,' said Cedric slowly. 'You know, I really begin to believe that something weird is happening, and it isn't just a trip. In the summer he was glad enough to take their money, wasn't he?'

'There might not have been much of it,' Stick concurred. 'But what they could, he and Rosie took. Today, though, the only people I've seen coming out of the Marriage were those two reporters.'

'Reporters?'

'Didn't you know? From the *Banner*, or so they said. The guy chatted me up a bit, and I mentioned you. Didn't he get in touch?'

The phone at the Court had rung an hour or so ago . . . but Cedric had been thinking about other matters. He shook his head.

'If he did, he must have spoken to my *belovèd* mother. What'll you have?' – as he pushed open the door.

'Cider, please.'

'Pint?'

'Pint.'

They drank under the baleful glare of Colin, which grew even sourer when Stick unwrapped and ate his sandwiches. Cedric's order of a pasty and salad mollified him, but only slightly.

'Know something?' Cedric said after long consideration.

'What?' Stick brushed crumbs from his beard.

'I promised Chris I'd have a word with Colin about not letting the pilgrims in. Think I dare?'

'You can always try it on. I mean, he's not likely to bar you from the place, is he? And if he does, *you* can always go over the road.'

'I know,' Cedric said unhappily. 'That's what's wrong with this bloody country . . . Excuse me! Colin! My – uh – my friends Chris and Rhoda said you aren't letting them in here, or the people who've come with them. But you never minded back in the summer, and it's more or less the same lot, you know.'

Colin exchanged glances with Rosie, then advanced to lean on the bar with folded arms.

'Back then,' he said, 'we didn't know what was going on. Now we do!'

Cedric jerked his head, for the words hit him like a slap. He said feebly, 'I don't understand!'

'We do. We've been working it out. Now we've been here five years. It's our third pub, and we've done well in all of 'em. We bought this one in good faith, knowing it had a brisk summer trade and a steady one, at least, in winter. And for the first two years it was like that – wasn't it, Rosie?'

She nodded until her much-powdered dewlap wobbled.

'But lately it's changing. Trade's dropped off. We don't get half the casual custom that we used to, nor half the regular neither. Do we, Rosie?

'And we've been thinking back, working it out. The drop began just about the time these – these pagan folk that you're so friendly with started arriving on their ungodly so-called pilgrimages!' A snort. 'No thanks to Mr Draycock for suggesting that that's what they call 'em!'

Cedric's mind filled with counter-arguments: inflation, unemployment, the impact of television, the opening of a drinks counter in the back room of Jacksett's, more young people owning cars so they could go to pubs in Chapminster or Powte or Fooksey where there were discos or other entertainment . . . He was too slow, for Colin was saying with immense deliberation, 'It's been like a leak.'

'A – what?' Cedric ventured.

'A gas leak!' Rosie said, pushing her ponderous body off

her stool and coming to stand with one arm across her husband's shoulders.

'That's exactly it,' Colin said. 'We've been discussing it, working it out. First you get the odd smell, and you don't know what it is. Then the leak gets worse. Then, if some expert doesn't come and tell you, you find out the hard way, don't you? Everything blows up!'

'And Mr Phibson had told us what's going on,' Rosie stated firmly. 'And I've been saying to Colin: we should have listened to Joyce Vikes before! *That's* why we're not letting in your pagan chums!'

There was a dead silence. Eventually Stick and Cedric met each other's eyes and by mutual agreement drained their tankards and headed for the door.

On the threshold, though, Stick turned back and said in the mildest possible tone, 'There's just one point, Colin.'

'Yes?'

'Rosie said you ought to have believed Joyce long ago.'

'Yes!'

'How do you square your complaint about declining trade with her calling your pub a den of vice? Are we to take it that you'd have been happy keeping it that way so long as your turnover stayed high? Come on, Ced. Leave them to work it out.'

And he slammed the door with quite un-Sticklike force.

Why did I never have that damned drive tarmac'ed? The grind of wheels on gravel gets on my nerves!

Fuming, Basil Goodsir flung wide the front door of the Court and strode out to confront the driver of the Sierra that was pulling to a halt.

'Who are you and what the blazes do you want?'

'My card, sir,' said the driver as he got out. 'Donald Prosher, of the *Globe*. This is my associate Mr Spout. It will make him blush as red as his hair when I mention it, but you

128

may recall that last year he won a major award for his photography. Would you by any chance be Basil Goodsir?'

Basil had been about to order them off the premises. The *Globe*, however, was one of Britain's three most highly regarded Sunday papers, albeit not the one he read himself. Taking the card, he admitted, 'As a matter of fact, I am. But' – he recollected something Helen had said earlier after answering the phone – 'I thought it was that rag the *Banner* that had sent reporters to Weyharrow!'

'Well, one never wishes to decry a colleague,' Don said in a tone of deprecation. 'But ... Yes, I'm afraid you're right. And some of the other – let's be blunt – the other scandal-sheets also have plans to invade this lovely village. I'm just hoping against hope that something can be done to prevent it being smeared nation-wide.'

'Really?' Basil growled.

'Yes, really! The way some of our contemporaries are likely to exploit a parson who has claimed from his pulpit that the Devil is at work hereabouts ...! Why, it beggars belief, doesn't it? That's why I'm appealing to you. My paper, as I trust you know, doesn't deal in that kind of crude sensationalism. But we do have a first-class record of investigative journalism. I'm much afraid that in tomorrow's press there will be at least a scattering of ill-founded rumours about Weyharrow ... My editor sent us here with an eye to setting the record straight on Sunday. An extra twenty-four hours ought to lend the necessary perspective to what's going on. That is, of course, provided we can obtain sufficient information to counteract the absurd rumours that no doubt you've heard.'

He waited, smiling. He could read Basil's face like a four-column headline. It was no surprise when he turned indoors, beckoning them to follow; nor when he met a thin fair woman in the hall – that would be his wife Helen, an ex-model, some of whose pre-marriage photos survived on the file, including a few nude shots – and said, 'These gentlemen are from the

Globe. They want an interview!'

The woman's expression had been glacial. At once it melted.

'Come into the drawing-room!' she exclaimed. 'I'll ring for coffee. Or would you care for something stronger? I remember from my modelling days ...'

Don suppressed a sigh. It was going to be one of *those*.

But he forced a smile, that broadened when Marmaduke limped from one of the rooms leading into the entrance hall, stick thumping on the stone-flagged floor, demanding what the row was all about.

He'd heard about Marmaduke. He wanted to know more. What a shame that the boy Cedric, on inquiry, proved to be elsewhere. Still, this lot between them should be good for most of the background data that he needed.

His smile threatened to become a grin. He substituted a look of gravity befitting an underling permitted access to the haunts of his superiors, and followed the effusive Helen, recorder at the ready.

Unfortunately Marmaduke proved to be a dreadful let-down.

This morning Vic Draycock had missed the excitement caused by the arrival of the hippie bus and the planting of tents on the village green; this was because he and Carol lived across the river on the Chapminster road, and he drove to work in Powte while she walked Tommy to Weyharrow primary school.

But he found out, as of the moment when he called the roll and asked why Harold Ellerford was absent.

His question was met with giggles.

'Didn't you hear?' one of the pupils said eventually. 'His mum's gone off her rocker!'

Someone else said. 'Serve 'em right! Him and that horrid Paul!'

'Know what Eunice Hoddie said to Paul?' interjected a third voice – a girl's – and the entire class rocked with laughter.

When he had sorted out a bit of sense from the kids, Victor felt duty-bound to inculcate a trace of social empathy instead of concentrating on the next stage of Britain's conquest of Canada. He had never approved of imperialism, even though probably three-quarters of his pupils would still have liked to celebrate Empire Day.

That was how he found out about Mrs O'Pheale's accusation concerning Miss Knabbe, and Tom Fidger driving on the wrong side of the road, and Eunice's put-down of Paul Ellerford . . .

Feeling as though he had spent the past day on another planet (and perhaps he might as well have done), he swallowed his initial fury and asked for further information.

He obtained it, but he didn't like it. Although of his over-large class only those who had so far spoken hailed from Weyharrow, the rest, while they shared the common detestation of the Ellerford boys, were already *au fait* with the scandal. They knew the parson had gone crazy, knew about Ken Pecklow fighting Harry Vikes, and Mary Flaken throwing eggs all round the Blockets' kitchen, and the rest. And they declared it was no more than Weyharrow deserved because it was full of wicked people.

'What makes you say that?' Vic challenged, expecting to hear that these children had been indoctrinated thanks to the publicity accorded to last summer's drug-arrests.

But the answers amounted to: *we've always known it*.

Gradually Vic came to the conclusion that he had tapped into a folk tradition. His pupils must have been told that Weyharrow was a scene of evil-doing long before they came to school. That meant the tradition must go back to the earliest incursion of Christianity!

The bell rang.

Exultant, during the morning break and over lunch Vic tried out his theory on his colleagues, most of whom were local, or had at least been in the area much longer than himself. Far from impressing them it was rebuffed by sour ripostes. Had he not considered the prosperity of the Slaking House and the jealousy it must have generated, for instance at Trimborne when the once-rich mill was falling into disuse? Had he not thought about the impact of the manor being inherited by Reverend Matthew, that notorious bigot from the distant north, who wanted to deprive the local people of their ale and cider? And how about the fact that Weyharrow had formerly been the highest navigable point on the Chap, so that it marked the limit where smugglers could dispose of foreign goods brought from the coast by water?

'We thought you'd been boning up on all this stuff!' said one of them.

Seething, Vic was more than customarily rude to his after-noon classes . . . though in his heart of hearts he was relieved to think that his article was not after all going to appear in the *Chronicle*, at least in the form that he remembered.

He'd promised it to Jenny Severance. He must get in touch and apologize.

Luckily, this term, he had arranged to have no extra duties on Friday. He was able to pile into his car immediately the final bell rang and head for home.

Or, more precisely, for Weyharrow Green. He wanted to talk to the returning pilgrims.

It was going to be another rainy night. Chris was much relieved about that; it would discourage people from coming out later on and messing with the camp-site. A good few of the younger locals, met last summer, had dropped by to say hello – some visibly tempted by the idea of cutting loose from their roots and taking to the road rather than hanging around here where there was neither work nor fun to be found – and some had warned of exactly what he feared: an attack on the hippies under cover of dark.

On the other hand, the drizzle did make it hard to keep the fire alight . . .

Such problems, though, paled into insignificance when he saw a familiar orange car draw up behind the bus, a baby Renault. He exclaimed aloud.

'That's Vic's car, isn't it? Vic Draycock's?'

Indeed it was. Hair tousled, looking harassed, Vic emerged to shake their hands and kiss some cheeks. He still looked excessively respectable in suit and tie, but one had to make allowances; it was because of his headmaster's stuck-in-the-mud attitude, and he stood to lose his job if he gainsaid the guy.

The pilgrims had debated the problem last summer, and come to the conclusion, if reluctantly, that it was better on the whole for there to be some people like Vic around, who might help to open children's minds a bit.

But when they invited him into the shelter of the bus, the first thing that he said was most unpromising: 'I daren't stay long, I'm afraid. Carol's expecting me for supper. I just dropped by to say hello and find out what's going down.'

Going down? Oh, well . . .

Chris shrugged. 'We've spent all day talking about it. We think the ancient power is stirring again. We don't know why, but it could be to do with the weather, or the pattern we created when we came here in the summer . . . What do you think?'

After a pause Vic muttered, not looking at him, 'I'm almost ashamed to admit how out of touch I've been. I had to be told what's been happening by the kids.'

'Well, you do remember we performed some rituals . . . Say, we were talking earlier to Cedric. Have you seen him this afternoon?'

Vic shook his head. 'I've been in school.'

'It's very odd. He went off to try and talk Colin and Rosie into letting us in the pub – they're putting up barricades – and Stick went with him, and we haven't seen either of them since . . . Speak of the devil!'

Stick himself was banging on the door of the bus, grinning like the proverbial Cheshire cat. Now the rain was thickening; Rhoda made haste to let him in.

Shaking wet from his hair, he climbed aboard and sat down, bestowing smiles and greetings. 'Hi! Hi, Vic! Hi! Listen, Cedric said you'd asked if I'm holding, and the answer's yes, so –'

'But what's become of Cedric?' interrupted Rhoda.

'Chickened out.'

'What?'

'After we left the Marriage he got back on his bike. Went home, I suppose. *I* don't know why! I don't think it was anything I said . . . I'll make a guess, though.'

All faces looked expectant.

'There's been a crisis at the stately home. His old man took leave of his senses yesterday, just like the parson, right?' Stick gazed seriously at each of his listeners in turn. 'And if I know Cedric, he got scared. He found Colin and Rosie treating this bit about the Devil literally. That hadn't crossed his mind before. I don't know for sure if that was it, but it could be. Could be.'

He sat back, linking hands around one upraised knee.

'That's not what I came to tell you, though.'

'Then what?' – from half a dozen throats.

'You got some hangers-on. Some steaming nits who think they're holy beggars. Seems a few of them decided this is the bit of the world that owes them a living today. So the fuzz are back. In force.'

Chris started. 'We didn't hear –'

And at almost the same moment Vic said, 'Where? I didn't

see them.'

'Down by the river. Didn't have the lights or sirens on. But I was on my way home and I saw them picking up a bunch of *samideanoj* –'

'What?'

'It's Esperanto.' Stick was forever coming up with improbable scraps of information; sometimes people pestered him with questions about his past, but he never talked of it, not even to Sheila. 'Means "people with the same ideas". I remember someone suggested we ought to invent the word "milver" so as to have a rhyme for "silver", which there isn't ... Where was I? Oh, yes: the fuzz.

'I had a word with Joe Book and apparently Tim – the chef at the hotel – caught them raiding his larder.'

'Not our lot!' Chris exclaimed.

'Nobody I recognized,' Stick concurred. 'But Joe said they'd taken a side of beef –'

'We don't eat meat!' Rhoda cried.

'I know, I *know*! And this lot weren't planning to eat it either. Said they wanted it for a blood sacrifice at midnight. Not that I see how that could work, do you?'

Rhoda said in a dead tone, 'Sounds like the lot we didn't let come with us to church this morning.'

Chris bit his lip before remembering how swollen and tender it was. He heaved a sigh.

'You could be right. Shit! That's going to get us the worst possible publicity. Here we are trying to be non-violent and respect other people's ideas, even if we don't hold with private property, and ... A sacrifice? Oh, *shit*! I knew the vibes were bad round here, but this is worse than any of us thought. Right?'

A chorus of agreement followed.

'Maybe we should sort them out,' someone proposed.

'Too late.' Stick spread his hands. 'The fuzz already did.'

There was an empty pause. Vic broke it by rising to

his feet.

'I'll see you in the morning, friends. There's a lot I want to talk about. Right now –'

'Right now,' Stick interrupted, 'why don't you tell the people about tomorrow's meeting?'

Vic shook his head, one hand on the bus's door.

'Why is it that I always seem to be ahead of everyone with news?' Stick pulled a face. 'It's set for eight, in the village hall. All we've got to do is survive the next twenty-four hours. You planning any rituals?'

Chris and Rhoda exchanged glances. She said at length, 'Maybe a private one.'

'My advice is: keep it private. After what those nitwits did . . . Well, I'd best be on my way.'

'Me too!' Vic said, as though released from mental bondage. 'Want a ride home? It's raining pretty hard.'

'Sure, thanks . . . I'll see you in the morning, gang.'

The door slammed shut. Despondent, Chris said, 'I knew the vibes were bad. I said so, didn't I? But this is *bad*. We better work the rite. There's power loose, and I don't like it much.'

'It isn't something you can like,' said Rhoda darkly. 'More something that you have to suffer. But it's loose.'

On the slippery bank of the river, as one of the police-cars drove away with the thieves, Chief Inspector Chade called out, 'Constable Book!'

Joe made towards him cautiously.

'A right lot you got on your hands, hmm?'

'They're not all like that,' Joe said after a pause. Mr Chade was new here since last summer, working out of Hatterbridge.

'No? A fight in the church this morning – complaints of smoke and nuisance from that fire of theirs – complaints about them begging door-to-door – last night a lady driven crazy, today another found dead in her bed . . . ! Isn't that enough for you?'

Joe muttered, 'It's more to do with Parson than with that lot.'

'Oh, right enough!' Chade slapped his wet leather gloves against one palm. 'But he's been claiming they're devil-worshippers, hasn't he – the parson? And what did they say they took that side of beef for? A sacrifice! Now I don't know about you, but I'm a God-fearing sort of person, and I'm more inclined to side with Mr Phibson than with them. Well?'

Joe said uncomfortably, 'They're a right bunch, yes.'

'I'm glad to hear you admit it.' Chade had a sharp tongue when he cared to use it; he was doing so. 'I think we ought to see them off our patch, don't you?'

'Soon as they find out there's nothing happening –'

'But there *is* something happening! Is it every day that a respectable maiden lady takes her own life, after being plagued with slanderous accusations? That reminds me: I'll want a word with this Mrs O'Pheale tomorrow. It's an Irish name, right? For all I know she may have IRA connections.'

Joe's jaw dropped. But before he could object, Chade had resumed.

'No, my mind's made up. At first light tomorrow we'll move them on. I'd do it now, but it would make a rumpus, and given that half of them are no doubt stoned I wouldn't care to let them loose on any public road by night.' He turned away, seeking one of his subordinates.

'Just a moment, sir!' Joe burst out. Chade scowled at him, but he ploughed on.

'Sir, there's something that you haven't thought about.'

'Such as?' Chade curled his lip.

'Reporters in the village, sir. Two of them at least, on top of our own local one. One's from the *Banner* and the other's from the *Globe*.'

Chade said slowly, 'All right, Constable. I think you have a point. Any suggestions?'

'There's going to be a public meeting tomorrow. The new doctor is supposed to speak, along with Mr Phibson. Mr Mender will be in the chair. I don't know much about Dr Gloze, but people keep saying he's very level-headed. I bumped into Penny Wenstowe – that's the daughter of our local builder – and she was over the moon about him. Mr Mender thinks quite highly of him, too. Wouldn't it be better if . . . ?'

'If what?'

'If we let these people be persuaded by the meeting that there isn't anything happening here after all? I mean, even though a few people have taken Parson's claims at face value, a visitation from the Devil isn't something they can go on crediting for long.' His confidence was growing as he realized that Chade was paying serious attention.

'I gather that the archdeacon may be coming, who can put Mr Phibson in his place from the Church's point of view. With him, and the doctor, and Mr Mender – chairman of the council – all setting their minds on clearing up the matter . . . Well, oughtn't that to disappoint them enough?'

'You mean you think that after tomorrow night they'll pack up and leave of their own accord?'

'I'd bet on it,' Joe said boldly. 'Particularly if a few people poke fun at them. They're like most of us: they like to be taken seriously, and if everyone around is laughing at them – well!'

Chade pondered for a while. Joe added diffidently, 'Besides, both the reporters are from Sunday papers. If we move them on by force tomorrow, it'll make headlines. If we let them drift away on Sunday . . . See my point?'

With unexpected cordiality Chade said, 'You have a head on your shoulders, don't you? All right, you've convinced me. They can stick around till Sunday. But if anything else

138

happens like that theft from the hotel –'

'Sir!' Joe said. 'The bunch that are left – I happen to know this for a fact – are vegetarians. They're very strict. They don't even wear leather shoes. The ones that we've knocked off weren't part of the same group.'

Chade considered a moment longer, and then shrugged.

'Very well. It's your patch, and you say you've met 'em before. I'll take what you say on trust. But bear in mind that if you're wrong I'll have your guts for garters!'

What a day it had been! That incredible morning surgery – and the evening one that had been nearly as busy – the death of Miss Knabbe – that damned photographer – the need to organize a post-mortem and an inquest, though the police took care of most of that – and now this approach from the parish councillors, half bribe and half threat . . . Hoping that his supper at the Weapers' wouldn't have been spoiled by keeping warm so long, Steven emerged from the bar of the Bridge Hotel pondering the implications, and halted in the porchway on realizing with dismay that it was raining hard. When he left the Doctor's House it had been barely drizzling, and in any case he had been piled into a car. Now his own – not his, but Dr Tripkin's, which he had the use of during his stay – was a good half-mile away.

Maybe someone here could lend him an umbrella.

He was about to turn indoors again when Jenny's Mini pulled up and she called to him.

'Steven! *Steven!* It is you, isn't it . . . ? Do you know where Wallace Jantrey is – the reporter from the *Banner*? I thought lots of pressmen would be here by now but he seems to be the only one who's bothered to turn up!'

She was leaning across to the passenger window. The light above the hotel entrance revealed an expression of anxiety and discontent on her pretty face.

'Apparently he's been trying to contact me, but some idiot

in the office forgot to tell me! I only found out by accident when some of us were having a drink after work!'

'I don't know where he is,' Steven said stonily, 'and I don't much care. Not after what his photographer did.'

'Steve –'

At precisely that moment a Ford Sierra drove past from the direction of the bridge, braked abruptly, and reversed until its tail was almost in contact with the Mini's nose. Heedless of the rain, both driver and passenger jumped out.

'Miss Severance?' the former inquired. 'Oh, good! I've been looking out for your car – I was given its number.'

'Are you Wallace Jantrey?' she exclaimed excitedly.

'Ah ... No. My name is Donald Prosher.'

'From the *Globe*? Goodness me!' At once her expression was all sunshine. 'How do you do?'

Shrugging, Steven turned to go inside and ask about that umbrella. Catching him by the arm, the Sierra's passenger said, 'Are you Dr Gloze, by any chance?'

Reporters!

But the *Globe* was a cut above the *Banner*, after all. With a sigh Steven admitted his identity.

'I'm Wilf Spout. Don and I have been looking for you too. Don, I found the doctor!'

'Great! Look, let's all go inside, shall we?'

Jenny was prompt to jump out. But Steven shook his head.

'Sorry. I've had enough of the press for one day. Besides, I'm late for dinner.'

Darting to join the others in the shelter of the porch, Jenny said, 'You can't be looking forward that much to Mrs Weaper's cooking – not after what you said about it yesterday.'

Steven was obliged to give ground. He said, 'Anyway, I've just been talking to some people in there, and I said I wanted to go away and think things over. It's going to look pretty odd if I go straight back in. And what with one thing and another I've had a hell of a day.'

'I have an idea,' Don murmured. 'Doctor, are you on call?'

'Ah . . . No, not tonight.'

'When we came through Chapminster this morning I noticed a Chinese restaurant. Suppose both of you let my paper take you out to dinner.'

'Oh, you mean the Silver Moon!' Jenny exclaimed. 'Yes, it's very good! Steve, come on! If you've really had such a bad day . . . And you can ring up Mrs Weaper when we get there.'

Abruptly it seemed like a very good idea. Steven gave a wan smile of agreement, and two minutes later the Sierra was swinging around the green and heading back towards the bridge with him and Jenny in the back seat.

He could not resist a mild gibe, though.

'You gave up pretty quick on your search for Wallace,' he murmured.

'Well . . .' Jenny bit her lip. 'He could be anywhere, couldn't he? And Mr Prosher –'

He'd been listening. Over his shoulder he said, 'Don.'

' – Don . . . He's not even from one of the papers that I got in touch with.'

She leaned forward, grasping the back of the driver's seat, as the car traversed the 'new estate' with its wipers slapping.

'So what did bring you to Weyharrow – uh – Don? Did you hear about it from someone I did ring up last night?'

To Steven it seemed that Don suppressed a faint sigh as he braked at the edge of the village before switching his head-lamps to full beam against the rain and gathering dark and making the left turn towards Chapminster.

'At the risk of disappointing you,' he murmured, 'I have to admit that we were on to the story rather earlier.'

'How?' Jenny demanded in dismay.

Steven snapped his fingers. 'Let me guess!' he exclaimed. 'That tour guide! The one who started talking about flying saucers at Stonehenge!'

'Precisely.'

141

'But –' Jenny began, then broke off. 'Oh. Her coach broke down near here, didn't it?'

'We passed the very spot a moment ago,' Don said. 'And the first person I talked to this morning was the mechanic who turned out to fix it.'

'Mr Fidger,' Wilf supplied.

'That's right.'

Jenny looked, in the occasional glow of oncoming headlights, as though she could have kicked herself. She said, 'What did Tom have to say? Or is it private?'

'Not at all,' Don said, slowing as they approached Powte and its thirty-mile limit. 'He confirmed what the coachdriver had already told us. Mrs Kailet was acting quite normally – apart from being a bit agitated, as you might expect. After all, her tour was hours behind schedule, and the people were getting somewhat stroppy.'

They passed Powte School and the end-of-limit sign, and he accelerated back to fifty.

'So what did you make of all that?' Steven ventured at length.

Don shrugged. 'That I was on to a non-story, of course. Matter of fact, I began to wonder why my editor had sent us here, because it looked as though the poor woman had simply broken down under overload. But that was before I heard about the parson. Then I changed my mind completely.'

'Quite a guy, is our editor,' Wilf grunted. 'Got *the* sharpest nose for news I ever ran across.'

'Right,' Don agreed. The lights of Chapminster loomed ahead, and he slowed abruptly. 'Jenny, do I go left or right at the next fork?'

'The restaurant is on the right but there's a no-entry further on. Take the left and I'll show you where to park, near an alley we can cut through without getting wet.'

'Fine.'

And none of them said any more of consequence until they

were seated and studying the restaurant's menu.

It was not, Steven feared, going to be a very jolly dinner. He himself was preoccupied; Jenny was downcast – whether she was in awe of Don because he worked for the prestigious *Globe*, or whether she was simply annoyed with herself for not insisting on being allowed to follow up the Weyharrow mystery instead of tamely agreeing to cover a funeral, or whatever – while Wilf was clearly taciturn by nature, and confined himself to brief utterances at extended intervals.

That left Don. And he transformed the atmosphere in two minutes flat, by handing his menu back to the waiter and addressing him in Chinese.

Astonished, the latter beamed, nodded, beamed again, and collected all their menus.

'Was that really Chinese you were talking?' Jenny breathed. 'Where did you learn it?'

'Hong Kong ... I hope you don't think I'm being high-handed, but in this kind of restaurant there are usually a few goodies not on the list. Even in a place like this they keep them for their special customers. I just told him to see what the chef can do for us, all right?'

It was indeed all right. Tiny cups of a fiery aperitif were succeeded by plates of something crispy and dark green – deep-fried seaweed, Don explained. After that came crabs with ginger, and after that chicken cooked four different ways, and after that two kinds of pork plus vegetables and straw mushrooms and, only at the very end, a dish of rice. Lastly, when Steven would have expected a dessert, there was a boiling-hot clear soup, so aromatic that it scented half the room before the waiter even poured it out.

Customers at other tables looked round enviously, wondering who these people were to merit special treatment.

'Would anybody care for a sweet?' Don suggested.

Steven leaned back and failed to repress a burp. He shook his head. A meal like that was capable of transforming the world, and for him it had done so; that was enough. The others declined as well.

'Tea?'

To that they all said yes. Waiting for it to arrive, Steven realized with a start that they had scarcely spoken as they ate.

Warmly he said, 'Don, thanks a million! I've only been at Weyharrow a week – no, less, because I arrived last Sunday – and I'd already forgotten what real food is like!'

Don gave a modest smile. For the first time Steven realized he was rather handsome: fifty, perhaps, but lean, with a craggy face and tightly-curling hair poised between light brown and grey. Reaching in his pocket, he said, 'Does anybody mind if I have a cigar? I'll try and blow the fumes well clear of you . . . Thanks. Anyone else care for one? No?'

When the cigar was lit – the waiter rushed up with a box of matches – he leaned back and breathed the first smoke at the ceiling. Still gazing upward, he said, 'Steven, what are you going to say at this meeting tomorrow?'

'I've no idea,' Steven admitted after a pause. 'I was going to spend this evening thinking about it.'

'I'd have thought something could be worked out along the lines of lies and damned lies. And . . .'

'Statistics,' Steven supplied automatically, sampling his tea and finding it still too hot to drink. 'I'm not quite sure I follow that.'

'Well, let's consider what we have.' Don set his elbows on the table. 'Suppose we start with our unfortunate tour guide. After all, that was what brought me and Wilf here.'

'You said,' Jenny butted in, 'she more than likely broke down under stress. And she'd been in contact with someone from Weyharrow who then did something silly himself: Tom.'

'I suspect you're thinking the way I was at one stage,' Don said in a warm tone that made her blush with pleasure. 'Some sort of contagious hysteria, right? How does a doctor feel

144

about that idea?'

Steven frowned. 'You mean the sort of thing they sometimes get in convents and girls' schools?'

'I suppose so.'

'Wouldn't wash.' A vigorous headshake. 'I mean, if we're still talking about what I can say at tomorrow's meeting.'

'I entirely agree.' The waiter brought an ashtray and Don tipped his cigar into it. 'The last thing people in Weyharrow want to hear is that some collective disorder is afflicting them. On the other hand, if it turned out that through some statistical freak an unusually large concentration of *individuals* experienced, in one small area, the kind of trouble that's going on all over the country all the time, but doesn't get widely reported because a single nervous breakdown, say, isn't material for headlines ... Are you with me?'

'I am indeed,' Steven said, nodding repeatedly.

'I'm not sure I am,' Jenny said obstinately. 'There is something collective about what's happening. It started with Mr Phibson, but it spread.'

'You mean the fact that even a hard-headed publican and his wife – let alone the religious fanatic wife of a hard-up farmer – fell for this yarn about the Devil taking over? Oh, I think that's about the easiest part of it to deal with, don't you, Steven?'

All of a sudden Steven's mind seemed to be working in top gear. He said, 'I can think of half a dozen ways to explain that away. I could start by poking a bit of fun at people who've watched too many horror films on telly.'

'That's the kind of line I had in mind,' Don concurred. 'Go on.'

'And when you consider every case in turn, forgetting for the moment about the others ... Yes, I like it. Don, I'm much obliged.'

'Spell it out!' Jenny insisted. 'I keep feeling like I'm left behind!'

145

'All right.' Steven tasted his tea again, found it cooler, and took a healthy swig. 'If you examine each separate case, you can find the causative factors perfectly easily. Start with Mr Phibson. If I have to do this in public, of course, it'll be rather cruel, but –'

'But better that than let the notion of a diabolic incursion fester,' Don suggested.

'Yes, exactly. Now I don't know all that much about the people who have been affected, but I did have quite a long talk with Mr Phibson, and I've also had a word with his housekeeper, Mrs Judger – whom he tried to turn out of the parsonage, by the way; did you know . . . ? Ah, you did, Don. I could have guessed. You really are a newshound, aren't you?'

That provoked Don to a modest smile. Another sip of tea, and Steven resumed, ticking names off on his fingers.

'Mr Phibson is an elderly widower and drinks too much sherry. The strain of coping even with an undemanding parish like Weyharrow has proved too much for him, just as her job proved too much for the tour guide we already mentioned. Ah – Miss Knabbe was a maiden lady probably going through the menopause, though I'm not sure how I can put that into words that won't drive half the audience away.' He hesitated.

'You, Jenny . . . No, you won't want your lapse talked about any more than I do.'

Cheeks like fire, she stared at the tablecloth. She said, 'I wouldn't like it noised around, no. But if you absolutely have to . . . I don't think people would care much about me, though. I've only been in Weyharrow six months. It's the local people and the long-settled residents that count. Mary Flaken giving way to jealousy, for instance.'

'Yes, exactly.' Steven counted off another name. 'And Tom Fidger is another such, isn't he?'

'Right. He's forever going on about how hard the times

are. You know they used to have a proper bus company, with three buses. All they have now is the one they use to take the kids to school. When that's off the road, they have to hire a replacement, and that means they're losing money.'

'And that's public knowledge,' Steven said. 'I mean, even I knew about that, after less than a week. So that leaves . . . Hmm! I haven't accounted for Basil Goodsir!'

'Broke,' said Don succinctly.

'What?' Steven blinked. 'But his family owns the Court, and half the land around here as well!'

Don breathed smoke gently towards the ceiling. 'I spent the best part of an hour at the Court today,' he said. 'I can recognize the signs when people are striving to keep up appearances. My bet is – and I've got friends in London checking this out for me – that your chum Basil is overdue for a trip to Queer Street. Does that take care of it?'

'Can I safely say that in public?' Steven whispered. 'He's bound to be there tomorrow night.'

'Tell him privately that you will unless he holds his tongue. He's a dreadful egoist. He'll do anything you want – support anything you say – if you just let him understand you know his secret.'

Steven nodded thoughtfully, his mind elsewhere. At length he said, 'Well, that provides a rational explanation for all the important cases, doesn't it?'

'You've missed out Ursula Ellerford,' said Jenny. 'But I can see how to deal with her. Widowed, husband didn't leave enough to send her sons to his old school, they're at Powte and thoroughly disliked because the other children call them snooty . . . Don, is something wrong?'

'This seems to be somebody I don't know about,' said the reporter slowly. 'Did you say Ursula Ellerford?'

Jenny nodded.

'Was she ever in Hong Kong?'

'I believe she was. Why? Did you know her there?'

147

'Was her husband's name Ted, by any chance?'

'That's right!'

'Well, I'll be damned . . . And what's become of her?'

'You'd better ask Steven.'

Who recounted the woman's plight.

'She has two sons, you say. How old are they now?'

Jenny pondered. 'Fourteen and sixteen, I suppose.'

'And who's taking care of them?'

Steven started. 'Christ! I've no idea. Does she have any relatives in the area, Jenny? Any special friends?'

'She's the secretary of the Weyharrow Society,' Jenny said. 'I don't suppose there's any need to worry.'

'No, I'm sure there isn't.' But Don was reaching for his wallet and glancing around for the waiter. 'Nonetheless, for old time's sake I think I should look in on them before I turn in. Speaking of which, it's time we settled up. I hadn't realized how late it's getting.'

Nor, said Steven and Jenny when they'd checked their watches, had they, either.

Back in Weyharrow Jenny asked to be dropped outside the hotel, where she had left her car, and suggested that she take Steven the last half-mile to the Doctor's House. Don made no objection; having asked precise directions to the Ellerfords', he seemed curiously eager to go there right away. After exchanging thanks and good nights, Steven and Jenny dashed into the Mini. It was still raining, though not as hard as earlier.

During the brief ride she said, 'Do you suppose Don is concerned about those boys because he really was friendly with the Ellerfords in Hong Kong?'

Steven glanced at her. 'What do you mean? What other reason could there be?'

'Well, Ursula seems to be just about the only person something funny happened to that he hasn't yet tracked down and interviewed. Apart, of course, from poor old Phyllis Knabbe.' She halted the car outside the Doctor's House.

'Oh, maybe I'm just growing prematurely cynical,' she went on. 'On the other hand . . . Well, when I was finally told that Wallace Jantrey was looking for me, I rang madly round all the numbers I could think of here in Weyharrow, and the only person I managed to reach was Moira. She was in Phyllis's cottage all alone and mourning. But – you know she works Fridays and Saturdays for the Jacksetts?'

'Did she go back there this afternoon?' Steven asked. It was all he could think of to say.

'Apparently yes. She said if she'd been left on her own she'd have gone crazy. Maybe she has, because she told me something very odd. The shop has a fine view of everything that's going on, doesn't it?' – with a gesture in its general direction. 'When I asked about visiting cars, she said that just after the ambulance took Phyllis away she saw Don's car – she knew it was his because they'd met when you turned up to look at the . . . the body . . .'

'I remember,' Steven sighed. 'He cornered Moira on the landing with a tape-recorder.'

'Yes. Well, later on she saw him driving out of the village.'

'He went to the Court and talked to Basil Goodsir. He said so.'

'Yes, but he also said he spent less than an hour there, and Moira said she didn't see his car come back. *I* don't think he came back until he cornered us outside the hotel. Now wouldn't you expect that if he'd passed the rest of the day around the village, asking people, he'd have heard about Ursula before we told him? Especially since it turned out to be a name he recognized?'

Steven was growing tired. As Don had said, they had spent an improbably long time in the restaurant. He said, more or less at random, 'Yes, but the boys would have been at school.'

'You think so?' she countered. 'Today? After what happened to their mother?'

'Well, maybe not ... Jenny, I'm sorry. I'm dreadfully tired. And I still have to figure out what I'm going to say at the meeting tomorrow.'

'I thought Don had solved that problem for you.'

'Well, he's certainly given me a line of argument ... Thanks for the ride. See you at the meeting?'

'Yes, of course.'

It was as though she half-expected him to kiss her goodnight, but he wasn't inclined. He opened the door. She checked him with a touch on his arm.

'Yes?'

'I can't help wondering whether it might not be worth inquiring where Don spent this afternoon. If you see him before I do, ask him, will you? And let me know?'

'Yes.' Insincerely thanks to weariness. 'Yes. Thanks again. Good night.'

His key poised at the lock, Steven glanced back at the green. In the dim glow of the street-lamps the hippies' tents glimmered, rain-wet, moving to the wind like living creatures under water. But there was scarcely any sound save the wind's, and even as he looked some of the last remaining lighted windows darkened.

Shivering of a sudden, he retreated indoors.

II

The rain continued. By midnight, from the tents on the green and from the back of the bus which had been partly converted into bunks, one could hear water splashing in the gutters like a series of miniature brooks. Despite Stick's efforts, here and there dead leaves gathered in quantities enough to block a drain-grating, and then one heard the sound of micro-waterfalls as it flowed on to seek another.

But it was soothing.

So too was the fact that a ritual had been performed, even though, ideally, it should have taken place out of doors, perhaps in the clearing Cedric had led them to last summer, which certainly had the air of an enchanted spot: enclosed on all sides, yet wide open to the welkin. Whether or not it was the true site of the ancient pagan temple – and ever since he came down from the trip he'd been on at the time, Chris had had suspicions on that score, though it hadn't stopped him liking Cedric – no one could deny that it was the *kind* of place the Old Believers would have felt was holy. Like Delphi, Rhoda was fond of saying, though not of course on anything like the same scale. She had hitchhiked to Greece once, long ago, and insisted that nobody could stand on that hillside and not at once conclude this was a proper place to meet the gods.

Even on the strength of postcard pictures, Chris was prepared to take her word.

But most soothing of all was the knowledge that the rain would discourage any local people who might have planned to descend on the visitors by night and tear their tents down.

Even the babes-in-arms slept well.

★

The strangeness that had overtaken Weyharrow was passing from the minds of its inhabitants like – as so many of them had said – the memory of a dream.

Cuddled close to Sheila, for the night was cool, Stick thought of his illusory conviction that her kids were boys, that they had seemed to share. On the brink of sleep, he murmured in her ear, 'I'm glad they're not.'

'What?' – drowsily amid the tangle of her hair.

'Not boys. Hilary and Sam. Makes me think of the kid who didn't like bananas.'

'*What?*'

'The kid who said "I'm glad I don't like bananas." You don't know that one?'

Muzzily: 'No . . . Why was he glad about it?'

' "Because if I did I'd eat them, and they're horrid!" '

'Oh, Stick . . . ! Did you have to wake me up to tell me that?'

'No. Just to say how much I prefer figs. Sleep well.'

But there were some places where the dream had left a deeper trace.

The lights stayed on late in the Ellerford house. Paul and Harold had been glad to seize an excuse for missing school, and for a while they had kept up a mutual front of feigned bravado. There was food in the house, and they found money in their mother's purse; also there was the key to the drinks cabinet, and by afternoon they were making a kind of celebration of Ursula's departure, saying what a lousy mother she had always been, forever telling them they must do this, or mustn't do that, or she couldn't afford to let them have the other – when bloody yobs and oiks from all around, off the farms for God's sake, were getting motorbikes and home computers and flashy clothes and summer holidays in places where the girls went topless!

But, subconsciously, they had both been expecting that

somebody would come along and take them in charge. Not until darkness fell did they truly realize:

We've got to manage by ourselves.

It was Harold who said awkwardly, 'I suppose we'd better let somebody know.'

'What?' Paul had been investigating the liquor even more enthusiastically than his brother, and the stock of cigarettes as well, that Ursula kept solely for guests, having herself given up smoking in order to economize after Ted's death.

'Well, money, for example. We can't last on what was in her purse. And we ought to visit her in – in hospital.'

Thanks to a call from Mrs Weaper, they knew about her transfer from Chapminster to Hatterbridge. They also knew, as did all the children in the village, that Hatterbridge was where they sent 'the mental ones'.

Paul's speech was slurring and his face was pale as he drew on the latest of too many cigarettes.

'If she wants to see us she can send a bloody taxi!' was his answer.

Harold sat down, clasping an empty glass in both hands. He said, not looking at his brother, 'She's not in any state for that, you know.'

'Then it's her own bloody fault!' Paul shouted, and in the same moment set his own glass on a nearby table, tried to stab out his cigarette in an adjacent ashtray – but missed, so Harold had to retrieve it smouldering from the carpet – and fled. Shortly after, there were loud retching noises from the bathroom.

Stupid ass!

Waiting, passively watching the television that had been on all evening, Harold realized it was cold in here. They had lit a fire earlier, but it was dying. He moved to put more coal on, and found the scuttle empty.

The coal-bin was in the back yard, and rain was pelting at

the windows.

Very slowly it began to dawn on him how much he and Paul had taken for granted.

After throwing up, Paul collapsed, groaning, on his bed, and shortly fell asleep. Harold, sighing, turned off the TV and started to clean up. Tomorrow, he resolved while rinsing the plates they'd eaten a makeshift supper from, things were going to be different. Paul was going to have to pull his weight –

The doorbell rang.

He was halfway to the door in high excitement when he realized he was dripping detergent suds on the carpet. A wave of embarrassment overcame him. He had been indoctrinated with very clear ideas of what a *man* did and what a *woman* did. Cooking was all right; weren't all the greatest chefs male? But it wasn't manly to arrive at the door looking like a housewife!

He retreated to the kitchen and dried his hands and rolled his sleeves down. The bell rang again.

But then, all of a sudden, he realized he desperately needed to pee. It must have been the effect of running water into the sink . . .

Visions of greeting a caller with his thighs clamped together horrified his tipsy mind. He rushed upstairs to the bathroom. When he dashed back down and flung open the door there was no sign of anybody, except a car he didn't recognize starting up and driving off.

He ran out, waving, but he was too late.

That night, for the first time since he was a little boy, he wept into his pillow.

Moira O'Pheale was weeping, too, though for a different reason.

She was infinitely grateful to the Jacksetts for letting her finish her day's work at their shop. Even if it meant enduring the curiosity of the customers, she needed some kind of distraction. But at closing time she had had to fend off their sympathy in order to be allowed to return to the cottage.

Where she sat in darkness, writhing with self-contempt, hoping against hope that the parson wouldn't drop in, or the doctor, or Jerry Blocket, or *anybody*.

When the phone rang she tried to ignore it, found she couldn't, and eventually answered, sighing. The caller was Jenny Severance. To Moira's immense relief she found herself required to talk about a stranger, the reporter from the *Globe*. She became almost loquacious, and Jenny uttered a flood of thanks when she rang off.

A little cheered, Moira allowed herself to answer the phone a second time, even though she was preparing to warm her supper – a canned steak pie. This time, though, it wasn't Jenny.

'Mrs O'Pheale, you don't know me,' said a man's voice. 'But I heard the dreadful news about Miss Knabbe.'

Christ. More bloody sympathy. Haven't I had enough?

'Are you there?'

'Yes' – in a dull tone.

'I thought I should convey my condolences ... Oh, my name is Ralph Haggledon. Of Mortis and Haggledon?'

'Oh, yes.' During the two years she had lived here Moira had often posted letters to Phyllis's lawyer, whose office was in Chapminster. He took care of all her affairs, including the exiguous income from the investments her parents had bequeathed.

'Well ... I hope I'm not talking out of turn, because traditionally one should wait until after the funeral to publicize the contents of a will. But I did feel I ought to let you know: there is no risk of your being displaced from your current residence.'

For a long moment Moira stood like a wax dummy,

phone in hand. She husked at last, 'You can't possibly mean . . .'

'I think you're ahead of me.' There was a dry chuckle at the far end of the line.

'She never left me the cottage?'

'As I said, Mrs O'Pheale, you're ahead of me. Let me just say that if in the future you feel the need for professional advice –'

'Oh Christ. Oh my God. You're trying to tell me that she left me everything.'

Her mouth was dry, her hands were shaking, her vision blurred. Swaying, she had to lean against the wall.

'Miss Knabbe had no close relatives and no direct heirs. So it can't have been entirely unexpected –'

You bastard. You're a smooth-talking bastard like my Declan! What you mean is: you've been taking a cut from managing Phyllis's money and you don't want to lose a penny of it now it's passed to me . . . !

You want your foot in the bloody door, don't you?

'Excuse me?' – in a frosty tone.

In horror Moira realized she had uttered the last sentence aloud.

She drew a deep breath, thought it over, and came to the conclusion that she'd been quite right to say it.

'I said,' she repeated more clearly, 'you want your foot in the bloody door, don't you? Well, don't hold your breath! I could give the bloody lot to charity!'

And slammed down the phone.

When she eventually ate her supper, it was salt with falling tears.

Tim Wamble slept well. After the loss of that side of beef this morning – which, even if it hadn't been retained as evidence, would have been spoiled by partial thawing – there hadn't been enough in the hotel's freezer to feed all the people who had suddenly decided they ought to pop over to Weyharrow for dinner and find out what was behind these extraordinary rumours. Not many of them had been satisfied on that score, but a good few had gone away telling Nigel Mender that his chef was a marvel because of the way he'd been able to cope at such short notice.

And all he'd done, really, was conjure up a few simple dishes from what he found in store: a Chinese 'soup for the gods' with chopped spring onion, *spaghetti alla carbonara* which called for pasta plus ham and eggs of which there were plenty, coriander mushrooms (luckily he had a good stock of button mushrooms and they took literally minutes to prepare), every vegetable he could lay hands on, cut small and stir-fried, and lots of salads with his own favourite dressing that included mustard and horseradish . . .

It was the first time since he went to work as a chef that his appetite had really felt tempted by his own productions.

And Nigel Mender had boomed as he returned from seeing off the last of the customers, 'Tim, my boy! You've worked wonders tonight!'

Tired, but very pleased with himself, Tim smiled across a pile of dirty pans.

'I try to do my best, sir –'

'Name's Nigel, old chap! We've known each other long enough! I think you deserve a bonus! When you're through in here, pop into the bar and have a drink on me!'

For a long second Tim imagined that was to be the bonus: just a drink.

But Mr Mender – Nigel – chortled.

'If all the customers come back who said they would I'll up your pay. Here's an extra fiver to be going on with.' He fumbled out his wallet.

'That's very kind of you –'

'Kindness has nothing to do with it! If you hadn't come up to scratch . . . Well, you can imagine how embarrassed I'd have been. Come on and have that drink. A brandy?'

Tim slept extremely well that night.

But Ella Kailet spent all night awake. She had been fired. Tomorrow she would have no work to go to.

Distraught, in the grip of powers she could not control, she left her London flat – she didn't even pack a bag – and walked the mile to the Chiswick roundabout where traffic divided on the main routes to the West Country. She had on a raincape over a short dress, with high-heeled shoes. As she had hoped, a good few lonely men pulled up for her. To each she said, 'Weyharrow?'

'Never heard of it!' was the routine reply. 'But if it's anywhere near –'

She couldn't recall where it was near. They left her in the cold, frightened by her lapse of memory, scarcely able to see for the rain that smeared her glasses.

Not until two long hours had passed, when traffic had thinned, did it dawn on her confused mind that she did now remember where Weyharrow was near. Names drifted back out of mental mist: Trimborne, Hatterbridge, Chapminster ...

'Chapminster?' said the driver of an open pickup holding second-hand furniture under a plastic sheet, halted at a pointless stop-light – pointless because the other entries to the roundabout were vacant. 'Yes, I'm going that way.'

'Do you pass Weyharrow?'

'I suppose so. There's a sign ... Jump in. Be quick! The lights are changing. No need to feel scared. I'm over fifty and I have four kids. But hurry!'

Ella obeyed.

Having made one stop and fed her on baked beans and chips and hot sweet tea, he left her at the promised sign. By then the rain had reduced to drizzle. She walked the rest of

158

the way, hating the shoes she had put on, not knowing why she wanted to be where she was going.

An hour or so past dawn she fell in with the hippies camping on Weyharrow green. On learning her name they pestered her with questions, but when they realized how tired she was they gave over. They hung her cape to dry, shared their breakfast with her, offered her a threadbare blanket, and left her to sleep in the back of their bus, promising to say some sort of prayer on her behalf.

She felt indescribably grateful. She was terrified of going mad.

So too had Mary Flaken been. How *could* she have done that awful thing to her best friend Hannah? How could she have imagined she was actually married to Bill Blocket, when she'd been Philip's wife for more than two years? She had kept saying over and over, 'It was like a dream! I can't have been myself!'

Fortunately the Blockets had been very understanding – more, she thought, than she could say about Phil. He was still snapping at her every chance he got. When they at last went to bed, he did the same as last night, even though he hadn't been out to the pub this time, and turned his back without so much as a good-night kiss.

She lay awake a long while, staring into darkness, hoping against hope that at tomorrow's meeting some explanation would be offered that would make sense of her terrible experience.

She shared that hope with many others: Tom Fidger, breaking out in a cold sweat each time he remembered how he had driven a busload of passengers on the wrong side of the road; Harry Vikes when he recalled turning his cows into the turnip field; Ken Pecklow on wondering again about the new chemical spray Harry had bought and he had not been able to afford . . .

And Jenny Severance, when she thought about the last public meeting she had been sent to cover, and the incredible nonsense she had seemed to recollect from it.

The whole episode now felt unreal. But for the appalling vividness with which it burned in memory, she could have believed it never happened.

The Reverend Mr Phibson, who had prayed more desperately than ever in his life, likewise found his memory of Thursday's ghastly morning service vague and distant. He wished he could have felt the same about the anathema he had pronounced on Mrs Judger, who had rallied loyally to him, cleaned the house and served his supper as though nothing had occurred amiss. He was very ashamed of himself, and wondering whether he should apologize for the anathema, or whether it was best left unmentioned, inasmuch as she had no idea he'd spoken it.

Up at the Court, Basil Goodsir felt more and more helpless in the face of Helen's sarcastic taunts, for how could one rebut what one was now convinced had not been real in the first place?

It was no use saying so, of course. Helen and Marge Grewsam were clearly in cahoots, and their joint efforts were winning round that bloody lawyer, Haggledon . . .

At the hotel Wilf Spout slept well and deeply. In the adjacent room, however, Donald Prosher lay awake and worried, thinking of the Ellerford boys. Presumably they'd gone out, to a friend's house no doubt, even though there had been a light behind the front room curtains; he had heard no noise. In the morning he must call again.

He had never said as much to anyone, and didn't intend to start talking about the matter now, but there was a good chance that the younger boy, Paul, was not Ted Ellerford's son, but his, fruit of a short and casual affair. Ursula had never tried to pin paternity on him, but after leaving Hong Kong he had seen a birth announcement in *The Times*, and counted backward month by month, and . . .

But he had other, more important considerations to contend with.

At the other end of the building, in bed with Lisa, who like Wilf was contentedly asleep, Wallace Jantrey tossed and turned and fretted. This Weyharrow scandal should have been tailor-made for the *Banner*'s readership! He had come down here with high hopes, intending to arrive ahead of the rush – he knew Jenny had phoned other papers as well as his.

What rush, though? Where was everybody else? Where were the people from the *Sunday Trumpet*, for example, or *The World on Sunday*? (He scarcely thought of the *Globe* as competition.) Almost, he had mentioned their absence when he phoned his editor this evening, but decided not to. There was a story here, he was certain of that, even if it wasn't of the kind he had expected . . . Why weren't the locals nailing crosses to their doors to keep away the Devil? Why weren't they besieging the church to pray for forgiveness? Why hadn't they attacked the hippies? Why was Don Prosher looking smug?

Suppose he had laid out fifty quid in drink for some of the local layabouts; could he not have talked them into overturning the hippies' tents? He should have thought of that before. Maybe tomorrow night, if the meeting was as dull as he expected . . .

He drifted into uneasy dreams.

Downstairs Nigel Mender was belatedly confronting a problem. Who was going to take charge at the hotel while he was chairing the meeting in the parish hall? He'd meant to sort that out earlier, but the sudden rush of customers had distracted him. He had a couple of extra waitresses and an extra barman organized, but he needed someone authoritative and responsible to stand in for himself. The hotel was going to be packed out; he had taken four more bookings this afternoon, which left only two vacant rooms.

He snapped his fingers. Of course! Jack Fidger would be perfect – Tom and Fred's father. Before taking over the garage from his own father, Jack had had it in mind to go into the licensed trade, and had actually worked for a while at the Marriage. Of course, that had been a long time ago, but he was an affable type and would no doubt do a favour for an old friend.

Assuming he wasn't planning to attend the meeting . . .

Nigel glanced at his watch. It was far too late to ring the old man up. But first thing in the morning –! And if not him, maybe Tom's wife, or Fred's . . . Something could be arranged.

Nonetheless, he had to calm himself with another stiff brandy before he could relax enough to go to bed.

Sleepily Yvonne called out, 'Is that you, Joe?'

Shaking the wet from his cape, PC Book assured her that it was, and joined her in the sitting-room where she was drowsing over a late film on TV.

'Is everything okay?'

'All quiet on the Weyharrow front,' he said around a yawn. 'Mr Chade promised to send a car by a couple of times during the night, but I told him there wouldn't be any trouble. Not unless our lot start it.'

'Think they will?'

'Not with it streaming down like this . . . Film any good?'

'Not much. I've been dozing half the time, anyway. Lost track of what's going on.'

'I'll turn in, then. It's going to be a long day tomorrow.'

'You got to go to this meeting?'

''Fraid so. Sounds like most of the village will be there.'

'Think I ought to come?'

'Up to you. But . . .' Joe hesitated.

'But what?'

'It could be,' he said slowly, 'kind of a major event.'

12

All during Saturday the atmosphere of Weyharrow was . . .
Strange? Peculiar? Out of the ordinary? All of those, and
something extra it was hard to put a finger on.

It wasn't just that people were exaggeratedly courteous to
one another, as if afraid they might have given offence even
though they could not recall having done so. That entered
into it, but it wasn't the whole story.

Nor was the way they closed ranks against the outsiders –
'foreigners', be they from as near at hand as Powte or Fooksey – who came into the village on this non-working day
ready to poke fun or gather scandal. Even Philip Flaken and
Bill Blocket – even Ken Pecklow and Harry Vikes – joined
forces to rebuff these sensation-seekers, first with scowls,
then with insults and at last with threats, until by lunch time
they were retiring disappointed . . . though others, unfore-
warned, tried the same again during the afternoon, and met
the same hostile reception.

By contrast, their treatment of the hippies was outway
polite, almost as though, having been here before, the latter
had become honorary citizens. That too was odd. But once
more it wasn't what counted the most.

Perhaps the real key to the strangeness of the day was to be
found in everyone's determination to make it as ordinary as
possible.

That, at any rate, was how it struck Steven. He said as
much to Jenny when they crossed paths after morning
surgery and went together for a drink at the Marriage.
The customers were returning to the pub, somewhat shame-
facedly, and no more reference was being made to sinks

164

of iniquity.

'I know exactly what you mean,' she muttered. 'I got up early and went to see if anything special was happening at the church. It was an ordinary service, except that Mr Phibson sounded extremely tired. There weren't many more people there than usual, though: about a dozen. Later on I bumped into Don Prosher, coming away from the Ellerfords. He said when he went there last night he couldn't get an answer, but he saw the boys this morning. Said they both looked ghastly. Got at Ursula's drinks-cupboard last night, apparently, and overdid it. I suppose you can't really blame them . . . But he said he was going to take them to see her at the hospital, which I thought was nice of him.'

'Last night,' Steven said caustically, 'you were more inclined to think of him as speaking with a forked tongue. Did you find out where he spent yesterday afternoon?'

Jenny shook her head. 'He clammed up when I mentioned it. I think he's on to something . . . Steve, you know something? I don't think I'm cut out to be a reporter. I don't have the right kind of – of antennae.'

'Isn't it something you've always wanted to do?'

'Oh, ever since I was about thirteen. But . . .' She shook her head, looking doleful. 'I seem to be still treating it as though it were some kind of school exercise. Almost as though I expect to have my work marked, with corrections in the margin! And I can't go on doing that for ever, can I?'

Her wide blue eyes fixed on Steven's face. He found himself at a loss. Instead of answering directly, he said, 'And what about the people from the *Banner*?'

'Oh, they're around somewhere.' Jenny shrugged. 'I met them earlier, but they seemed mainly interested in chatting up the yobs – Damn. I mustn't say things like that, must I? It'll turn them off for good, and I need to stay on the best of terms with everybody . . . Maybe that's what I'm not good at. What do you think, Steve? You seem to have made a tremendous hit in just a few days. I've been here over six months, and I don't seem to have made any real friends, and – and I'm annoyed with myself. Sometimes I wonder whether I'm behaving like the Ellerford boys, giving the impression that I'm too good for a place like this and only want to use it as a stepping-stone to Fleet Street.'

'Speaking clinically,' Steven said after a pause, 'isn't that true?'

'I suppose it is, really . . . Well, thanks for the drink. The *Trumpet* hasn't sent anybody down from London after all, but when I rang him earlier the editor said he is still interested in a story from me. So I'd better draft one. See you this evening . . . Oh, if only today weren't turning out so ordinary, like you said!'

'What were you hoping for?'

'I don't know.' Jenny shook her head unhappily. 'Except it wouldn't have been like what we've got.'

That remark was still ringing in Steven's memory when he walked across the green to the parish hall fifteen minutes before the scheduled time of the meeting. Half the village seemed to have decided to attend, perhaps because the evening was fine and mild and there was little worth watching on TV. Shortly he found himself surrounded by people he'd never met who beamed and greeted him by name. He had a wild and fleeting vision of Weyharrow as a 'dear octopus', a creature that once it had made up its collective mind could draw a stranger permanently into its toils, and wondered – not for the first time – whether succeeding to Dr Tripkin's practice was such a good idea.

But he had no time to worry about that. Constable Book was accosting him.

'Doctor, Chief Inspector Chade would like a word!'

Two regular police-cars in livery of blue and white, and another larger one, all black bar the county emblem on each side, were parked in a group across the road. Three constables and a sergeant were keeping a wary eye on the assembly, particularly the hippie visitors. The latter were standing at a discreet distance for the moment, but clearly intended to get into the hall if they could.

'Evening!' said the chief inspector curtly, proffering his hand. 'I gather you're one of the main speakers. I already told your chairman: we'll be standing by, and at the slightest sign of trouble . . . !'

'I hope there won't be any,' Steven muttered, and passed on.

There followed a somewhat confused reception in a poky anteroom, where he had to shake several more hands without registering most of the names, though he gathered he was being introduced to members of the parish council. In a corner, accompanied by Mrs Judger, sat the parson, a forced-looking smile coming and going on his face. Nigel Mender himself was bustling about, offering people half-filled glasses of South African sherry – 'compliments of the hotel!' – which Mrs Judger banned from Mr Phibson's reach. Looking especially unhappy, Basil Goodsir and his wife were chatting with some of the people whose names Steven was told but failed to hear properly, though he did take notice of one man, about forty, dark-haired, wearing a grey mohair suit that practically yelled, 'Bespoke!'

Its wearer's face, however, was so unmemorable it could have been a clown's, or a spy's; it was an international face such as might be seen on any of ten thousand streets in fifty countries. He, the Goodsirs and Steven exchanged platitudes about the weather while Nigel moved distractedly from group to group, pausing now and then to ask whether there was any news of the archdeacon. He did this in whispers, making sure to be on the far side of the room from Mr Phibson.

'It's six minutes past,' he announced at last. 'I don't think

167

we should wait any longer. We'll go in, if that's all right with everybody ... Steven?'

'What? Oh – oh, by all means.' Steven drained his glass. He had been seeking an opportunity to broach his private knowledge of Basil's plight, as Don Prosher had suggested. It had not arisen, and now there was no time.

'Give 'em hell, old chap,' said Nigel, taking him companionably by the arm. 'You know there are reporters here, I'm sure. We're all relying on you to make sense of this to-do.'

Sense?

Steven could scarcely refrain from laughing. But he composed his face and meekly followed Nigel and the rest.

He hadn't been inside the parish hall before. Someone had mentioned in his hearing that it had been built at the turn of the century because previously public meetings had had to take place either in the church itself – which the residents felt was inappropriate for discussing secular matters – or in a disused barn on ground adjacent to the Marriage. That, the gentry felt, was even worse; it meant meetings could too easily be packed with the pub's customers, bribed in advance with beer and cider.

Here was the result: a mock-Gothic edifice with pointed arches at its doors and windows, a timber roof with varnished rafters from which dangled cobwebs – Steven heard one of the councillors muttering about 'that fellow Stick' who should have been told to clean up the place! – and a grey, unwelcoming floor of lias flags. At one end was a dais, on which a table set with a carafe and water-glasses awaited the main speakers and the chairman; this was carpeted. In addition to chairs for the speakers, there was another row behind, on which the members of the parish council took their places.

Sitting down, on invitation, at Nigel's right, Steven surveyed the body of the hall. It was crammed with chairs. Even

168

though two aisles had been left, they were probably too close to be consistent with fire-safety regulations . . . but he dared not comment. Under wan, tapered bulbs on round black wrought-iron chandeliers hung from chains, the people of Weyharrow were gathering to hear their doom.

Plus sundry others from outside.

The front row of seats bore handwritten signs saying 'RE-SERVED'. Basil and Helen Goodsir occupied two, and the man in the mohair suit sat down beside them. (Who had they said he was? But Steven had simply failed to catch the name.) Mrs Judger, sniffing, took another one realizing that the hall was already almost full.

Also there were the press. Jenny was escorting them to their places. Not looking as though they enjoyed each other's company, Don and Wallace sat down either side of her, flanked by Wilf and Lisa respectively. That much was as Steven had expected. So, albeit somewhat less so, was the fact that Don had found places for the Ellerford boys immediately behind him. So too was the arrival of Chief Inspector Chade, to take the chair at the left end of the front row, near a door over which a lighted sign said 'FIRE EXIT'. Beside him was another man Steven didn't recognize, in a navy-blue blazer and regimental tie, with whom Chade exchanged muttered comments. Joe Book took station beside the fire exit, crossing his arms and looking official.

Speaking of muttered comments: it looked as though Don Prosher was acquainted with the man in the mohair suit. At any rate, they smiled insincerely at each other.

A couple of vacancies remained at the front. A dark, fortyish woman in glasses, walking as though her feet were sore, whose face struck Steven as vaguely familiar though he didn't recollect her as a local person, tried to claim one of them. But Nigel beckoned Mrs Judger and whispered to her, and the would-be intruder retired to the rear of the hall, obliged to join the hippie visitors who had filtered in last of all and were standing at the back, shifting from foot to foot as though uncomfortable among the more conventionally dressed, among Tom and Fred Fidger, Vic Draycock, the Jacksetts, Lawrence Ratch the pharmacist, the Flakens, the Blockets, Moira O'Pheale, Harry and Joyce Vikes, Ken Pecklow and his wife, and the rest.

With a start Steven realized: apart from those who had other obligations, such as the Jegges who had to keep the Marriage open, almost literally everybody he had met since his arrival in the village had assembled. Even Stick was here; they caught each other's eyes and exchanged waves. The pretty, long-haired woman next to him, presumably, would be Sheila Surrean, whom Steven hadn't met. Her children were sitting on her lap and Stick's.

And wasn't that Cedric Goodsir on Stick's other side?

His eyes ranged to the extreme far end, in search of the woman who had hoped for a seat at the front. It always infuriated him when he saw a face he felt he ought to recognize but couldn't. But her head was bowed, as though she were praying, and her features were in shadow.

Directly above her hung a clock of the kind Steven always associated with memories of school: a plain white dial and heavy black Roman numerals, with the conventional IIII in place of IV to mark the four. That same lecturer who had told his students about Ambroise Paré – was Penny Wenstowe here? No, though her parents were. Moreover there was scarcely anybody present, apart from Jenny, the Ellerford boys and the Surrean girls, younger than himself; this was a middle-aged gathering, inclining to the elderly – that same lecturer had explained that the mistake was deliberate, designed to help the astigmatic.

Assuming it was right, the time was ten past eight.

Beside him Nigel Mender rose and cleared his throat.

'Ladies and gentlemen! Friends! We *had* hoped that our gathering this evening was to be favoured with the presence of Archdeacon Thummage.'

From the corner of his eye Steven noticed that the parson relaxed a trifle, though his manner and his posture remained alike downcast.

'Unfortunately he must have been delayed. So rather than keep you hanging about any longer –'

At that precise moment there was a disturbance near the main entrance at the far end of the hall, and a woman's voice called out, 'It's okay, Nigel! Here he is!'

A tall, long-faced man, all in black bar a silver-grey silk front and a white band at his throat symbolizing the traditional 'dog collar', appeared in the doorway, bestowing smiles of apology on everyone around him as he made his way to the front row, and occasional glares on the companion who followed him: a much younger man in similar garb save that he wore a plain black front.

'Mr Phibson! Mr – Mr Mender, isn't it? A thousand apologies! I'm afraid my driver missed our way, or we'd have been here long ago. Do continue, since you decided to start without us. Quite right, too!'

Nigel leaned across to whisper, 'You won't have met Mr Thummage, Steven. He's the archdeacon of the diocese. It's not for nothing that they call archdeacons "the bishop's eyes and ears"!'

'Is that so?' was the only answer Steven could contrive.

'Pray continue, as I said!' said Mr Thummage, sitting down, crossing his legs and linking his fingers in front of him. Looking distinctly unhappy, his companion sat hunched forward with his hands between his knees.

'I need scarcely say how pleased we are that you have found it possible to join us after all!' Nigel declared heartily. 'So, now, even if we are a little late, I can call this meeting to order and introduce our speakers.'

His tone became self-consciously solemn.

'We meet together because certain strange events have

overtaken our village in the past few days. We are all anxious to get to the bottom of them. The elected members of your parish council, of which I have the honour to be chairman, are as desirous as anyone of solving the – ah – the mystery. That's why we've called you here.'

Someone roared past on a noisy motorcycle; apart from that, there was total silence.

'Now after considerable deliberation, the councillors concluded that the speakers you would most hope to hear from would be, on the one hand, our respected parson –'

The old man's face had been pale all evening; now it turned the colour of candle-wax.

' – and on the other, Dr Steven Gloze, who as you know is deputizing for Dr Tripkin who's on holiday. I hate to think what he's going to say – heh-heh – when he finds out how much excitement he's been missing . . .'

That was a false note. Nigel realized the audience was glowering, and changed tack.

'However that may be, and – I must stress this – without wanting to turn this evening's meeting into an argument, with people taking one side or the other, the council has decided that the various views need to be aired. I call on Mr Phibson to express his opinion of the matter.'

He turned to the parson with a flourish, and sat down.

But Mr Phibson simply sat there, immobile save that now and then he licked his lips. Renewed silence lengthened.

Eventually someone from the back of the hall called out, 'Ah, come on, Parson! You told everyone it was the Devil!'

That had been a man's voice. Steven, peering through the dimness, failed to identify the speaker.

A woman spoke up, equally loudly, and he knew who this was: Joyce Vikes.

'May God forgive you if you've told another lie! We all know what heresies you preached! Holy kisses! "The Father and the Mother and the Child"! Whoever heard such diabolical nonsense? It was the Devil's doing, and you said so!'

Nigel looked anxiously at the parson, who seemed finally to be summoning his courage. After another tense pause he forced himself to his feet; Steven's trained ear caught the sound of creaking joints, and he made a mental note to have the poor old fellow tested for bursitis.

He glanced at Mr Thummage. The archdeacon, hands still linked against his chest, was smiling benignly.

As he had told Mr Phibson, Steven had lost his faith. Suddenly it struck him as imperative to make as many other people as he could lose theirs, rather than remain prey to a sleek and smiling conniver like this archdeacon.

Speaking of sleek and smiling . . . who in the world *was* that person sitting next to Basil Goodsir, whom Don knew? What business did he have among the folk of Weyharrow?

And how about the man beside the chief inspector?

But Mr Phibson had found his voice at last. It creaked like the branches of an old oak in a gale; like an old and unoiled hinge; like his own painful knees . . .

Steven was assailed by waves of pity. How far in the future did a like fate await him – ? No! How *near*?

Abruptly reminded of mortality, he clenched his fists unseen beneath the table.

Mr Phibson said, looking at nobody: 'The archdeacon and I have spoken on the phone today. I wish him good evening. I know he has the pastoral care of all of you at heart. He knows that I was sincerely misled in what I said the other morning in this church – *the* church. And isn't that what God expects of us: sincerity?'

The audience was growing restive. He seemed oblivious.

'I'm told that shortly I shall be replaced. I shall miss the many friends I've made in this parish. I think with special affection of the babies I've baptized since coming to Weyharrow. I only hope that the pagan taint which infects your water and your very air, so that your appointed master – I mean pastor – is compelled to stand under the same roof as filthy loathsome immoral *disgusting* people like those that I see near the door . . .'

He had completely lost track of what he was saying.

Alarmed, Steven leaned towards Nigel. But already the chairman was signalling to Mrs Judger. She marched up the three steps to the dais, took the parson by the hand, and led him away. When the door closed behind him, Mr Thummage had taken the place he had vacated.

'With your chairman's permission,' he said in a resonant baritone, 'I shall claim the privilege of substituting for my unfortunate brother in Christ. Far be it from me to put words into his mouth, but it does so happen' – he glanced modestly down at the table – 'your chairman and I had a brief telephonic conference today, and reached a modicum of agreement . . . I do not deny, nor shall I ever do so!' – this time he banged the table with his fist and glared around the hall – 'that the Evil One exists! How could anybody claim that he does not, confronted with the reality of evil in our modern world?

'What I do say, though, is this!' He straightened in his chair, shoulders back, eyes blazing.

'It is not yet in a placid English village that one may seek his rule! Oh, certainly there are signs that it may one day come to pass.' His voice dropped. 'Immorality is rampant everywhere! There are countless persons who seek false happiness in relationships unsanctified by the Church! There are stupid people who resign themselves to the artificial gratification that can be got from drugs, when all such transient joy is but a shadow of what can be obtained through dedication to the love of God! Perhaps – I do not say this is the case, but certain evidence I've been given inclines me to suspect it may be – perhaps here in Weyharrow these forces, due less to evil than to mere stupidity, have overcome your parson and undermined his – *mind*. I say the poor man is overwrought. He needs caring for, and a long rest. I would

174

rather believe so than think that you, you ordinary decent English people, have consciously and voluntarily allowed that being whom we know as Satan to enter your hearts, your minds, and your souls ... despite your willingness to welcome pagans in your midst!'

He concluded with a glare directed at Chris and Rhoda.

Someone said faintly, 'You mean Parson was wrong? The Devil didn't take him over like he said?'

Smiling indulgently, the archdeacon said, 'Even those of us who have spent long years in the service of Christ are vulnerable, if not to the Evil One, then to human weakness. You can hardly expect Mr Phibson to be immune.'

Nigel tapped Steven on the arm. Leaning close, almost chortling, he said, 'He's doing our work for us, isn't he? Sounds as though I may not even have to call on you!'

Swallowing hard, Steven said, 'I'd like to speak anyway. I didn't really want to before. Now I do.'

Surprised, more than a mite dismayed, Nigel stared at him. But he said at length, 'Don't want to miss your moment in the spotlight, is that it? Well, I can understand that. How about now?'

It seemed like as good a time as any, if he hoped to make a rational contribution to the proceedings. Half the audience were sitting stunned, as though to have their parson contradicted was unthinkable. The rest were whispering among themselves, and from the susurrus of their voices arose a change in the formerly quiet mood.

'We – ah – we thank Archdeacon Thummage for his levelheaded appraisal of the situation,' Nigel said, rising and staring down the hubbub. 'Now I call on Dr Gloze, whom some of you – most of you, perhaps – already know despite the brief time he's been with us. Steven?'

He was on his feet, nodding acknowledgment of scattered applause ... and his mind was absolutely blank.

He said at length, 'Friends – I hope I may call you so

175

despite, as Nigel said, the short time I have been here . . . Friends, I'm sure you were as pleased as I was to hear the archdeacon ascribe Mr Phibson's actions to excessive stress and mental pressure, rather than to supernatural forces. Had I been called upon to voice a professional opinion' – thank goodness the poor fellow wasn't in the room! – 'that, I'm afraid, is what I too would have been forced to say. For a medical man, it's something of a relief to hear one's views confirmed by a theologian.'

He paused, hoping that there might be a smile or two, even a chuckle, in response to his sally. Instead there was silence, tense as a fiddle-string.

His mouth dry, his throat hoarsening, he launched into the carefully reasoned, statistically defensible, wholly and absolutely logical argument he had prepared in every spare moment during the day. He had a sheaf of paper in his hand, and every page bore solid data, authoritative and documented . . .

And no one, after the first minute, listened to it. He wound down with a weak statement that sounded more like an apology, even to himself: 'So, you see, what happened here could well have happened anywhere.'

There was a pause.

At length, beaming, Nigel Mender said, 'I hope that sets everybody's mind at rest. We could scarcely have hoped for a clearer exposition of the facts, could we?'

Was that going to be it? Steven stared out across the audience. From their expressions he could tell that they were as dissatisfied as he. But as Nigel went on to say something about a vote of thanks to the speakers, his fellow councillors started to shuffle and rise from their chairs. Obviously they were past masters of the art of sweeping dirt under the carpet. So . . .

Despondent, on the verge of renouncing once and for all any ideas of taking over from Dr Tripkin, he mechanically folded up his papers.

176

He would have liked to know for sure what had afflicted him. And Jenny, and the parson and everybody else. It looked as though he wasn't going to get the chance. Not tonight, at any rate.

And then there was a cry from the body of the hall.

'Oh no you don't! We didn't come here to be fobbed off with doubletalk! We still got questions – lots of 'em!'

Praise be!

13

That outburst had come from Mary Flaken, resisting her husband's attempt to restrain her. He might have succeeded but for the chorus of support that followed. Advancing down the left-hand aisle, Ella Kailet shouted, 'I came all the way from London to find out what happened to me here! For pity's sake, you can't stop us talking about it! *Something happened here that drove me mad!*'

'And a lot of other people too!'

For a second Steven didn't realize it was his own voice that had rung out from the platform. Then he realized that Nigel was scowling at him, and the archdeacon was looking like thunder.

And the parish councillors, *par force majeure*, were resuming their chairs.

He sought desperately for a way to excuse his intervention, and realized abruptly that there was no need. Shouts of approval were greeting it. Several people were on their feet, waving their fists. Loudest, and attracting most attention, was Tom Fidger.

'Doctor! We won't hold it against you that you had to spin that reassuring yarn! It's just what most of us have learned to expect around here! But you weren't enjoying it – were you? I could tell!'

Nigel was pawing at his arm again, but all of a sudden Steven felt reckless, as he had when he decided to take Jenny to the Marriage for a drink instead of treating her as a patient. He brushed the chairman's hand aside and rose to his feet.

What the hell difference did it make if he had to suffer another three weeks in this place? He need never return!

178

'You're right!' he bellowed. 'You're absolutely right! While I didn't tell you a single lie I don't believe I told you half the truth!'

'But that's only 'cause you didn't know it!'

Tom Fidger was pulling back his jacket and raising his hands as though to adopt the classic posture of thumbs in waistcoat armholes – only to realize he didn't have a waistcoat on. He covered his mistake by clapping.

'Now I agree with Mrs Flaken! We do have questions! And we want some answers! First of all!'

He thrust out his right arm, forefinger pointed, and his target was the man in the superbly-tailored mohair suit.

'Dr Gloze doesn't know you, but I do! You're from the factory at Trimborne! Eight-ten years ago I used to see you every day, back when people from Weyharrow worked at your place! You fired them one by one, didn't you? Our buses don't go up there any more! You don't have any more connection with our village! *So what the hell are you doing at our parish meeting?*'

The man in mohair looked disconcerted; Steven wished the people sitting behind could have seen the expression on his face. It being impossible to conjure up an instant mirror, words would have to suffice.

He shouted above increasing hubbub, 'And *I'd* like to know who's sitting next to Chief Inspector Chade!'

Beside him Nigel Mender buried his face in his hands.

'Would you permit a stranger to intervene?' said a mild voice that nonetheless carried to the four corners of the room. 'As it happens, I can answer both the questions that have just been posed.'

Rising from his seat in the press section, it was Donald Prosher who spoke. At the same time, Wilf Spout began to shoot flash pictures of the assembly. The man next to the Chief Inspector bridled and tried to object . . . but in the chair immediately behind sat Harry Vikes, who laid a hand on his shoulder and squeezed, hard. Wilf caught that.

'Well done, Harry!' called a voice from the other side of the hall – it was Ken Pecklow's. For a moment the audience was distracted by the improbability of those two becoming allies; then everybody realized, as one, that in this situation it was not just logical but necessary.

'Mr Chairman!' It was Vic Draycock on his feet at the back of the room; no doubt he had chosen to sit near the entrance to keep up his pose of befriending the 'pilgrims'. 'Some of us don't know who just spoke up, but if he does have any answers we'd all like to hear them!'

There was a rattle of applause.

Nigel Mender was looking around as though for guidance. Steven supplied it in a whisper.

'This isn't going to be a walk-over after all. Those people are scared, and I didn't persuade them out of it. I did try. You heard me. But they're right and I was wrong. Call on Don!'

'Who?' Nigel said foggily as the archdeacon plucked his arm and drew his attention the other way.

Not much future in that . . . !

Steven jumped to his feet. He shouted, 'Could we have a bit of hush for Mr Donald Prosher of the *Globe*?'

He glanced down at the press row again. Wallace Jantrey was pounding his forehead repeatedly with the heel of his hand, as though trying to punish himself for some sort of oversight. Like Wilf, Lisa Jopp was snapping pictures, flash-flash-flash, but she was scowling.

And where the hell was Jenny? Her chair was empty!

Uproar subsided as Don's identity sank in. Attempting to preserve the conventions, Steven turned to Nigel.

'Does the chair recognize Mr Prosher . . . ?'

The only answer was a wave. Steven concluded it was up to him to get this particular bit of the show back on the road. He caught Don's eye and spread his hands and sat down. That was enough.

In a didactic tone Don said, 'Traditionally it's no part of a reporter's job to influence the news, but only to report it. During my brief visit to Weyharrow I've been driven to the conclusion that unless I do more there won't be any news. And there must be. There needs to be. You see . . .'

He drew a notebook from his pocket and flipped its pages. He had left his tape-recorder on his chair, its cassette turning on battery power.

'You see, Mr – Mr Fidger, isn't it? We spoke yesterday morning when I stopped to fill up the car. The person you asked about is Dr Walter Frass of Helvambrit Pharmaceuticals. I met him yesterday afternoon.'

Steven's fingers clenched into his palms as he recalled Jenny saying that it would be worth finding out where Don had passed the time between his visit to the Court and his return to Weyharrow.

Where was she? Why the hell had she ducked out on this tremendous scoop? His own mind was running ahead of Don's words, and so should hers be!

Don was continuing. He composed himself to listen.

'The reason I went to Helvambrit was to ask about the leak that occurred late on Wednesday night . . . Don't let him run away!' – with sudden force.

Of a sudden there were grins all round the hall. Stick jumped up and took station between Dr Frass and the exit. As two or three other husky young men copied him, he called out, 'Not to worry, man! Keep rolling!'

Joe Book looked uneasy, but made no move.

'Thank you . . . Naturally, Dr Frass claimed there had been no such leak. The evidence is against him.'

'Can't hear you!' shouted someone from the back. Don glanced around. Nigel had his head buried in his hands again, and the archdeacon was scowling and signalling to his aide. That left Steven, who shrugged and beckoned. Don climbed up on the dais.

'Better? Okay, I'll carry on. There *was* a leak from Helvambrit on Wednesday night. A compound escaped in significant quantity – "significant" in this case means just a few grams, very finely dispersed – and it may not have been the first time. However, you see . . .' He drew himself up.

'On that particular night there was an inversion above the valley of the Chap: that's to say, warm air was trapped under a colder overlying layer so that mist was formed. Anybody here – ? Wait! Let me test my theory!'

Steven saw the man next to Chade starting to his feet. He signalled to Stick with a tilt of his head. At once the stranger was scowled back into his seat.

'If I'm right,' Don went on, 'everybody who was affected must have been in the open air, and near the river. Let's start with one person who definitely was. Mrs Kailet?'

The tour guide's eyes were closed and she was breathing hard. Some of the nearby hippies were growing alarmed and offering assistance. Brushing their attentions aside, she glanced up in response to Don's mention of her name.

'Yes! Yes! I stood in the mist for nearly two hours, and afterwards I slept at a hotel with the tourists and in the morning I did this stupid thing!'

'What about the passengers on your coach?' Don stabbed.

'They stayed inside. The driver too.'

'But Mr Fidger was with you?'

They looked at one another, and both nodded.

'That fits,' said Don with satisfaction. 'Being inside the coach was enough to protect the tourists. But others were less lucky. Like the Jeggses. I happen to know they were up late. And haven't they been acting oddly?'

'So what happened?' shouted someone from the back. It was Cedric, impatient as ever.

'Hold your horses,' Don advised, turning another page of his notebook. 'I still haven't quite figured out all the implications . . . but let's start with the people up here on the

182

platform. Doctor!'

Steven started. 'Yes?'

'Were you out and about around midnight?'

'Why – why, yes, I was! And so was Mr Phibson!' A sudden wave of relief overcame him. 'We went to see Mrs Lapsey because she thought she was dying . . .'

I shouldn't have said that!

But the response from the audience was a laugh! Someone said, quite loudly, 'Oh, no! Not again!'

He leaned back in his chair, ignoring Nigel, ignoring the archdeacon. Don was in charge now. Let him get on with it. He obviously knew far better how to manipulate an audience than anybody else in the hall –

Including Wallace, who was scribbling frantic notes.

But where was Jenny?

'What about the other people who were affected?' Don continued. 'Were you all out at Wednesday midnight?'

'I wasn't!' Stick objected at once. 'Nor were Sheila's kids! We had the effect you're talking about, but – No, I was indoors, and the kids were both in bed.'

'Ah!' Don raised his hand. 'But I know where you live. Doesn't your flat overlook the river?'

'Well, the living-room and the kids' room do. But . . . Oh!'

'Go on!'

'It could be right,' Stick admitted. 'I dozed off in the living-room, and the windows were open.'

'*And* – ?' Don stepped to the front of the dais.

'And Sheila's room is the other side of the flat, next to the kitchen and bathroom.' Stick drew a deep breath. 'Man, do I ever see what you are driving at! I got the whole load of it and thought Sheila's kids were boys when in fact they're girls. The kids sleep in the next room, on the river side, and they –'

There was a wordless cry from Hilary.

Stick said, 'Sorry, kids. You've got to learn this is a cruel world. But I'll just say they both did silly things at school on

Thursday morning. Though not half as silly as a pair of boys that I could name, much older . . .'

The Ellerfords flinched and stared around for a way of escape, but there was none. Without words, it had been decided that nobody should leave this hall before the mystery was solved.

Paul hunched forward as though wanting to vanish into thin air. Harold, though, braced himself for the worst.

He said in a clear voice, 'Paul and I were out late on Wednesday. But what did the mist have to do with it?'

'The inversion over the valley that brought it on,' Don said, nodding encouragement, 'was also what prevented the vapour from dispersing as quickly as usual . . . I can think of at least one other person who most likely got caught in it. If my explanation is correct, there must have been several more.'

There was a numb silence. But Don seemed to be prepared for that. He fixed the Ellerford boys with a chill gaze.

'What about your mother, for example? What was she up to on Wednesday night?'

Silence again.

'What time did you get home? Where had you been?'

'You haven't any bloody right to ask!' Paul shouted, leaping to his feet. 'You're starting to sound like her, you are! And we don't even bloody know you! I never saw you before today!'

'No. That's true. But your brother did, though he won't remember the fact. He was still a baby when I met your parents in Hong Kong.'

The audience drew in collective breath.

'And I remember how Ursula used to fret about him. One of the reasons I liked her was that she didn't leave her son all day in the care of a local nanny, the way most Europeans did out there. Even the loss of your father can't have changed her so much that she wasn't worried about where you were and what you were doing!'

It was a master-stroke. All of a sudden he had the whole audience on his side against the boys, and there were cries of confirmation.

'That's right! Every time they stay out late she paces up and down – in the garden, on the road – watching for them to come home! And when they do they shout at her for interfering! We've seen it! We've heard it!'

Those who had called out exchanged nods and glances, their expressions grim, and sat back in their chairs. All bar one. Moira O'Pheale remained on her feet, very pale, hands clenched tight on a black leather purse.

She said, 'Phyllis was up late on Wednesday, too. I could hear her from my room, calling Rufus. That's the cat. I don't know what time she actually turned in – I was asleep by then – but ... Oh my God!'

Her face crumpled like tissue paper and she dropped back into her chair, bowing her head.

In Weyharrow people were unaccustomed to displays of naked emotion. They were still shifting and stirring when Judy Jacksett exclaimed, 'Roy! Wasn't it on Wednesday that Boyo didn't come home? That's our dog,' she added. 'He's still not back and the kids are getting frantic.'

Starting, Roy said, 'Why! So it was!'

'So you were out late looking for him. And next day all those orders were filled wrong ... That explains it!'

'And something else as well!' called another voice. 'My father was up late on Wednesday night, too! My grandfather heard him walking up and down on the terrace at midnight! The terrace overlooks the river! And – well, I don't have to remind you what happened to him next morning, do I?'

The speaker was Cedric, hair tousled, clutching the back of the chair in front of him. Furious, Basil turned to glower at him, shaping a retort, but before he could find the right

185

words Joyce Vikes shouted, 'My Harry was up late that night too! With a sick calf! I knew he weren't truly out of his head!'

Someone – a man – said maliciously, 'No, just full of devils, warn't he?'

Was that Ken Pecklow? Steven started and glanced in the direction the words had come from, but realized instantly it couldn't be. Ken was in the wrong part of the room, and what was more he was rising to his feet.

'I agree with Joyce! Harry and me – well, we've been at odds a good long time, but I never thought he were crazy, and I never thought he got the Devil in him, either. What I did think . . .' He paused meaningly, glancing from side to side to make sure everyone was paying proper attention.

'What I did think, and maybe I still do, was this. Did it have to do with one of they chemical sprays he talked about all spring and summer – the very latest, the very newest? Is that what they brew at Trimborne now? Is that what got loose and did the harm?'

Dr Frass jumped up.

'No, sir! We do not manufacture industrial or agricultural chemicals! We make pharmaceuticals – medicines! And I am bound to warn Mr Prosher that if he continues with his unfounded accusations he will be hearing from our lawyers!'

'And from me,' rumbled the man beside Chief Inspector Chade. 'You said you knew who I am, didn't you, Prosher? Then I take it you know why I'm here, as well.'

Don was very pale, but stood his ground. He said, 'Of course I do. To threaten me with the Official Secrets Act, because the stuff that got loose from Helvambrit is being manufactured and tested under government contract–'

'Stop! Stop at once!' the man bellowed.

'I will not!' Abruptly Don was furious. 'There's no way that you can shut me up – *not now I've seen what you've done to my friend Ursula!*'

186

There was an astonished pause. Then, moving in front of the platform, Stick said loud and clear, 'Damn right, man!'

And collared the stranger with help from Chris, while Ken and Harry stood over Chade, and Bill Blocket and Phil Flaken closed on Dr Frass, making it wordlessly clear to Joe Book what would happen if he tried to intervene.

Also the villagers sitting nearest to Basil Goodsir invited him, politely, to hold his peace.

'This is a scandal!' Helen fumed. 'This is an outrage!'

'No it isn't,' a voice called behind her, intending to be heard. 'It's an inquiry!'

It sounded like her son, but when she glanced back she found no clue to who had spoken.

'It's too late anyway, Mr Pipton,' Don said quietly. 'This gentleman, friends, is from Military Intelligence. The substance that escaped from Helvambrit's factory –'

Pipton was struggling madly. Two of Chris's friends came to add their strength to Stick's, ignoring his threats about obstructing him in the execution of his duty.

'The substance,' Don went on, 'is probably the one known as Oneirin, from the Greek word for dreams. We've been hearing rumours for some while, but this is the first time we ever had solid evidence of its effects. What it seems to do is affect the faculty in the brain that distinguishes between what you've dreamed and what you actually remember. In other words, it makes the memory of your dreams more vivid than your memory of the real world.'

He paused, very tense, with sweat pearling on his forehead. At once there was a susurrus of comment, in which Steven wished he could have joined. All those affected were saying, 'Yes! That's exactly what it felt like!'

'Oneirin was originally intended as a battlefield gas,' Don resumed. 'Hence its presentation in vapour form. When it proved unsuitable for disorienting enemy soldiers, a new contract was entered into for its development as a means of

187

interrogating spies and prisoners of war. On the basis of what's happened here, it seems obvious that Helvambrit has again failed to come up with what was promised. What on earth would be the good of trying to extract information from someone who had lost the ability to distinguish dreams from reality? But Helvambrit doesn't want to admit defeat – for the good and sufficient reason that the contract is worth more than half a million pounds a year of the taxpayer's money. *Your* money!'

Basil Goodsir emitted a strangled cry. Helen turned on her chair and slapped his face, her own a mask of rage.

'Right, now you know,' Don said, his tenseness fading. 'And so, tomorrow, will the public. Mr Pipton, I said you were already too late.' He glanced at the clock on the far wall. 'I don't imagine you were able to close down every public phone in the county, much as you would probably have liked to. By now Miss Severance must have been able to get through to at least some of the numbers I gave her, along with the information I've just imparted. Wallace, why don't you grab your chance of getting out of here, too? My paper has a clear beat on the story, but it's too damned important to be kept to ourselves, and I shan't mind in the least if the *Banner* gets it into its late editions. You spell Oneirin O-N-E-I-R-I-N.'

'You bastard,' Wallace said under his breath. 'You son of a bitch!'

But in response to Lisa's frantic urging, he left the hall, people making wary way for him. Silence attended his departure, near complete . . . until abruptly it was broken by the sound of weeping.

It was Moira who began it, fighting to say amid her tears, 'Poor Phyllis! And it wasn't my fault after all!'

'Oh – *Mum*!'

That was from Paul Ellerford, barely audible. He buried his face against his brother's shoulder, racked with sobs.

Within seconds Harold was crying too.

But from some there was a more violent outburst. It broke all at once from half a dozen places in the hall, as people rounded on Dr Frass, Mr Pipton, and Chief Inspector Chade, the handiest targets. Clearest to be heard was Joyce.

'I'll murder them!' she shrieked. 'I'll kill them all for what they done to my Harry!'

Leaping to his feet – Nigel still seemed dazed – Steven shouted, 'Order! Order!'

After a fashion the archdeacon echoed him.

For a dreadful moment he thought they were too late. The furious villagers were turning on the strangers in their midst as though preparing for a lynching party. But help emerged from a completely unexpected quarter.

'Shut up, you bloody fools!' roared a tremendous voice. 'And bloody *grow* up while you have the chance!'

It was Chris the Pilgrim: his beard and hair in a tangle as ever, wearing stained jeans, scuffed boots and a sweater with one elbow out, but taking charge. He jumped up on the dais without bothering to use the steps, and Don retreated to make way for him.

'Who is this ruffian?' Mr Thummage whispered to Steven. 'One of your local yobbos, I suppose!'

'Do as he says and shut up,' Steven muttered wearily. The archdeacon blinked as though not believing anyone could address him in such terms, but after glancing at the councillors ranked at his back he yielded and listened.

'We've been conned!' Chris blasted. 'You lot, and us as well!'

For some reason Steven's gaze had fallen on Cedric, who had looked briefly apprehensive, fidgeting as though he were planning to slip away. He changed his mind and settled back into his chair.

'You worse than us, maybe, because we don't earn enough to pay taxes for the government to take away – and *throw* away, like you've been told! Mr Reporter, sir, you're a brave man! You're going to wind up in court, aren't you? At any rate if this guy Pipton has a say in it!'

Don shrugged and spread his hands. 'We have a fighting chance, according to our lawyers. It's nice of you to call me brave. But I'm not foolhardy. And now the horse is gone they may not want to shut the stable door in case it makes things worse.'

Chris gave a sour grin. 'That figures . . . Like I was saying!' His voice rose to full volume again. 'We were conned the same as you! And Ella! And Cedric's dad – what's your name? Ah, there you are . . . Basil! Yes!

'But we weren't conned the way you were.

'Oh, sure! We were fooled into piling into our bus in the middle of the night and making for Weyharrow because we were convinced the ancient forces were on the move again. We've been hassled by the police and we've been insulted by the locals and some people who got wind of what was going on followed us down here and made incredible idiots of themselves by stealing a side of beef from the hotel to make a sacrifice . . . God *damn!* If there are people who can be that silly anyhow, what's the point of inventing this stuff Oneirin?'

Cedric chuckled; his amusement proved contagious, and even those of the audience who had been most inclined to get up and walk out rather than listen to this outsider decided it could be worth hearing him to the end.

'But even though we were conned, we weren't duped as badly as you lot!' Chris thundered. 'You see, at bottom, we were right! We believed the ancient forces were stirring . . . *and of course they are!*'

There was a half-hearted objection from Mr Thummage, but no one seemed to notice except Steven and Nigel.

'So it wasn't the Devil, like your parson claimed? So it was actually a chemical that leaked from up the river? *So what*? It's a manifestation of the ancient powers anyhow! This world we live in *is* a dream! Or maybe more of a nightmare! Isn't it? It isn't the neat and tidy world of seasons that are always how they should be – mild spring, hot summer, autumn harvests, white Christmases with everybody gathered round the fire and singing carols . . . No!

'No, it's a stinking, disgusting, horrible, loathsome world full of food that's been tainted with chemical sprays and acid rain killing trees and lead from cars that poison your children's minds and make them backward! It's full of terrorists and hijackings and H-bombs and Doctor Xs making drugs to stop you telling truth from falsehood!'

He was shaking with the force of his tirade. For a second he seemed to be overcome, and there was a risk of the audience shouting back at him. Steven found himself clapping to forestall that; quick on the uptake, Don copied him, and others did the same. He thought the next was Ella Kailet, followed by the hippies, but almost immediately all the people who had been affected – no, make that 'afflicted!' – were applauding too.

They were not in the majority, but knowledge of what had happened to them made the rest of those present hesitate and defer. By this time, too, Mr Pipton and Dr Frass had resigned themselves to what was going on, even though their expressions were as thunderous as the archdeacon's. The same applied to Chade. As for Joe Book – *poor Joe*! Steven thought – he had left his post and sought Yvonne's company on a row-end near the middle of the hall, standing beside her and clutching her hand.

What training, in any police-force, could prepare a decent ordinary man like Joe for an invasion by the hideous outer world that had just been so graphically described?

'Well, it sounds as though one sweet little racket has been torpedoed!' Chris barked. 'But how many others are there? How many hundreds, how many thousands? How many farmers like Mr Pecklow are secretly afraid of what the sprays they use may do to people? How many – ?'

'Yes! Yes!'

The shout came from near the fire exit. All eyes turned, and – amazingly – it was Mrs Judger who had spoken, returned from escorting Mr Phibson back to the parsonage.

'Yes!' she said a third time, not so loudly but nonetheless with force. 'I've been with Mr Phibson since he came here, and I know. He's a good man, kind and sensible even though – Never mind! Losing his wife must have been a dreadful blow . . . What counts is this!'

She drew herself up to full height.

'I knew it couldn't be the Devil at work in a righteous soul like his! Even if he thought it was, himself! *I* knew it was those blasted chemicals!'

Nigel had recovered sufficiently to try and regain control of the meeting. He said, 'Thank you, Mrs Judger. I'm sorry you had to miss the main – uh – thrust of the contribution from Mr Prosher, and also from Mr – uh –'

Steven whispered, 'Pilgrim!'

'Mr Pilgrim! But after these extraordinary revelations, and particularly in view of the fact that some among you have laid – uh – hands on two official visitors, an action I'm sure the rest of us greatly deprecate . . .'

He was floundering, and everybody knew it. He gazed round desperately for guidance. It came from Vic Draycock, who leapt to his feet, brushing back a lock of hair.

'Mr Chairman! I've been as overwhelmed by these revelations as anyone! It isn't exactly public knowledge, but I too was out late on Wednesday night – couldn't sleep and took a walk along the river – and in the morning . . . Well, that's not important. Suffice it to say I shared the strange experience so

192

many of us underwent, though luckily with relatively few after-effects . . .'

His listeners were growing restive. Realizing, Vic cut his confession short and came to the point.

'But if you're about to close the meeting, I'd like to move a vote of thanks to Dr Gloze, and Mr Prosher, and – uh – our last speaker, Chris, who put into words what so many of us feel and often can't find the right way to express.'

He sat down.

Nigel was back in command of himself. He said, as by habit and reflex, 'I feel we ought to add Mr Thummage to the vote of thanks. With that amendment I put the motion to the meeting. Seconder?'

There was a frozen pause. Mrs Judger broke it.

'No!'

Nigel blinked at her, appalled.

'No!' she said again. 'Mr Thummage wouldn't take me seriously when I phoned him and asked for help for Mr Phibson! He was rude to me! He talked to me as though I was some giddy girl! *I* don't want to thank him!'

'I second the motion as originally put!' shouted Tom Fidger. At once there was a chorus of approval.

'Any further amendments?' Nigel asked, for the sake of formality. But the objectors, including the chief inspector, Mr Pipton and Dr Frass, were voting with their feet and leaving the hall. The archdeacon, snapping his fingers at his companion, did the same. No one any longer tried to bar their way.

'So moved . . . And passed by acclamation.' Nigel drew a handkerchief from his pocket to wipe his perspiring face. 'I declare the meeting closed. Mr Prosher' – in a lower tone – 'what is it the Americans say about a can of worms? Was that all true, what you told us?'

'All of it,' Don answered grimly. 'And if Chris hadn't stepped in, I'd have gone on to say pretty much what he did.

Doesn't it make you *sick?*'

Abruptly he slammed his fist on the table; people at the doors glanced round, but they went on filtering away.

'Doesn't it make you sick?' he said again. 'This is one of the most beautiful villages in England! Lord, the times I've seen pictures of it in BTA brochures!

'And even here you can't escape the loathsome reality of modern times! That bastard Pipton would love to put me in jail! Thanks to Jenny, I got the story out before he could clamp a lid on it. Wallace must have done the same by now, praise be. Do you realize those idiots have squandered ten million quid on a project that can never work?'

He glared at everyone around, including the baffled parish councillors.

'Even if they had made it work – well, wouldn't it have been just another proof of how sick our society is?'

That was from Chris, whom Rhoda had come up to hug, and Cedric, while the rest of the hippies hovered in front of the platform.

'Yes! Yes!' Don turned to Chris and shook his hand warmly. 'Your intervention was timely, to say the least. I'm much obliged ... Cedric! You are Cedric, aren't you?'

'Uh – yes.'

'I saw your photo all over the drawing-room at the Court when your parents invited me in. Lord, I wish you'd been there when I was! I'd have – No, forget it.'

He drew a deep breath.

'I am wiped out. Not even when I was a war correspondent did I feel this exhausted ... Ah, there's Wilf!'

The red-haired photographer was pushing his way against the flow at the exit. Raising his hand, he made a ring of thumb and forefinger.

'Did Jenny bring it off?' Don called.

'Yep! The story's broken like a scrambled egg! It's on the wire to *everywhere*!'

'Praise be,' Don said softly. 'Now let me depart in peace ... Nigel, we have to rush back to London, but all of a sudden I'm starving hungry. Can we still get something to eat at your hotel?'

Nigel, who had been conversing with departing councillors, turned round. He said after a moment, 'Of course. My chef's a wonder. He proved it last night. I think you ought to be my guests – you and Wilf, and Steven, and ... Chris, how about you? And – uh – your good lady?'

But Rhoda shook her head. She said, 'We don't live like that. You ought to know by now. And there are thirteen of us, a coven.'

'Oh, for God's sake!' Cedric, hovering in the background, exploded. 'Every night the hotel throws out enough to feed a bloody family! I've seen it! Give me the leftovers and I'll carry them across the road myself!'

Stick was eavesdropping. He said nothing, but stretched out one long arm and tapped Cedric on the shoulder. When the latter turned around, he met a broad approving grin.

Then Stick was gone in the wake of Sheila and the girls who had imagined – as he had – that they were boys.

The parish hall was empty but for themselves and the volunteers responsible for tidying up.

Nigel said at length, 'I only asked you, Chris, because I didn't realize before that people like you could talk so much good sense. Will you and Rhoda come to dinner with us if what Cedric takes to your friends isn't leftovers but – say – a good big pot of soup and bread and cheese?'

'Not if the soup has meat in it,' said Rhoda firmly.

'Oh, hell ... All right! I'll see what Tim can do –'

'Forget it,' Chris interrupted with a sigh. 'That's what's wrong with you. All of you. That's why the world's in such a stinking mess. It's because of people who can say what you just did.'

'What do you mean?' cried Nigel, bridling.

'You didn't say: "I'll see what *I* can do!" ... Come on, Rhoda love. Let's get our show on the road. Ella, want a ride to town?'

'Yes please. If you've got room.'

'We'll make some if we haven't. Come along.'

14

The night was dry and mild. But when they left the hall they might as well have walked into a whirlwind.

Weyharrow was fermenting like a brewer's vat. A hundred parsons claiming to be possessed each by a thousand demons could never have created such a stir. Some of those who had been at the meeting were dashing from house to neighbours' house to spread the news; others were on the phone, calling up friends outside the village; others yet had headed for the Marriage or the Bridge Hotel in search of drinks to calm their nerves and eager ears to pour their charge of gossip into.

A few of them even remembered how to spell Oneirin.

As for the police, they had vanished in the wake of Mr Chade and taken Mr Pipton with them, apart from Joe, who stood like an uneasy statue in the middle of the green, watching the hippies as they folded their tents and loaded them back aboard the bus. Prior to departure, Chris came over to him.

'Nothing personal, man,' he said. 'You understand?'

Joe nodded miserably, and as soon as the bus had trundled off across the bridge he made for home. In the past he had been inclined to agree with Yvonne when she complained about the location of the police house they were obliged to occupy: why couldn't it have been beside the river with a decent outlook? Tonight he was immensely glad it wasn't.

What would a policeman have done who thought his dreams were real? Worse than a teacher or a schoolkid – worse even than a parson, maybe!

Lord, he might have gone around arresting people like Stick!

Shuddering at the notion, he closed the door and bent to hug his kids as they rushed towards him for a belated good-night kiss.

Wallace Jantrey and Lisa Jopp had left for London; they had said goodbye to one or two people. The archdeacon and his driver had simply gone. Nobody seemed to have noticed when, or to care. The same applied to Dr Frass, while the Goodsirs had driven back to the Court, Basil in a filthy temper and Helen in a screaming tantrum. The only thing they seemed able to agree on was the need to sue Helvambrit.

'Fat chance of beating bastards like that!' was Cedric's jaundiced view.

But of course it would make a field day for lawyers . . .

He had stood a long while in shadow near the churchyard wall, the metal of his cycle's handlebars cold under his trembling hands. He was wondering whether he ought not to have asked Chris and Rhoda to wait while he went home and packed a bag, so he could join them on their pilgrimage.

At length, though, he had sighed and thrown his leg across the saddle, and set off up the steep and winding road for home.

Next year, perhaps. Next year . . .

But in his heart of hearts he knew what that meant.

Never.

Moira would have liked a drink. She was shaking from head to toe. But the cooking-sherry bottle was empty and she couldn't face the people to whom she had accused Phyllis of all sorts of dreadful deeds. She retreated to the cottage, where she found Rufus waiting for his supper.

She didn't like him much. She had never liked cats. But, mechanically, she poured milk into a saucer and shook dry catfood into his usual dish. When there was a ring at the front door she ignored it. When there was a knock at the back door, she couldn't.

It was Jerry Blocket, saying awkwardly, 'Moira, I don't know if I ought to say I'm sorry . . . Should I?'

Unable to answer, she shook her head.

'Well – well, I don't really want to. I'd rather say thanks . . . Look, I thought I might find you down at the Marriage –'

She had raised both hands by reflex before he uttered the next word, reaching in his jacket pocket.

'– because after what you've been through I felt you might need a drink. I still do. Here.'

He set a half-bottle of whisky on the table, and turned to go.

A thousand images flashed through Moira's mind. Was she being paid off, like a tart, for last night's pleasure? Well, there hadn't been much of that about it. Was Jerry trying to buy a lien on her future favours? If so, his standards couldn't be very high . . .

But all these fugitive ideas evaporated, quick as dreams. She heard herself saying, 'Don't go away. Let's drink to Phyllis. I want somebody to know how much I'm going to miss her, *and how much I hate myself!*'

Grave, Jerry said (and how could she never have noticed him properly before, even last night?). He had a nice face, too young to be lined like hers, spared the bitterness of a disastrous marriage, spared the burden of knowing that a friend had taken her own life . . . he said, 'After what you told us in the pub last night, I think we all began to understand you better.'

'What did I say?' she cried.

'You told us about Declan hitting you. You never said that before.'

'I did to Phyllis!'

'Yes, but she wouldn't have passed it on, would she?'

No. Naturally not. What was it Ursula once said? 'She doesn't have an ounce of malice in her body?'

She was crying. Jerry took her in his arms.

There wasn't, obviously, any future in it. But it was very nice to find a man who worried about her.

Under roof after roof after roof around Weyharrow: people saying to one another, 'So *that's* why!'

Sometimes it led to reconciliation: 'You said it was my fault we got the orders mixed up!' Roy Jacksett snapped at Judy. 'Well, now you know it was something that I couldn't help, how about saying – ?'

He had been going to add, 'you're sorry.'

But at that optimal moment there was a whine from the back door. As one, they erupted to their feet and ran to open it.

And there was Boyo, covered in mud, limping on his off front paw, with a great raw wound around that leg. He hobbled into the kitchen and made straight for the water-bowl.

'He's been caught in a trap!' Judy cried.

'Yes! That's why he didn't come home! It wasn't a bitch after all . . .' Roy bent on one knee, patting Boyo's back. 'You poor beast! I'm going to find out who's setting illegal snares!'

There was a cascade of feet on the stairs. The kids had woken.

'Boyo! You've come home! Where've you been? Goodness! Your *leg*! You poor old thing!'

When finally they got everything sorted out – Boyo fed, his injury dressed, the kids packed off back to bed – they looked at one another . . . and thought awhile . . . and finally they broke down laughing.

Contented, arm in arm, they went upstairs.

Sometimes, though, it led to the opposite:

Waiting in the hallway, Carol Draycock rasped, 'So you finally decided to come home!'

Blinking as he crossed the threshold, Vic said, 'But you've

no idea what's been going on! The meeting was – '

'I heard all about the meeting! People have been ringing up for the past hour! Why didn't you come straight back and tell me yourself? Did you think I wasn't interested?'

'I got detoured,' Vic muttered, hanging up his coat. 'I was asked to stop off at the pub and talk about it. Some people seem to value my opinion, even if you don't.'

'That's right!' she blazed. 'I don't!'

He blinked at her. 'Now, Carol darling – '

'Don't you "darling" me!' She advanced on him, fists clenched. 'You're a bloody hypocrite, that's what you are! Always looking for someone to pity you!'

'What the hell do you mean?' Vic blasted back.

'Just this!' She drew herself up, breathing hard. 'While you were out, what you often said might happen, did. Tommy managed to jump up and catch hold of the rope that pulls down the attic ladder!'

'Christ! Did he do much damage?'

'None at all. I was up there straight away; I'd heard it go clang . . . But have you forgotten that before we got married I worked – worked hard – to earn my own living in an office? I wasn't just a secretary, I was PA to a managing director!'

'Of course not!' Vic moved to lay a placating hand on her arm. 'That's why I have such respect for you! That's why I wanted to marry you – '

She interrupted. 'Respect? Hah! About as much as I have left for you!'

'What on earth do you mean?'

'You told me that *grand* and *wonderful* article of yours had been deleted from your disc!'

'It had!' Vic cried.

'The hell it had!' If there had been a spittoon handy Carol would have used it, to express her contempt. 'Since you obviously weren't going to come home in a hurry, once I'd packed Tommy off to bed I decided to investigate your word processor.'

'If you've mucked it up – !' Vic shouted.

'Oh, don't give me that,' Carol sighed. 'Ever since you bought it you've been telling me how easy it is to use – and that, at least, is true. It took me twenty minutes to find out.'

Vic's face was pasty-pale. He was backing away from his blazing-eyed wife, until at last the door met his back.

'Big man!' she said mockingly. 'Boasting about how marvellous you are because you can run a system that took me less than half an hour to get the hang of. It's a terrific manual, by the way – the best I've seen. And what did I find when I loaded the disc you wrote your article on? There it was! It hasn't been deleted!'

She turned her back with a grimace of disgust. He followed her, his expression pleading.

'I know what must have happened!' he cried. 'It must have been because I was out late on Wednesday night and caught a dose of this damned chemical from Helvambrit – '

Pointing at the stove, she disregarded him.

'There's your supper, what's left of it. It was overdone half an hour ago and I haven't looked at it since. I don't want to. I don't want to look at you, either – you fake, you hypocrite, you *stupid braggart*!'

'But, Carol – !'

'Here I was' – she seemed not to have heard him – 'fooled into thinking you can do things I can't! Why? Why did I think marrying a teacher was a good idea? I must have been insane! I knew damn well that all the time I was at school my teachers lied to me, or fed me their own personal obsessions ... Don't come near me! You sleep downstairs! If it wasn't Sunday tomorrow – if it wasn't for Tommy's schooling – I'd leave you right a-bloody-*way*!'

Dissolving into sobs, she rushed upstairs and slammed the bedroom door, leaving Vic to explain to empty air, 'But it wasn't my fault! It was a nightmare that suddenly came real!

You know, like the one I often told you, the one where I wind up in class on Monday morning and find I don't know anything about the subject I'm supposed to teach!'

True or not, it did no good for him to say it.

And sometimes it made not a blind bit of difference: 'What did you think of the meeting?' Sheila asked.

Hilary and Sam exchanged glances. Hilary shrugged and answered for them both.

'Something bad came through the window the other night. It made Stick imagine we were boys.'

'That's all?' Stick prompted.

'Well . . .' Hilary bit her lip and gave a mischievous grin. 'Maybe we thought we were boys, too. Just for a bit.'

'Would you rather?'

'Be boys? No! We'd grow up to be men, and men do stupid things.'

'Such as . . . ?'

'They build bombs and fight wars and kill people,' Sam said with utter certainty. 'That's sick!'

'True,' Stick said. And repeated, almost breathlessly, 'True . . . Okay, you lot! Cocoa! Bed! I'll go and warm your milk!'

Later, when Sheila came to join him in the living-room and share a joint, she was giggling.

'What's the joke?' Stick inquired, proffering a match.

'Know what Sam said when I kissed her good night? She said, "Is Stick really a man? I mean, I know he has a beard, but is he *really* a man?"'

Already chuckling, Stick said, 'So what did you say?'

I said, 'Of course! Why should you think he isn't?'

'And . . . ?'

'She said, "Because he doesn't go about hitting people."'

There was a pause. Eventually Stick said, putting his arm companionably around Sheila and groping inside bra and sweater for her breast, 'That's good. Let's keep them feeling that way, shall we?'

'Long as you like.'

She turned and nuzzled through his beard, seeking his mouth with hers.

'What's going to happen here now?' Steven said.

Those at the table with him had been waiting for the question. The Bridge Hotel was packed, not just with the usual Saturday trade that occupied the bar, but also because several of Nigel's fellow-councillors, and their spouses, had decided to grab a bite or a drink before going home. Everybody seemed to need the chance to talk to someone else about tonight's revelations. Snatches of conversation had come their way, many directed at Nigel.

'The Goodsirs should never have been granted their planning permission at Trimborne!'

'That's right! Wasn't it enough to let them cut down all the woods along the valley? When I was a boy . . .'

'Of course the rot set in when they allowed a garage on the green instead of down a side-road. Have another?'

'As chairman of the council, Nigel should have – Where the hell's he got to? He was here just now!'

Nigel was out of earshot. He had other problems on his mind. Jack Fidger had stood in as best he could, but not only were there more tables booked in the restaurant than there was time to fill and empty and refill and clear by closing time, but seemingly there was a double room that had been double-booked, and two visitors were voicing their complaints for all and sundry . . .

With vast relief Nigel recognized the number of the room.

'No problem!' he crowed. 'That was the one the people from the *Banner* had. They've gone. We only need to change the sheets and towels . . . Do forgive us!' – to the guests. 'But it's been a most unusual day. Has anybody told you yet about this gas that leaked from the Helvambrit factory. . . ? No? Well, not to worry! It's been taken care of! But here you're in the midst of history, you know! Have a drink on the house and I'll explain!'

Despite his declaration of hunger Don Prosher displayed little appetite when food was finally set before him in the hotel restaurant. He seemed to welcome Steven's question as giving him an excuse to push aside his plate and echo it while lighting a cigar.

'What's going to happen here?' he repeated. 'Well! I'm flattered to be asked, but the person you ought to apply to is our landlord . . . No, he's far too busy, isn't he? Let's ask someone who knows your village better than I do. I mean, all I did was walk in and apply a few standard principles, you know – plus a trace of inside information. And here she comes, for goodness' sake!'

He and Wilf, who was seated at the other end of the table, jumped to their feet. Approaching from the door was Jenny, looking radiant. She embraced Don so warmly it made Steven briefly jealous.

'How does it feel to have filed your first international beat? Don't tell me – I remember when it happened to me! Sit down! Grab a chair from somewhere, anywhere! Steve, make room! Don't you realize how well the cause of freedom of expression has been served today by this pretty friend of yours?' He patted her affectionately on the bottom.

'Now sit down, Jenny – have a glass of wine, you deserve it more than most of us . . . Find her a menu, somebody – ah, there we are. I don't know what's left this late – '

'I'm not hungry. Too excited.'

'Well, that's understandable. I was just talking about you, you know. Steven asked what's going to happen in Weyharrow now, and I said he ought to ask someone who knows the place better than I do, meaning you.'

'But I don't really,' Jenny said after a swig of wine. 'Steve knows that.'

There was a pause.

Abruptly Steven crumpled his paper napkin and tossed it to the middle of the table.

He said, 'It was stupid of me to ask anyhow, wasn't it?'

'What? What do you mean?'

'I know the answer. And it's sweet FA!'

'That's ridiculous!' Jenny exclaimed. 'Things will never be the same again! This affair has changed people's lives!'

'I'd have said so,' Don confirmed, eyeing Steven sidelong. 'For instance, there's been a grand reconciliation between two feuding families – '

'You mean Ken's and Harry's?' Jenny butted in. 'Yes! And that's probably only the start of it! You know, since time immemorial this village has had the full-scale squire-and-parson bit, but after Mr Phibson started talking about the Devil and Basil called for that boy to be hanged...!'

'And by the time the world's press has converged on the pharmaceutical factory,' Don supplied, 'and acres of paper have been devoted to the story of how people at Weyharrow were accidentally turned into guinea-pigs for the Ministry of Defence, or Ministry of War as it should properly be called ... Steven, I'm not convincing you, am I? Why not?'

'Because last night you led me up the bloody garden path – *that's* why!'

Don was silent a moment. Then he shrugged. 'I have to plead guilty. But I was using you as a kind of touchstone. Knowing, or rather guessing, what I did, I wanted to hear how someone like yourself, rational but unaware of the facts, would counter all these claims about possession by the Devil. I'm sorry I upset you. How, though, does this prove that Jenny's wrong? *My* life's been changed! I never meant to speak out at your meeting! It was seeing Ursula in hospital that drove me to it.'

The last few words were almost inaudible; he gulped more wine.

'Ah, you weren't on the platform during the meeting proper,' Steven muttered. 'You didn't sense what I did about the councillors –'

'Wasn't it amazing how well that fellow Pilgrim spoke?' Don cut in. 'I had my eye on Cedric, who's supposed to be a friend of his, and the schoolteacher too: what's his name?'

'Vic Draycock,' Jenny supplied.

'Yes, him. I swear they were both as astonished as I was.'

'My guess is,' Steven said sourly, 'they never met Chris before when he wasn't stoned.'

'Oh, come on!' Don exclaimed.

'No, I'm serious!' Steven drew a deep breath. 'You may think of this evening's meeting as a great event – proof of fundamental democracy in Britain, your role in it, and Jenny's too, as evidence that we live in a free society, truth will out, and all that kind of crap. But do you know why I was put on the platform?'

His voice had risen. All around people were interrupting their own conversations, including several councillors, two at least of whom had joined in Nigel's attempts to persuade him to settle here in the room of Dr Tripkin.

He was pleased about that. The same recklessness was overtaking him as had supervened more than once already. What he had it in mind to say might give offence; too bad!

'I was put on to talk people out of believing that anything extraordinary had happened! You heard the drivel I was forced to utter! Damnation, you fed me half of it! And I went along with the idea, because I've always dreamed of a country practice and it was made very clear that if I co-operated I'd have one within my grasp.

'And then after I'd given my talk and seen how it affected people, I felt ashamed! Don't you understand? I felt I'd been bought and paid for!'

He drained his glass and slammed it back on the table.

'Thank heaven for Mrs Flaken and Mr Fidger! If they hadn't spoken up, everybody would have been fobbed off with the official lie that nothing had actually happened, and the first they'd have known about how serious it really was would have been when they read about it in your paper! If any of them take the *Globe*, that is!'

'As a matter of fact,' Wilf said mildly, 'we sell over twenty copies here. I asked.'

For a second Steven was thrown off-stride. But he recovered swiftly.

'And I suppose the *Banner* sells a hundred! That's not the point, is it?'

'The point is,' Jenny said in a firm clear voice, 'that the truth *has* come to light. A bit late, maybe, but it's out, and all the Piptons of the world can't stuff this bit of toothpaste back in the tube.'

'Good girl!' said Don, and squeezed her hand.

Steven seized the wine-bottle and poured the last into his glass. He said, 'That still isn't the point!'

'Then what is?'

'They called tonight's meeting to put a damper on the matter! To try and shut people up!'

'But it didn't work!' Jenny cried.

'No thanks to the people of Weyharrow!'

'Nonsense! You just said it was because of Tom and Mary – Wait a moment!' She hunched forward, elbows on the table, her keen blue gaze on Steven's anguished face.

'I just thought of something. Don, are there any after-effects from Oneirin?'

'The only ones known are the ones reported from right here ... Hmm! I see what you're driving at!' He whistled under his breath. 'But you're in a better position to answer that than I am. How do you feel now?'

By this time the entire dining-room was paying attention,

including the waitresses. Nigel, returning, was brought up to date in whispers by one of his fellow councillors, and thrust forward to eavesdrop too.

'Well . . .' Jenny was flushing to find herself the focus of the gathering. 'Well, I felt terribly ashamed of what I'd come so close to doing, naturally. But – '

'But what?' Don demanded.

'But that's over. Now I know it wasn't really due to any fault in me. I did think it was! I told you, didn't I, Steven? I remember saying – '

' "I don't have the right antennae for a reporter." Yes.' His voice was gravelly.

'Now what I'm mostly feeling is – I don't know how to put it – maybe a sort of grief? Yes, that's it. Grief. I don't feel ashamed any more, but I regret that the world is as it is, and I feel sorry for everybody in it. Including me.'

'On that basis,' Don suggested softly, 'it seems you, Steven, are still in the first phase. Maybe you were hit with a stronger dose.'

'Oh, I'm not sorry for myself!' Steven rasped. 'That I promise you! But I'm sorry as all get out for the people who tried to stop this evening's meeting from digging out the truth!'

He jumped to his feet. 'Thanks for the dinner, what I was able to eat of it! I'm off home. I have patients to look after in the morning – '

'On Sunday?' Jenny exclaimed.

Steven checked in mid-movement, looking foolish.

'Before you go, I have a question for you,' Don said, tilting back his chair. 'Did your experience with Oneirin make you doubt your competence as a doctor?'

Steven's forehead was gleaming with sweat. He muttered, 'When Mr Ratch phoned me from the chemist's, yes. But only for a moment! When it turned out that Mr Cashcart thought my prescription had done him more good than all the pills he'd had before – '

'Thought?'

Don inserted the single word with the subtlety of a hypodermic needle.

For a moment it seemed that he had got through to Steven. Then the young doctor shook his head and gave a harsh laugh.

'That was a good try, Don. No one can doubt that you're a bloody smart guy. But I'm thinking along very different lines. Just as a for instance: what's the betting that tomorrow their precious archdeacon – or someone very like him – will be sent here to preach reassuring sermons in Mr Phibson's place? As of this moment, I think I'd *prefer* a world beset by devils to the one we have, poisoned by chemicals that drive you mad! You can exorcise devils, can't you? But what the hell can anybody do about the muck those careless bastards let escape?'

And he stormed out.

'Spoken like a doctor,' Don said when the resulting uproar had died down. 'That guy has his head screwed on.'

He tapped ash from his cigar. Catching sight of Nigel, he added, 'It'll be damned silly of your people if you let him get away. Speaking of getting away, though, may we have the bill?'

Ignoring that, Nigel said, 'What do you mean? You heard what he said about us! Think we want someone with that kind of attitude in Weyharrow?'

Jenny too was staring at Don in disbelief, though Wilf was sitting back in his chair and inspecting his nails as though afraid of finding country dirt beneath them.

'Yes,' Don said after a pause. 'That's exactly who you need. I don't think you can have been listening.'

Nigel reddened. 'I came in late on the argument because I had to sort out a problem.'

'But you heard me say: "spoken like a doctor"?'

'Ah . . . Well, yes, of course.'

'And a proper doctor is exactly what you need! Do you believe in devils – actual objective devils taking over people's souls?'

Disconcerted, Nigel shook his head.

'I should bloody hope not! On the other hand, now you know there's been at least one major leak of Oneirin from Helvambrit, *and* that the stuff has after-effects lasting days or more, I hope you're very worried indeed! That's what Steven meant! You can't argue with a chemical poison in your blood and bones! It's *there*, and because the stuff is secret you can't go and buy an antidote from the chemist's! *That's* what Steven saw at once, that none of you lot seemed to have cottoned on to yet! I'll lay a bet that the only people here who've even started to think about suing Helvambrit are your lords and masters the Goodsirs who so much hate the firm because they bought the Trimborne mill instead of paying rent for it, which would have kept Basil and Helen in luxury for the indefinite future! Did none of you notice their faces when I said the Oneirin contract is worth over half a million pounds a year?'

He drew on his cigar and found with a grimace of disgust that he would have to relight it.

Nervous, Nigel produced and struck a match. He said, 'But you can't expect us to invite someone here who feels the way Steven does about us.'

There was a rumble of agreement from the rest of the company.

Blowing smoke, Don shook his head.

'He won't if you do.'

There was a puzzled silence. At length one of the other councillors strode forward.

'All right! I suppose we're obliged to you for telling us what really happened – though I don't like your paper, or its pinko politics! But you don't have any right to tell us what we ought to do! You march in, all the way from London or somewhere, and start giving orders like you own the bloody place!'

Don fixed him with a level gaze. He said, 'I think you missed my point. What I meant was that if you drive Dr Gloze away you'll wind up with someone else to replace Dr – what's his name? – Tripkin, who either won't know or won't believe that some of the nervous cases he has to deal with stem from leaks at Helvambrit. He'll just scatter tranquillizers around the way your farmers do the sprays that Mr Pecklow is concerned about!'

Thrusting back his chair, he rose to his feet.

'Speaking of whom! How is it that *I* – who've only been here since yesterday – realized how amazing it was when he took the same side as Mr Vikes?'

He stared down any answer, and went on: 'I'll tell you! It's because Dr Gloze noticed! Who had only met them when he had to dress their bruises after they got in that fight the other morning! Think a reporter from outside, like me, can catch up that quickly on what's going on? Nuts! All I could do was watch Dr Gloze's face during the meeting . . . and from his expression I figured out what I just said. And I'm not wrong, am I? You really were surprised when the Vikeses and the Pecklows turned into allies *even though you too were closing ranks*!'

'What do you mean?' said the former speaker uncertainly.

'Against him! Against me! Against anybody who would tell you what was going on was due to anything but devils!'

Once more there was a pause. Don ended it with a glance at his watch.

'Nigel, I asked for the bill. It isn't here yet.'

There was a pause before the response came.

'Oh! Oh, I thought you knew you were invited . . .' Nigel drew himself up, with a glance at his fellow councillors.

'And, you know, I said all along he'd be a good doctor for

Weyharrow . . .'

Realizing that wasn't going to wear, he added hastily, 'Not of course for the reason you just spelled out. Just because – well – I got the impression he was *sound*.'

Sound was a good word. Nods greeted it.

'For what it's worth, I think so too,' Don sighed. 'Thanks for your generosity; I hope it may already have been repaid, because I took special care to mention your hotel in my story, and that's a bit of free publicity if nothing else, though I hold no brief for what the subs may have done to my text . . . Wilf, are you ready? I want to phone in an update from the car.'

The redhead spread his hands, as if to say: 'Can't be too soon for me.'

'And thanks again to you, Jenny,' Don concluded, bending to kiss her cheek.

But she avoided him, looking elsewhere. She said, 'You know, there's one thing I still don't get. This is the age of the information revolution, right? Everybody has access to floods of it all the time! More newspapers are sold – there are more news programmes on TV – more people have typewriters and photocopiers and word processors than ever before . . . Yet these people here' – with abrupt defiance, glancing at Nigel first and then the rest of the customers – 'let a scandal like this one carry on right under their fucking *noses*! Why? Why did it have to be *you* that broke the story?'

Abruptly her large blue eyes were full of tears.

While the onlookers were still recovering from the shock of hearing a pretty girl use a crude term they might have passed over had it emanated from almost anybody else, Don laid a friendly hand on Jenny's shoulder.

His answer was almost a whisper, though no one missed it.

'I've been in this job longer than you've been alive . . .'

He briskened. 'Right! Thanks again! Wilf, got the carkeys? Fine! And – oh, yes. Someone will keep an eye on the Ellerford kids, won't they? Make sure they don't do anything

213

stupid like set the house on fire? You know I met their parents in Hong Kong; if there's anything I can do to help I will.'

Mechanically Nigel said as he followed Don and Wilf to the front entrance and signalled for their coats to be returned, 'Yes, it's in hand. Tomorrow – no, not tomorrow because it's Sunday – next week a lawyer I know, who takes care of lots of people's affairs around here . . .'

'Ralph Haggledon?' – with a suspicious cock of his head.

'Any reason why not?'

'Because unless I'm completely off my rocker he's going to be preoccupied for the immediate future with the suit the Goodsirs are liable to bring against Helvambrit. I'll find out whether my solicitor in London has a correspondent in the area. And I'll pass on details to you. If your chef wants to sue, he'll need a neutral lawyer . . .'

He grew suddenly aware that most of the customers from the dining-room had decided that this was the best time to end their meals and follow him. Rounding on them, he cried: 'Yes! I am talking about the Goodsirs who sold the woods along the Chap valley for lumbering and the Trimborne mill to Helvambrit and now are more than likely getting set to sue before you even think of it in spite of the foul way you were treated! Mr Draycock told me that hereabouts "Goodsir" is a nickname for the Devil! Take my advice and don't look any further for the power of evil in your village! No matter what your parson says! Good *night!*'

A little after the door had closed on Don and Wilf, the company dispersed, as gloomy in its different way as those who had quit the Marriage under threat of demons.

Seeming to match their mood, since the public meeting ended clouds had overrun the valley from the west.

On the riverside terrace of the Court, Marmaduke watched

them blotting out the welkin. He was sitting on a stone bench that, despite the blanket wrapped around him, seemed to suck the warmth from his scrawny, aged hams. When he heard Basil's car on the driveway, he found he was too tired to rise.

He was weary, but not uncontent. All the precautions that were his to take had now been taken. Awareness of that fact remained to comfort him when he realized that something more than cloud was cutting off his vision of the stars.

Until the last he fought to keep his eyes ajar. They were fixed open when he ceased to breathe.

15

There had been noises from outside the Doctor's House: cars roaring past, perhaps – Steven thought bitterly – after their drivers and passengers had stayed longer than he at the hotel or pub.

He had eaten the hors-d'oeuvre of his dinner, plus a few mouthfuls of what followed. Also he had taken at most two glasses of white wine. Yet he couldn't remember what the main course had been; he might as well have been drunk to the point of amnesia!

Next time someone asked him, 'Are forces of evil at large in Weyharrow?', he was resolved to answer YES!

This damned village was unbearable!

He had changed into pyjamas in the sparsely-furnished guestroom, washed, brushed his teeth, gone through the standard nightly ritual, when it dawned on him that he was hungry. Preparing his speech had drained him of energy – delivering it, for what little it proved to be worth – and then taking over from Nigel Mender when he broke down under pressure . . .

He what?

He was already heading downstairs – he had made a mug of hot Bovril and a slice of toast to fill his belly – he had disposed of this exiguous nourishment . . . when he stopped and thought again.

And the word that haunted his mind was: *after-effects*.

He shook his head abruptly. He was in the kitchen with an empty mug before him and a plate that bore dry crumbs. He rose, glancing at his watch and realizing with dismay what time it was, to put the used crockery in the sink.

216

A car pulled up outside.

He ran water over the plate and mug, mechanically.

There was a tap at the front door.

He ignored it.

There was a ring at the bell.

That was loud enough to be heard next door. Annoyed, he marched into the hall, set to say, 'Dr Hastoby in Hatterbridge is on duty this weekend – '

Instead he said, blinking, 'Jenny?'

She confronted him, hands on hips, glaring. 'Yes, it's me!' – kicking the door to with her heel. 'And you're not bloody going to turn me out! Come here!'

Once more engulfed by recklessness, he did so.

'Why didn't you stay?' – spelled out by wet lips against his neck. 'Don was right! And he's been in his job longer than I've been alive!'

What am I doing here? I'm in bed, not alone! This is incredible! What became of my pyjamas – her clothes?

But he did know, if only vaguely. He recollected, when he set his mind to it, how his hands had met the sleekness of her inner thighs as he drew down her jeans.

Who? Not possible for it to be Jenny ...

It was.

What, though, was she saying? It had to do with the after-effects of inhaling Oneirin –

'I'm not a dream! Damn you! I'm *real real real*!'

And his mouth remembered shaping foolish words.

But not as keenly as the rest of him remembered her.

'I knew if someone didn't do this right away it would be too late for bad and all and I'm so glad I figured it out right because I've made so many crazy mistakes ...'

It was Sunday morning. There was light behind the close-drawn curtains, grey and misty. Steven stretched and turned over, and finally convinced himself that someone real was talking to him.

He had thought it all imagination.

But she was rolling him on his back, her hand exploring his crotch, erecting and straddling him, speaking as it were with both her mouths as her breasts bobbed up and down. She was saying again, 'I wish you'd stayed to hear what Don said about you! He was right! If a place like this doesn't have a doctor that can tell the difference between the Devil and a leak of chemicals – !'

He cried out, a blast of over-long chastity overcoming him. (Last night . . . ? But last night was a veil of dream.)

She fell beside him, snugglingly content, one arm across his chest, and carried on with what she was saying.

'*And* if a place like this doesn't have someone like me whose business it is to watch and listen and take notice, people like Frass can get away with murder!'

He yawned tremendously. When he could, he said, 'I'm not sure I follow.'

'Don't you see?' She sat up, arms linked around knees, head turned away from him. 'We shouldn't have had to wait until Mr Phibson went off his head before finding out what was really going on. Don said as much last thing before he and Wilf got back in their car and drove away. He said – and I'm absolutely sure he's right – that but for the lucky accident of there being a reporter on the spot, who . . . No, I oughtn't to repeat the rest.'

He caressed her back. 'Go on.'

'Well' – biting her lip – 'he made it sound as though I'd done something special. All I did was make a few phone calls.'

'And turn down my invitation to dinner,' Steven murmured. He was waking up by degrees, and discovering that he felt much better than he had during the past few days. His mind felt normally alert.

'Yes. Sorry about that . . . But, you see, I did it for my sake, not the sake of the people here. Do you know what I mean?' She turned a troubled gaze on him.

'Same reason I made that godawful speech.'

'I suppose so.'

There was a pause. Eventually, sitting up, Steven said, 'Well, things did turn out better than I expected.'

'I know. But I think Don was right when he said – Of course, you weren't there when I preached my little sermon about the information revolution. I was saying roughly that when everyone is supposed to be better informed than ever in history it doesn't seem to make much difference. And just before he and Wilf left Don said it's because we don't make use of it. People who want to be reporters – he was aiming this at me, and I promise you I got his point – think they have to go to London or some other big city, or places where there are riots or crimes, because all the news is happening there. He said it isn't the right way to go about it any longer. He said it's a hangover from the old centralized pattern due to the invention of the railways, and the pattern's changing, so that a major news story can break even in a hole-in-the-corner place like this. And what's happened here is going to have national repercussions, which is typical of the way the future's likely to develop. At least,' she concluded doubtfully, 'that's more or less what he said. I think.'

'Heavy thinking this early in the day has never been my forte,' Steven sighed. He turned over to glance at the bedside clock and discovered it wasn't nearly as early as he had imagined. He sat up.

'Goodness! We shan't be able to find a *Globe* anywhere within miles! They'll have been snapped up!'

'It's okay, it's okay! They keep all the papers for me every day! But' – her tone altered – 'we ought to find out how much of the story actually got into print.'

She swung her legs to the floor, looking around for her

clothes. He too rose from bed.

'I'll go and make some coffee.'

'You do that' – drawing on her panties. 'I'll get the papers.'
Jeans – sweater, not bothering with her bra – and shoes.
'Back in five minutes!'

'Right!' – seizing his dressing-gown from the peg behind
the door. Tying the sash, he was struck by a sudden thought.

'Uh – does anybody know you're here? I mean, I suppose
your landlord knows you were out all night . . .'

'Oh, Steve!' In the doorway, she blew him a kiss. 'As Don
said, the old patterns are changing! Even in Weyharrow!'

Alone in the kitchen, filling the kettle and setting it to boil,
Steven pondered the implications of the past few days. Last
night, he remembered, he had spoken with great bitterness
about the determination of the local Establishment to make
people believe nothing had really happened – that it was all a
storm in a teacup.

Nonetheless, it had turned into a whirlwind.

*Don is right. Every community nowadays needs a reporter, or
someone who can be relied on to blow the gaff, at least. Every
community needs someone who can look beyond the comfortable
habits of the past and say, 'This might be dangerous – this might
be fatal!'*

As though to underline his thoughts, the bell for morning
service began to toll from the church. He wondered whether
his prediction had been right, and the archdeacon – or someone sent by him – would be preaching hollow comfort and
false reassurance yet again.

It must not go on! The ancient pattern – yes – was breaking
up.

He began to think in terms of giving an interview to the
Chapminster Chronicle when he took over Dr Tripkin's practice. Now it was known that the village's misfortunes were
indirectly due to the Goodsir family, and their greed, it

220

wasn't likely that people here would much respect the old squirearchy in times to come. After Mr Phibson's breakdown they would doubtless have less respect for Parson, too. Who was to fill the void, if not the doctor for his knowledge, and the reporter, for being in contact with the greater world beyond the limits of the village? It was a parallel . . .

Not, of course, that one could make it quite exact. But it was a most intriguing prospect. Weyharrow might set a useful trend.

A tap at the door: no doubt Jenny. He went to answer.

And it was, arms full of newspapers, but face downcast.

'What's wrong?' he demanded. 'Didn't they run the story?'

'Oh, it's all over the front page,' she muttered, pushing past him. 'Questions are likely to be asked in the House – people from the Ministry of Defence are going to be hauled over the coals for wasting public money – everything I dreamed of is happening.'

'Then what's wrong?' he repeated, following her into the kitchen where she dumped the papers on the table.

'Marmaduke died in the night. Marmaduke Goodsir. I don't suppose you met him. I did, two or three times. He was the only one of that ghastly family worth a spit in the bloody ocean. Apparently Basil and Helen got back last night and found him dead in his chair. Know what that means?' She fixed him with a blue glare. 'Now Basil can do what he likes – break up the library and sell it to America – turn the Court into a hotel – anything could happen! Everyone in the village who leases a house or land from the Goodsirs is scared stiff! This is *awful*!'

Mechanically he handed her the promised cup of coffee; mechanically she accepted it and made to sip, but it was still too hot.

He said at length, 'You know something?'

'What?'

'I suspect you care for Weyharrow.'

Hand on cup, she checked. After a moment's thought she said, 'I think you're right. And I think you must, too.'

'I just discovered that I do. Sit down. I'll tell you what I've been thinking while you were out . . . Eggs and bacon? You didn't eat anything last night.'

'Please don't tempt me. I'm on a diet, as usual . . . Oh, all right: an egg. Poached, though, not fried. Dry bread.'

'Speaking medically, I approve.' He hunted among the kitchen cupboards for a poacher, found one, and poured in water. Over his shoulder he said, 'Old Mr Goodsir's death is another part of the way the pattern's breaking up, isn't it? Life in a village like this must once have been very certain, very predictable, very secure. I mean there've been no civil wars, let alone invasions, for centuries –'

'Invasions, yes,' she said absently, perusing the *Globe*. 'Chris the Pilgrim and his bunch.'

'Hmm! You're right. I hadn't thought of it that way. But that only adds to the force of my argument.'

'You haven't told me what it is yet . . . Oh, see what Don said about you!'

He bent over her shoulder, one hand tousling her hair, and followed her pointing finger. She read aloud: 'Dr Stephen Gloze, 28, the young GP deputizing while Weyharrow's resident doctor is abroad, summed the matter up by saying, "I would have preferred devils because they can be exorcised, while we know of nothing that will drive this poison from our blood and bone." Steve, that's marvellous!'

'He spelt my name wrong,' Steven grunted, turning back to the stove. 'It's with a "v".'

'That's probably the sub's fault . . . Oh, you're pulling my leg!' She jumped up to embrace him. 'But aren't you proud?'

The phone rang.

'I'll go!' Jenny exclaimed, and was in the hallway before he could stop her.

222

Let it not be a medical emergency . . .

It wasn't. She was back, flushed with excitement.

'It's Nigel Mender! He says the rest of the council have been on the phone to him all morning, and he wants a word with you, so would you drop by the hotel at lunch-time? He says everybody he's been talking to thinks you were wonderful last night. And – and he said . . .'

'Something about you?'

She nodded, eyes bright. 'He said that if I hadn't thought of calling in the nationals it could have been ages before we found out about the leak from Helvambrit.'

'Did what's-his-name – Wallace – get his story in, too?'

'I haven't looked yet . . . What shall I say?'

Steven glanced at the kitchen clock. 'Say one o'clock.'

'They open at twelve – '

'It'll give us time to make love again and have a bath together.'

She stared at him for a long moment as though unable to believe her ears. Then she grinned enormously and dashed back into the hall.

As he set her breakfast before her a minute later, he said in a musing tone, 'Squire and parson . . . Doctor and reporter could make a bloody sensible replacement.'

'What?' She glanced up, uncomprehending.

'Just something that's been going through my mind. I'll explain later. Eat up.'

'Okay.'

When he did get around to explaining, on the way to the hotel, she listened intently and at last gave a firm nod.

'You're right, of course. There's only one thing I don't like about it.'

'What?'

'I've never been the sort of person who wanted to take charge.'

'Nor have I. I never wanted to be a consultant, or head of a teaching department. I want to be a country GP, that's all . . . But you want to be a Fleet Street reporter.'

'Not any more. Like I said, I don't have the right antennae. I found that out last night. What I want to be is what's most badly needed.'

'Say it.' He squeezed her hand.

'A communicator. A link between a place like this and everywhere else. So that what happens there won't be so awful in the future, and what happens here won't ever again become a national scandal.'

'Let's say that to Nigel and the other councillors. If they understand what we're driving at, we're in.'

'Agreed.'

Contentedly, she linked one arm with his. With her other hand she waved at Stick and Sheila, emerging from the Marriage after a Sunday noontide drink. Stick excused himself and came rushing over.

'You heard about Marmaduke?'

'Yes!' Jenny's sunny mood clouded again. 'Isn't it awful? When one thinks of what Basil may do now – '

'That's it! He can't! Cedric was here a while ago and told us!'

Both Steven and Jenny blinked at him; Steven said, 'What do you mean?'

'The estate's been left in trust to him! Basil and Helen can go on living at the Court, but they can't sell anything – the library, the house, the land – without squandering a fortune in lawyers' fees to challenge Marmaduke's will! That's what he's claiming, anyhow.'

'Oh, wow,' Steven whispered. 'I hope that's true!'

'So do I!' said Jenny fervently.

'It isn't going to be much fun for Ced,' Stick observed. 'I mean, living with those bastards that he has for parents and all the time bombarded with demands to gimme, gimme – as though they were the kids and he the daddy! But you know something?'

He fixed them with a serious gaze under his bushy eyebrows.

'If anything can make that guy grow up, this'll be it. And there are more people on his side than he imagines . . . Well, I best get home. I promised Sheila and the kids a special lunch and left it in the oven. *Au revoir!*'

All of a sudden Weyharrow felt like not too bad a place to be.

Though something would have to be done, eventually, about the distinction between the patrons of the pub and those of the hotel . . .

Time enough for that, though. Time enough, if in the world of the information explosion enough people could be told often enough about the horrors being conceived beyond their personal horizon, and learn to stand up and shout aloud, 'You stop that! Stop it now! And that means NOW!'

Postlude

Later, the weather at Weyharrow turned cold again. In Wearystale Flat Sheila complained to Stick about the way he left wide open the windows that overlooked the Chap. She was shivering, she said; so were the kids.

Sighing, resigned, he closed out the dense autumn mist that was gathering along the valley.

'Shame . . .' he murmured into his beard.

'What do you mean?' Sheila demanded.

'They say there aren't going to be any more leaks.'

'You think that's a shame?'

'Well, it was cheaper than pot, wasn't it? No trouble about growing it. No hassles with the fuzz, either!'

Sheila erupted into a noise between a giggle and a gurgle; she was in bed, sipping a mug of Ovaltine.

'Stick, how often do I have to tell you? Don't make me laugh while I'm eating – I mean drinking!'

'Ah, it's because I·plan to do away with you and wreak my wicked will on your two lovely albeit not-yet-nubile daughters!'

His boots he had already kicked aside; now he peeled off his sweater. He was pushing down his jeans when he realized Sheila was staring at him strangely.

'Did you say "daughters"?'

'Sam and Hilary, who else?'

'Daughters?' She set her empty mug aside.

'Yes, of course!'

'But Hilary and Sam are boys . . . Stick, how much have you been smoking lately?'

He only grinned at her, and scrambled into bed. As she

turned her mouth up to greet his, he thought: *No more leaks, hmm? You could have fooled me!*

I wonder what tomorrow has in store!

Also available
in Methuen Paperbacks:

JOHN BRUNNER

The Compleat Traveller in Black
A fantasy classic

Chaos ruled throughout the universe in this time of the far future – or perhaps the unguessably distant past. The scientific laws of cause and effect held no power and men could not know from one day to the next what to expect from their toil. Even hope seemed foolish.

But there was one man entrusted with the task of bringing order and reason forth from Chaos. A black-clad traveller, who had many names but a single nature, and who carried with him a staff made of light. Wherever he went the forces of Chaos swirled around him, buffeted him and tested him. But he fought them, and little by little he drove them back.

For the first time available in one volume, here are all the Traveller in Black stories in the definitive edition.

BEN BOVA

Privateers

It is early in the next century. The Soviet
Union controls the heavens and holds the
world hostage through superiority in space
weapons. Dan Randolph, former astronaut
and engineer, as famed for his romantic
conquests as for his vast fortune made
through the mining of space, is driven from
the USA by the collapse of its space programme. Establishing himself at a new base
in Venezuela, he plans to tap the untold
wealth of the asteroid belt. But the Russians
are willing to take brutal measures to preserve their power. Soon Randolph is pitted
in a deadly cat-and-mouse game against
Vasily Malik, the ruthless Commissar of
Space. Forced to operate outside the law,
Randolph becomes a latter-day privateer, a
buccaneer striking back at the Russians to
raise the stakes in this deadly game. Here is
a riveting tale of high adventure on earth
and in the stark reaches of the space fron-
tier, by one of the great futurist writers of
our time.

C. J. CHERRYH

The Faded Sun
An epic of quest and fulfilment across the Cosmos

The Faded Sun shows C. J. Cherryh at her awesome best. A trilogy of epic scale, published for the first time in one volume, *The Faded Sun* plots the fates of three individuals against a vast background of war, alliance and treachery across the stars.

Two are members of a far-flung people, the *mri*-mercenary explorers and warriors, and currently deadly enemies of humanity. But with Melein, their last priestess-queen, and Niun, last of the true-bred warriors, is a human: Sten Duncan, who has renounced his own loyalty to serve them. They set off on a quest for the half-legendary *mri* planet Kutath.

Around this trio, mighty actions swing, and great destinies hang in the balance. C. J. Cherryh proves herself yet again to be an imaginative writer of exceptional power and invention.